IN THE
zone

a novel about championship golf

BY
GARY M. CRIST

DOWN THE MIDDLE PRESS
JUPITER, FLORIDA

IN THE ZONE

Published by:

DOWN THE MIDDLE PRESS
1150 S. U.S. Hwy. # 1
Suite 401
Jupiter, FL 33477
Gary M. Crist, Publisher
Phone: (561) 745-8748
Fax: (561) 745-8756

Prepared and Produced by
CRONOPIO PUBLISHING
John Sammis, President

Design and Electronic Page Makeup by
JAFFE ENTERPRISES
Ron Jaffe

Cover image based on AP/Wide World Photo image
and used courtesy AP/Wide World Photo.

© Copyright 1998, Gary M. Crist
All Rights Reserved
First Printing: Fall, 1998
Printed in the United States of America
ISBN Number: 0-9664366-1-X

This book is dedicated to the memory of George and Mary.

PREFACE

The world of sports recognizes a rare state of mind, which is reserved for athletes whose concentration during competition overcomes all apprehension, anxiety and self-doubt, that would otherwise inhibit their performance. It is sometimes called "the Zone."

This is a story about a professional golfer who rediscovers his way into the Zone, while competing in the PGA Tour's showcase event, The Players Championship, resolving in the process many of the conflicts in his past, and unlocking the doorway to his future.

Prologue

The fortyish, athletic-looking man sitting at the gleaming, brass-railed bar was reflecting on how he loathed Orlando. In his view, nearly everything there was a tourist trap, disguised thematically to look like something it was not. The hotel he had just checked out of, for example, was called The Polynesian, because of its fake teak facade, and the fact that the staff wore leis around their necks, while fleecing young families out of some $200 per night, to experience the country's premier example of profiteering off the fantasies of youth: Disney World. Having grown up in the 50's and 60's, the man conceded the original genius of Walt Disney. Nevertheless, he was convinced that if old Walt could have foreseen how the MBA's would transform his legacy, he would have been sure to take Mickey with him to the grave.

The bar was another monument to what the man perceived as Orlando's gaudy and phony motif. It was called The Outlaw's Dallas Saloon and was located in the Church Street Station section of the city, a four-block square dominated by garish, blinking neon signs, which directed those who read them to bars, restaurants, night clubs and manufacturer outlet merchandise shops. Each establishment was, as applicable, dedicated to selling tourists over-priced drinks, mediocre meals, second-rate talent shows, or polyester tee-shirts emblazoned with some presentation of the word Florida, or depicting Floridian local color, such as a flamingo or a gator.

It was a late Friday afternoon in October, and the man stared into the almost empty beer mug in front of him with obvious dejection. Looking up and catching the attention of the bartender, he put aside his dark thoughts for a moment and said politely, "Another Michelob please." It would be his fourth.

Apparently hearing him order the additional beer, an elderly lady the man had noticed seated a few empty bar stools to his right spoke up: "Aye, young man, ye look as though ye've lost your last friend. Can it really be so bad?"

The man looked over in the direction of the voice, somewhat irritated at first by the prospect of his private brooding being interrupted by some uninvited and unwelcome interloper. But something about the woman's voice and appearance piqued his curiosity and caused him to return her invitation to conversation. She looked to be well into her seventies, but her eyes radiated a youthful energy. She seemed to be overdressed for the still muggy central Florida weather, and her accent was distinctly and attractively English. The man had always been fond of English people, particularly their manner of speaking and tendency to dry, understated humor.

"I lost my job," the man replied, dimpling his right cheek slightly in a half-smile. He was referring to the fact that approximately two hours earlier he had missed the 36-hole cut at the Disney World Golf Classic, bringing to a close the worst season of his 23-year PGA Tour career.

"I know," the woman said, much to his astonishment. "I watched you do it." The energy radiated from her sparkling green eyes again. "Do ye mind if I join ye for a round?"

"Please do," he said after a moment, astonished again by her forwardness. As she got up to move to the bar stool next to him, the man returned his gaze to the beer mug. *Missed the cut, drinking $5 beers in a fake saloon, getting picked up by a septuagenarian*, he thought glumly... *only in Orlando.*

Little did he know that the conversation he would have over the next couple of hours would begin the process of turning his life around.

By the time the lady had positioned herself on the stool next to the man, the bartender was removing the now empty beer mug and replacing it with a frosty new one. Turning to his newly found companion, the man reassumed a pleasant countenance, and, looking directly into the lady's bright green eyes, asked "What'll you have?"

"Oh, thank you young man, but I'll be sticking with this," the lady replied, gesturing to a half-full shot glass of what appeared to be some kind of whiskey. The bartender had moved away already anyway, apparently knowing, thought the man, that the lady would not be ordering anything more. The two sat silently for a moment as the man started to sip the fresh Michelob. His thoughts began to darken once again.

Detecting the lapse back into dejection, the lady spoke up brightly, like she had before. "So tell me how you lost this 'job' of yours. You seem far too accomplished and attractive to be unemployed."

"I thought you said you watched me do it," the man replied.

"Aye... aye, in a way I did, the woman allowed hesitatingly... But I'd like to hear your description of it. I fancy you've got your own tune to play."

"Pretty simple, really," the man said after a moment. "Three-putted one from 10 feet for bogey, to get things going sideways right off the bat; blocked the tee shot at four out of bounds; made triple; and couldn't get it up and down from the collar at eighteen. All in all, a smooth 75 for the day, missed the cut by two shots, and I'm, as they say, 'down the road.'"

"To where?" the woman asked.

"West Palm Beach," the man replied. "My season's over; nowhere to go but back home... How about you? I can tell by your accent you're not from around here. What brings you across the pond to Orlando?"

"Orlando? ... Is that where we are?"

The man returned his attention to the beer stein, his mood further depressed by the thought that not only had he managed to hook up with a septuagenarian, but with a disoriented one at that. One who didn't even know where she was. He took another long pull at the beer, and decided to resume the conversation anyway. The effects of the alcohol were beginning, as they usually did, to make him enjoy the sound of his own witty commentary.

"Yep, you're in Orlando all right. Can't you tell from the looks of this phony-baloney saloon?"

"Is that what you see here?" the woman asked.

"I'm afraid so... Don't you?"

"No young man, can't say as I do. In fact," the woman said, looking around over her shoulder for a moment into the restaurant behind them, as if to confirm the positive perceptions she was about to relate, "I see a rather nice place, where a whole variety of people seem to be enjoying themselves quite nicely... If you'll pardon me for saying so, young man, the 'phony-baloney' may be a layin' on the other side of those nice brown eyes of yours..."

"Look here at my glove," the lady continued, holding her left hand up in front of her face, the palm facing outward. "What do you see?"

Beginning to be intrigued by the woman's frankness and energy, the man decided to play along. He looked closely at the brown leather glove she now held up for his inspection. It was faded and wrinkled and had a small hole just below the center of the palm, where the lady's ivory white skin showed through.

"A worn-out glove," the man responded... "But you can get a new pair across the street. How would you like some with little pink flamingos stitched between the fingers? How about a pair with gold sequins spelling out 'Florida' across the knuckles?" The man chuckled at his own cynical remarks, which were typical of the black humor he lapsed into after a few drinks when he was feeling depressed.

Unaffected by the man's sarcasm, the lady smiled and grasped his arm, her green eyes continuing to peer into his. "No," she said with some insistence, holding the glove up again and rotating her hand slowly so the palm now faced her. "What I see here... and what you could see, if you looked with a bit of appreciation... and understandin'... is a wonderful, comfortable glove... a glove that fit so well... and warmed so completely... it was worn, and worn... and worn yet again...

"You see young man," she continued after a moment, "what we see in this world, and how we interpret and record it, is up to each of us to decide. There's good and bad in nearly everythin'. I find happiness in appreciatin' the good; I've learned that it's a waste of time and energy to wallow in what's bad.

"Life is life," the woman continued after a moment. "But how we package what we see and do in that life, is something each of us can control."

The man nodded, as if to concede the woman's point, and continued to stare into her eyes. Glancing off to the still half-filled jigger of whiskey on the bar, he began to understand that, for whatever reason, the old woman was on a mission to teach him something. And her style in doing so made him want to listen, and learn.

"I see what you mean," he finally said... "I see what you mean."

"Take your round of golf today," the woman said, continuing to hold onto his arm, increasing the pressure slightly. "You described it like it was torture; all you chose to recount were the things that didn't go well. You recorded in your mind and published to the world your failures, and skipped right over the good things, concentrating on them not a whit!... What about the eagle-2 you made at the 16th? I didn't hear anything about that from you, although before you came in there was a chap down at the other end of the bar, going on and on about how it was one of the finest shots he had ever seen. Said it reminded 'im of the 2-iron you knocked stony at the Road Hole at St. Andrews, the year you won The Open."

"That was a long time ago," the man said, gesturing to the bartender for another drink, "a long, long time ago... Did he say whether the four-footer I missed at 17 reminded him of the three straight I missed at the Belfrey in '89?"

The woman offered no response to the man's instinctively negative comment.

The two sat in silence for a while as the man thought back to the prime of his career, some 20 years ago. He had won the British Open and three other Tour events that same year at the tender age of 22. In those days he had expected to win every tournament he entered. Now, he acknowledged glumly, shaking his head slowly in the process, he was struggling just to make the halfway cut in the events he played. With few exceptions, he hadn't seriously contended for a tournament win for several years. He had become a journeyman player. One with an impressive past, but not much of a future.

"Can you ever do it again?" the woman asked, reaching toward the whiskey glass and interrupting the man's unhappy reminiscence. "Can you ever again focus on the success you're capable of, rather than the failure you're so afraid of?... Can you ever win again?"

"I don't know," the man said after thinking for a moment. "What do you think?"

"I think that's up to you to decide... My husband, who was quite a sportsman in his day, used to say that 'success is always an option, all you have to do is have the guts to choose it.' He said that accomplishment was a personal vision that each has to capture in his own mind's eye. He called the process 'concentration.'"

The conversation continued and the man allowed himself to be drawn further and further under the old woman's spell. The glow from the drinks, her positive philosophy and wonderfully expressive manner all combined to drift them along as the afternoon turned into evening.

An hour or so, and a couple more Michelobs went by, and the man decided it would be unwise to attempt to head back to West Palm. He excused himself, telling the woman he needed to call to check back into his hotel, and went to the telephone in the hallway at the back of the bar.

When he returned, the woman was gone. The man sat back down and looked around for her, but she was nowhere to be found. The half-filled whiskey glass on the bar was the only evidence that she had ever been there at all.

Only in Orlando, the man thought again as he summoned the bartender for the bill. But this time he didn't mean it derogatorily, as he had only a few hours before. And as he left the bar he noticed that the people there really did seem to be enjoying themselves.

Driving back to West Palm Beach the next morning, the man's thoughts returned to last night's strange encounter with the old woman. The dryness in his mouth and his mildly aching head confirmed his overindulgence in reaction to missing the cut yesterday at

Disney. It was the eleventh straight time he had failed to qualify for weekend competition, and a paycheck.

But despite the hangover that gripped his body, and the financial insecurity that troubled his mind, the man sensed positive, optimistic feelings as he motored east on I-4, headed toward the Florida Turnpike and the two-hour cruise home. Psychologically, he felt somehow refreshed. The woman's simple message had seemed to cleanse away the debris that had been tarnishing his attitude, and his skills for the last several years.

"Success is always an option," she had said. "All you have to do is have the guts to choose it." The man repeated the phrases from time to time as he drove along. The more he thought, the more he appreciated how they pointed the way toward the resurrection of his career, and his hope for the future.

The Turnpike mile markers counted down as he sped south. The man set the car's cruise control on 75 and relaxed with the pleasant thoughts that seemed to be springing into his mind, from where he wasn't sure. He recalled his grade school and high school teachers, one by one. He thought about his parents, both dead now, and how his childhood had been a good one. Rather than lamenting his mother's death, which had occurred earlier in the year, he spent several moments remembering the strength and beauty she had given to the world, and to him. The focus of his thoughts was on what a truly remarkable lady she had been, rather than how bad and unfair it was that at age 80 she had passed away.

He thought about his coaches, and big games his teams had won and lost. He thought about the first golf tournament he had played in, at age 11, the junior club championship at his father's country club in rural Indiana. He smiled remembering how his basketball career had ended some 25 years ago, with him lying flat on his back on the varnished hardwood, having failed in his attempt to draw a last-second foul, and looking up at the final scoreboard: River Grove 67 Southside 66. How many restless nights since then, he wondered, had he tossed and turned, feet sweating, wondering if he could have made those foul shots, had the referee blown the whistle. Thinking again of the old woman's teachings of the night before, he had a warming sense that yes, he would have made them. Back in those days, he almost always chose success; he was too young to be distracted by the fear of failure.

Arriving at the West Palm Beach exit, the man eased the car off the Turnpike and along the looping ramp to the toll plaza. As the attendant handed him back his change, she stated a perfunctory "Have a nice day." Looking her in the eye and smiling, the man said "I have chosen to do so. You have a nice day too."

The woman thought the response was a little overstated, but at least the man was pleasant. Half an hour ago, in response to her salutation an overweight, silver-haired fellow driving a Lincoln with New York plates had told her to "Go fuck [herself]." The man was back in South Florida.

Chapter 1

Jeff Taylor slipped the new Wilson golf glove from its package and began the methodical process of working it onto his left hand. Standing in front of his spacious oaken locker at the Tournament Players Club at Sawgrass, at 7:30 on this Thursday morning in late March, Taylor was preparing to compete in the first round of The Players Championship. The Players is regarded by many in the golf world as the sport's fifth Major championship, outranked in terms of prestige only by The Masters, the U.S. Open, the British Open and the PGA Championship.

In terms of prize money, The Players is the richest event in golf. Earlier in the week, the PGA Tour's Tournament Policy Board had announced that the total prize money for this year's event would be raised to $6,000,000. A cool $1,080,000 would go to the winner. Even the players who failed to make the 36-hole cut would each go home with $5000, approximately the amount David Graham had earned by finishing tenth in the inaugural Players Championship in 1974, then known as the Tournament Players Championship. This year, tenth place would pay in excess of $160,000.

The white leather glove felt smooth and cool, within the air-conditioned quiet of the locker room. After cinching the red "W"-labeled Velcro fastener snugly, Jeff spread his left hand open and tried to pinch leather from the palm of the glove with his right thumb and index finger. There wasn't any excess leather to pinch, indicating that the fit was just right.

"Show time," Jeff whispered, lightly slapping his bare right hand against the freshly-gloved left hand, "show time."

Emptying his pants pockets, except for two silver sixpence coins and the back pocket-sized, florescent orange contestant "book," which diagrammed the contours and yardage of the Stadium Course, Jeff closed the heavy locker door, and turned to head out to another day in the rarified air of competitive professional golf.

The spikes of his black leather golf shoes clanked along the stone-tile floor as Jeff walked toward the door leading from the clubhouse to the golf course. As he walked, Jeff caught a glimpse of himself in the wall-length lavatory mirror to his right. Yielding to the introspective mood he almost always experienced before the first round of a tournament, Jeff approached the mirror and placed the heels of his hands on the edge of the marble sink cabinet. He glanced around quickly, to make sure he was alone in the locker room with his thoughts, then put his face up close to the mirror and peered into his own brown eyes. Jeff felt good about what he saw, all things considered. But there was a trace of apprehension in the weathered stare the mirror returned.

The Players would be Jeff's fifth event in the still-young season, and his game was showing signs of rebounding from the depths it had reached last fall. He had made the cut in all but one of the four events he had played so far, and had finished a respectable 12th two weeks ago in Fort Lauderdale at the Honda Classic.

But at age 43, there was no denying that Jeff was in a difficult period of his professional career. Seven long years away from the less competitive but still financially-bountiful Senior Tour, Jeff often worried about how much longer he could remain competitive on the Regular Tour, the "Big Tour," as the players themselves called it. More and more, he struggled with the realization that he was beginning to have more in common with the silver set than with the limber backs he would be competing against over the next four days, assuming he played well enough today and tomorrow to make the cut and continue playing over the weekend.

The primary reason for the tension Jeff often felt was the fact that he was in the last of the 10 years of "exempt" PGA Tour status he had earned by winning the World Series of Golf. This meant that beginning next year his eligibility to continue playing the Tour would need to be based on some other, more current achievement, such as a tournament win or at least a "top 125" finish on the official money list. The frightening reality was that in neither of the last two years had Jeff played well enough to meet even the seemingly modest standard of making the top 125. Indeed, last year he had made the cut in only six of the 24 tournaments he had entered, earning barely $60,000 in prize money, not enough even to cover expenses. Such lackluster performance would have to end, if Jeff was to keep his "card," i.e., eligible status to compete in Tour events. Closing his eyes as he continued the self-searching process in front of the mirror, Jeff whispered the words "sixty-five," and attempted to visualize himself, sitting in the media center later in the day, explaining to the working press how he had managed his championship-leading round... "Good drive on one... 9-iron, pin-high right... 15-foot putt, that I knew would die left at the hole... made a good, smooth stroke... easy four... killed the drive down the left center on two... great 3-wood to the front collar... almost made eagle, easy birdie four..." He continued, methodically visualizing the shots that would be necessary on each of the 18 holes to shoot 65 on the challenging Stadium Course.

Some minutes later, his positive meditation process concluded, Jeff reopened his eyes, made a final tug at the bill of his visor, and turned to head out to the golf course.

As he walked along in the crisp, morning air, Jeff noticed the rose-colored sun rising over the eastern horizon off to his left beyond the ninth tee, and reflected on the advice he had received from an elderly English woman, one Polly Whitson, last fall in a bar in Orlando: "Success is always an option," she had said. "All you have to do is have the guts to choose it." She had called the process "concentration." Jeff knew that Polly's wisdom was really only her own version of the power of positive thinking, hardly a revolutionary idea. But her charm, and her interest in him that mystical evening in Orlando had affected him profoundly. And since Jeff had rededicated himself to the discipline Polly recommended, he had seen some improvement in his play, and his enjoyment of life in general. He was sensing every now and then that things were coming back together.

Sand Wedge, Jeff's long-time caddie, was waiting for him, smoking a cigarette while sitting astride Jeff's Wilson Staff golf bag, alongside the putting green. Not being much of a morning person, and wincing at the smoke drifting from Sand Wedge's cigarette, Jeff mouthed a cursory "good morning," and quickly reached into the bag for his putter. Unlike most pros, Jeff had recently taken to starting his pre-round warm-up process by stroking putts first, moving on to the practice range as a second step. Rising from his impromptu seat on the huge golf bag, Sand Wedge handed Jeff three new Titleist 3's. Jeff accepted the balls and walked onto the practice green.

The early morning air was fresh and dry, foretelling a beautiful spring day in north Florida. Jeff looked to the trees off to the left of the putting green, to see if any wind was beginning to stir. The thing he liked most about his 8:34 starting time was that he would probably be finished before any serious breezes started to blow. The Players Championship, like all of the Florida swing events played on Tour every year during March, was infamous for high winds, which usually equate to a golf pro's principal nemesis: high scores.

Jeff dropped the three golf balls on the green, about five feet from one of the practice cups. Assuming his usual reverse-overlap grip on the putter handle, he stroked one of the balls smoothly. The coordinated movement of his arms and shoulders felt good and he savored the sound of the ball thumping the back center of the hole, and rattling into the bottom of the cup. He repeated the process on the two other balls. The third ball, although finding the hole, slid a fraction to the left before disappearing from sight. The first inkling of negativity, such that all professional golfers have to deal with every day, crossed Jeff's mind momentarily. *Accelerate*, he thought, attempting to note positively the fundamental key to good putting. It was a seemingly simple concept; but one that had become increasingly difficult for Jeff to execute, particularly in pressure situations. Like all veteran athletes, his nerves had aged under the pressures of the many years of constant competition, jangled by the thousands of times what looked to be good putts had gone over the cup's cellophane bridge, or died a centimeter too short in the jaws of the hole, or hit a spike mark at the last millisecond, veering the ball to the left or right. Each miss added another stroke to Jeff's scores, scores he depended upon for a living. "Backstroke low and slow," Jeff whispered; "accelerate through the ball."

Sand Wedge, who had positioned himself behind the hole Jeff was targeting, picked the balls from the cup and rolled them back into position at Jeff's feet. This time Jeff gripped the putter in a cross-handed style, placing his left hand below the right, and again stroked the three balls toward the hole. Each ball hit the center of the cup and disappeared cleanly. Jeff smiled inwardly as he felt more comfortable with the feel the cross-handed grip seemed to be delivering. He decided that the putting strategy for the day would be to use a conventional grip on the longer putts and to go cross-handed on the shorter ones. He paused for a moment, emphasizing in his mind that the decision was a positive one, based on the better feel of the unorthodox grip. Not so long ago he would probably have recorded the same decision as a concession to failure, an unhappy admission that he could no longer putt his best with a conventional grip. The discipline of repackaging his thoughts in a positive way was one of the things Polly had emphasized that evening in Orlando.

"Good God, Taylor, you going cross-handed on the freakin' practice green these days? Man, you gotta lighten up. They still count, you know, even if they don't go in the exact center of the hole."

Jeff looked up to the familiar sound of his buddy Skip Florine's wisecracking conversation. "Just trying to hit it on the right twitch," Jeff joked, noting immediately that his instinctive remark was inconsistent with the positive mental discipline he was rededicating himself to employ. "Just wait until you're old enough to shave everyday, even you might eventually miss one."

"Oh, I know I'll miss one some day," Skip acknowledged. "Matter of fact, I think I already have... YEAH, now I remember, missed a six-footer at Doral two years ago, doncha know."

Jeff noted Florine's youthful confidence and exuberance, and recalled for a moment his own bulletproof attitude about his golf game, particularly his putting, when he had come out on Tour, more than 20 years ago. He remembered how he would often envision the putt he was stroking going into the hole, before he even hit it. Jeff longed for some way, any way, to get that super-confident feeling back. And he thought that thanks largely to Polly and his providential evening with her last fall, he was again moving forward on the right track.

"Hey Skip, I wanted to ask you, you going to the player meeting tonight?"

"I don't know," Skip responded. "Depends on what I shoot. If

I break 70, I'll be there. If I don't break 80, I'm going to the Homestead and get drunk, and maybe try to get lucky. By the way, Sandy's tending bar there again, and she was asking about you... Anyway, if I'm somewhere in the 70's, I'll think about it. Why do you ask, anyway?"

"Cause they're going to talk about the new world tour deal that was announced yesterday, and I think it's important that we see for ourselves exactly what's going on... How's Sandy seem to be getting along? She seem OK?"

"Seems to be fine... and she looks great, man ... absofreakinlutely great," Skip answered, looking for any reaction from Jeff. Skip knew that Jeff and Sandy had been an item for quite a while, up until about this time last year. Not seeing any evidence of Jeff rising to the bait, Skip continued, "OK, if I break 80, I'll be there. But if I don't, I don't need to know about no damned world tour anyway."

"OK man, play well," Jeff said, satisfied that he had impressed the importance he saw in tonight's meeting successfully on his young colleague.

"You too," Skip replied.

With that, Skip walked on across the practice green to find his own practice cup to finish up preparation for his dewsweeper first-round starting time of 7:54.

After stroking 20 or so more putts, of varying lengths, employing the day's previously determined putting grip strategy, Jeff told Sand Wedge to get the bag and the two of them headed off to the practice range to continue getting ready for 8:34.

Chapter 2

Since it was still very early in the morning, it was an uninterrupted walk from the practice green to the TPC's expansive practice tee. As he and Sand Wedge ambled wordlessly along, Jeff was thinking that he hoped his walk back to the clubhouse from the scoring tent later that day wouldn't go so placidly. He hoped it would include several stops, to sign autographs and respond to eager questions about how his tremendous first round had gone. Although trying not to, he was also thinking about Sandy. Maybe he'd drop by the Homestead later in the week, and see how she was doing. Then he thought it might be wiser just to give her a call.

His focus returning to the business at hand, Jeff asked Sand Wedge, "How we gonna shoot 65 today?"

"That be the number, boss," Sand Wedge responded, speaking with his ever-present cigarette bobbing comfortably between his lips. "That be the number all right... yessir... My man, you knows this place. Keeps the ball in play. Keeps it below the hole. Be patient. Sixty-five... yessir, that be the number...

"And don't be hittin' no damn driver on number four!"

The emotional wind-up to Sand Wedge's advice was in reference to Jeff's mistake in yesterday's practice round, when he hit driver off the tee on the relatively short par-4 fourth, finding the deep rough through the fairway on the left side, nearly out of bounds. As a consequence of his poor judgment, (Sand Wedge had urged him to hit a more conservative tee shot with a 1-iron), Jeff made a triple bogey-7 on the hole, spoiling what otherwise would have been a solid practice round score of 70.

Arriving at the practice tee position identified by a Players Championship placard inscribed with his name, Jeff took out his lob wedge and swung the club a few times in ultra slow motion, holding his position at the top of the back swing for a moment, and also at the finish of the follow through. Jeff's basic theory of the perfect golf swing was all tempo, the slower, the better. He knew that 95 percent of his shot execution mistakes were due to his tendency, particularly in pressure situations, to get too quick with his swing, causing him to go over the top of the shot, pull-hooking it to the left, or block out, pushing the direction of the ball far to the right of the target.

After a full five minutes of slow motion practice swings and stretching exercises, Jeff reached the head of the lob wedge into the pyramid of brand new golf balls that had been meticulously arranged for his use by the volunteer committee responsible for the practice facilities. He flicked out the first ball of the 60 or so he would hit in his ritual-like preparation for 8:34. Positioning the ball on a perfect lie on the closely cut, beautifully manicured Bermuda grass, he executed his first serious golf swing of the day. The wedge contacted the ball solidly, sending it soaring straight toward the pin on the target green Jeff had selected, some 60 yards away.

Sand Wedge noticed that the tempo of Jeff's swing and the club's contact on the ball were perfect. Jeff reached with the club head for another ball, positioning it on the grass immediately behind the perfect divot the club had made on the previous shot. He swung the lob wedge again, aiming for the same target green and pin. The ball followed a seemingly identical flight pattern to that of the first shot.

"Yessir, boss," Sand Wedge said, "65 be the number."

Looking back toward the practice green as Jeff continued his warm-up, Sand Wedge thought he recognized one of the two ladies standing in front of the three-sided Rolex clock tower that stood in the area between the practice green and the practice tee. The two appeared to be sipping coffee as they consulted a pairing sheet which indicated the starting times of the players. *Yeah, that Sandy all right,* Sand Wedge acknowledged with some alarm, as he continued his gaze for a few moments. *She a looker all right; smart too,* he thought. *But we don't be needin' her pretty her pretty lil' ass 'round here now; my man need to be thinkin' 'bout 65.* If he would have had a time machine, pre-set to next Monday, Sand Wedge would have tried to figure out some way to get Sandy to climb into it.

Returning his attention to Jeff's practice routine, the caddie hoped Sandy would have the good sense to steer clear of his player, at least during the championship. Sand Wedge didn't know what the deal was currently between Jeff and her, but he did know that they had some kind of bad falling out, right after last year's Players, and that Jeff had played very poorly throughout the rest of the spring, missing the cut at New Orleans, Greensboro and Atlanta. And when Jeff missed the cut, so did Sand Wedge.

The summer and fall hadn't gone much better. In fact, a couple weeks after Disney, the last official money event of the year, Sand

Wedge had called Jeff and told him he didn't think he could stay on the bag next year. Tom Cooper, who Sand Wedge had caddied for on an off before beginning to work exclusively for Jeff some 15 years ago, had turned 50 and was poised for a rebirth of his professional career on the senior tour. Tom wanted Sand Wedge to come out on the senior circuit with him and had driven to Sand Wedge's home in Belle Glade to make him the offer.

Cooper's proposition had put Sand Wedge in a quandary. He retained a sense of commitment to Jeff, whom he believed still to have the potential to win, if he could ever get his head screwed on straight. But Cooper's offer was very attractive. Most thought he was a cinch to win at least two or three tournaments in his rookie senior tour season, and probably well over $1,000,000. Sand Wedge's share of that would go far to replenish savings that had dwindled to almost nothing as Jeff's performance had spiraled downward, particularly during the last couple of years. Also, the courses on the senior tour are shorter and Sand Wedge would be allowed to use a golf cart. Nearing age 50 himself, the idea of spending next year mostly riding, instead of always walking held great appeal.

So Sand Wedge had called Jeff in West Palm Beach to advise him of Cooper's offer. Jeff had suggested that they get together for dinner to discuss things and they had met at Fat Boy's Barbecue in South Bay. Jeff's thesis during the dinner and conversation, which had gone on for nearly two hours, was that perhaps, under the circumstances, Sand Wedge should go with Cooper. Jeff also believed Tom would be an instant success on the senior tour, and wanted only the best for his long-time partner. But Jeff had gone on to say that he was feeling much better about his own game, and was looking forward to the coming year with a new sense of optimism and purpose. He recounted for Sand Wedge the Friday evening session in Orlando with Polly and said that during the off-season he had been playing every day and hitting a lot of balls. Jeff said he felt his game was now better than ever; even better than it was back when he and Sand Wedge were winning three or four events a year, and not worrying about how to pay bills.

Sand Wedge was impressed with Jeff's conviction, although a little suspicious of this Polly person, or whatever. He wasn't entirely sure whether Jeff had truly "found it" or maybe "lost it" altogether. But in the end, the caddie had decided to stick with his man, at least for one more year. And so far, it was looking like he had made a good decision.

It was Jeff's practice tee routine to hit four balls with each of the 13 clubs he carried in the bag, in addition to the putter. He had just handed Sand Wedge the 6-iron and was reaching for the five when he noticed Norm Thompson walking toward him at what appeared to be too brisk of a pace for early morning.

"Hey Jeff," Thompson called out, "you going to the player meeting tonight?"

"Yeah, I expect so," Jeff responded. "But Florine and I decided that if we don't break 80, we're going to blow off the meeting and go to the Homestead for some upside-down margaritas."

Ignoring the invitation to levity, Thompson approached closer and said in a lower, yet insistent voice, "Really man, I think you need to be there. Everybody's telling me you're against the world tour deal, and I, for one, want to know why. I think it's the best damned thing that's come along in a long time and if you're going to be against it, it's by God your duty to explain why. You know all the young guys still follow along pretty much with whatever you do, and frankly, I think its chicken shit for you to oppose this thing if you're not going to come out publicly."

"Hey, Norm," Jeff responded, "lighten up, man. I'll be there, all right? I was just joking... Hey man, I'm shooting 65 today."

Thompson seemed to relax a little, and stepped back, cracking a half-hearted smile at Sand Wedge. "Think he's still got a 65 in him Sand Wedge?"

"Sure he do," Sand Wedge replied in his deep, melodic voice. "Sixty-five be the number."

"OK," Thompson said, redirecting his words to Jeff and turning, apparently to head back to the clubhouse. "I don't play until this afternoon," he continued, as he began to walk away. "But I wanted to talk to you about the meeting before you started your round. See you tonight then, Jeff. Play well."

"You too," Jeff said, as Thompson strode off in the general direction of the clubhouse.

"Weird," Jeff said, a moment later, to nobody in particular, furrowing his brow slightly and shaking his head. He couldn't readily understand why Thompson would go to all the trouble of looking him up, at this hour of the day, just to ask if he was going to a player meeting.

It seemed very peculiar.

Getting back to his own purpose for the morning, Jeff returned to the 5-iron. Sand Wedge noticed that Jeff's first 5-iron swing was a barely perceptible fraction quicker than all of the previous swings. The shot still sounded and looked majestic to the casual observer, the ball soaring straight toward one of the medium-length practice greens some 185 yards away. But as it descended, the ball drew somewhat to the left, landing a good 40 to 50 feet away from the target pin.

Sand Wedge's experienced eyes perceived the tension from Thompson's confrontational remarks creeping into his player's swing. That, and the hands of the three-sided Rolex advancing toward 8:34, were beginning to work on Jeff's mind. Sand Wedge stood quietly, as his player continued putting his game-face on. Looking again back toward the clock tower, Sand Wedge noticed that Sandy and her companion had apparently moved on. He hoped they had elected to blend into the anonymity of the gallery, rather than follow Jeff's early round play.

After finishing his warm-up, by hitting 10 pitch shots to the end of the practice tee, Jeff said, "Grab the bag Sand Wedge; let's go hit a few more putts, and head for the tee. Like you say, 65 be the number."

As the two walked away from the practice tee, Jeff added, "By the way, remind me to have that 5-iron regripped after the round. I think we need to take a layer of tape off the shaft under the grip. It doesn't feel quite right."

Sand Wedge acknowledged without comment his player's positive attitude-preserving diagnosis of what had caused the somewhat erratic performance of the 5-iron on the practice tee.

It would soon be 8:34.

Chapter 3

The Stadium Course has a smaller, secondary practice green positioned 15 or 20 yards to the right of the first tee. During the Players Championship, it serves as a sort of staging area for the group of players awaiting the next starting time. When Jeff and Sand Wedge arrived, the first tee announcer was calling out the names of the players in the 8:26 group.

Designed to be the PGA Tour's premier "stadium golf" facility, the Stadium Course's first tee is located within a natural amphitheater, allowing literally thousands of spectators to view the players hitting their initial drives. Clad in his scotch-plaid, two sizes too small, Committee of 100 sport coat, which denoted him as a past Players Championship Chairman, Quentin Farley resembled a circus barker as he called out the names of the players in the threesome playing ahead of Jeff:

"Ladies and gentlemen, please welcome the players in the 8:26 starting time... From Albany, Georgia, the second place finisher in the 1995 PGA Tour School Qualifying Tournament, please welcome Gene Belcamp." The 500 or so spectators already encamped in the first tee amphitheater clapped respectfully.

"From Moline, Illinois," Farley continued, "a former winner of the Texas Open and third-place finisher in this year's AT&T Pebble Beach National Pro-Am, please welcome Jerry Swisher." The introduction drew another round of mild applause from the onlookers.

"And from Jacksonville, Florida, winner of four PGA Tour events, including the Westchester Classic and the Kemper Open, please, ladies and gentlemen, give a special homecoming welcome to our own Randy Hartsfield." The applause level rose several octaves as the spectators acknowledged one of the local favorites. Born and bred in Jacksonville, Hartsfield was well known and admired by nearly all of the Players Championship fans.

While all this was happening on the first tee, Jeff was routinely stroking putts on the adjacent practice green. The balls were rolling true. Jeff would stroke each of the three Titleists toward one of the practice holes, 12 or 15 feet away. Usually, one, two or all three of the balls would disappear into the cup. Standing immediately behind the hole, with a large white golf towel draped across his shoulder, Sand Wedge would bend down, retrieve the three balls, wipe them back to their pristine brilliance with the towel, and toss them back to the vicinity of Jeff's feet.

As Jeff had previously noted on the other practice green, the early morning weather conditions were comfortable, perfect really. The temperature felt to be about 70, and a high overcast sky was slightly muting the rays of the morning sun, as it began to climb over the functional, pyramid-shaped TPC clubhouse off to the right. And, most importantly, there was not even a hint of wind. The Players was Jeff's favorite tournament on Tour and he was beginning to really believe in the 65 he had been spending the morning talking himself into; capturing it in his mind's eye, as Polly would say.

"Not bad, for an old man," Jeff heard as yet another practice putt plopped into the hole by Sand Wedge's feet. He looked up to the smile and offered handshake of one his playing partners, Trent Blalock. Jeff liked Trent and was glad to be grouped with him for the first two rounds. In addition to this morning's round, they would be playing together tomorrow, in the afternoon.

"Yeah, I just hope the holes on the course are as big as the ones on these practice greens," Jeff responded, grasping Trent's hand to acknowledge the greeting. "But what the hey, sure beats working for a living. How've you been, man?"

"OK, OK," Trent replied, "had some neck spasms earlier in the week though, so I may not be 100%. But who knows, maybe it'll make me swing better. Had 71 yesterday, so we'll see. Guess we're next, see ya at the tent."

Jeff stroked a couple more putts as Trent walked away, then announced to Sand Wedge, "Let's go on over and start working on that 65." He handed the caddie the putter and also headed for the tent by the first tee, where the officials give the players their scorecards, and introduce their official scorekeeper and young standard bearer, each of whom would accompany them throughout the round, advising central scoring and showing the gallery how each player was faring in the quest against par 72.

When Jeff got to the starter's tent, the officials were asking Trent if he had seen Elroy Robinson, the other player in the 8:34 group. Trent was saying that he had not, and it occurred to Jeff that he also hadn't seen Elroy. Right then, Nat Fleming, Robinson's manager, entered the tent and advised that Elroy was withdrawing, for medical reasons. Fleming said that Robinson had suddenly wrenched his back on the practice tee and was at this moment in the mobile fitness and medical treatment facility that follows the Tour from week to week. It appeared that Jeff and Trent might be playing a twosome, unless an alternate player could be located and brought onto the tee within the next five minutes. Jeff felt bad for Elroy, whom he also liked a lot. But he reminded himself that now was not the time to begin worrying about Elroy Robinson, or anything else. Now was the time to finalize preparation for the first of the 65 golf shots he planned to hit during the next four hours or so.

As Jeff approached the starter's table, he heard the familiar and welcome voice of Earl Schoenberger, the honorary starter for this year's championship. Jeff had gotten to know Earl and his wife Fran over the years and was glad to see him apparently rising through the tournament volunteer ranks, to better and better assignments. One usually started out as a tournament volunteer at about age 30, on the ecology committee. This meant, basically, that you emptied trash cans on the weekend, for no pay. If you stuck with it, as Earl apparently had, and were lucky (or well connected socially or in the business community) you could eventually work your way into the starter's tent, or some other plum assignment, by about age 60.

"How ya doing, Jeff? How's our favorite former neighbor?" Earl beamed. "We're just delighted to have you back at the Players Championship." Earl's greeting alluded to the 10 years Jeff had lived in Atlantic Beach, just 10 miles up A-1-A from the Stadium Course, before he had moved to South Florida in 1989.

"Glad to be back, Earl," Jeff responded. Leaning closer, he continued in a whisper, "hope to hell I'm back again next year," acknowledging to Earl, and again to himself, the coming expiration of his exempt status, if his competitive fortunes didn't continue their recent improvement.

Earl smiled back, and proceeded to go over the preliminaries with Jeff and Trent, handing each the other's scorecard, and introducing their volunteer scorekeeper, Mrs. Alma Feathers, and their standard bearer, 12-year-old Tommy Lawson. Trent and Jeff shook hands once again and gave each other the customary competitor's salutation: "Play well."

For the seemingly one millionth time, Jeff felt the adrenaline begin to flow throughout his body. His stomach began to flutter as his gaze became more vacant. He was focusing inwardly on the challenge at hand. His game-face was now completely on. He could puke, if there was somewhere to do it, without anyone seeing.

The hands on the three-sided Rolex pointed to 8:34.

As Quentin Farley did the introduction of Trent to what was now a much larger number of first tee onlookers, Jeff stood quietly beside Sand Wedge by the right-side tee marker. Sand Wedge held Jeff's golf bag upright at his feet. He had removed the head cover from the metal 3-wood and was holding the shaft of the club in his left hand, indicating to Jeff silently the caddie's judgment that the 3-wood was the right club for Jeff's first tee shot.

The first hole on the Stadium Course, a 395-yard par-4, was a particularly difficult driving hole for Jeff. It calls for a straight, or slightly drawn tee shot to get into good position in the left center of the fairway to approach the small, bunker-protected green. The challenge of the shot, combined with Jeff's historically jittery first tee emotions made for a bad combination.

Farley's introduction complete, Trent touched the brim of his visor to acknowledge the spectators' reception and proceeded to execute his drive. He made what appeared to be a somewhat uncomfortable swing, and struck what by Tour standards was a mediocre drive, some 240 yards, down the right center of the fairway. Trent winced slightly as he bent down to pick up his tee, indicating, as he had told Jeff on the practice green, that he was not at his best physically.

"Next on the tee," Farley resumed, "from West Palm Beach, Florida, and playing out of the Palm Beach Polo Club, winner of 27 PGA Tour events, including the U.S. Open, the Western Open, the Tournament of Champions, the British Open and the World Series of Golf, a five-time member of the Ryder Cup team, and the first-round leader in last year's Players Championship, ladies and gentlemen, please welcome Jeff Taylor."

Jeff acknowledged the enthusiastic applause of the spectators by removing his visor and extending it with his right arm as he smiled toward various sections of the gallery. As the applause died away, he replaced the visor and stepped back alongside Sand Wedge, reaching over for the 3-wood.

The club now in hand, Jeff moved to the middle of the tee, and, as was his custom, took two lazy swings of the 3-wood as he stood facing the first fairway, focusing mentally on his target landing area, down the left side. His final preparations for the first shot he would have to count on the scorecard were now complete.

Having decided to draw the tee shot from right to left, Jeff moved to the left side of the tee and reached down to tee up the Titleist 3. He teed it a fraction higher than he ordinarily would when using a 3-wood, in begrudging deference to the insecurity he still felt about the shot. Jeff had topped a low-teed opening drive at the Greater Hartford Open last summer, hitting an embarrassing grounder, which the gallery had reacted to with a collective "ooooooh," followed by an uneasy silence. The negative mental imagery he carried from that experience had dogged him on nearly every first tee since. It was a mental scar that even his rediscovered positivism had trouble overcoming. As he addressed the ball with the head of the club, Jeff attempted to dial in his conservative, auto pilot swing, the one he resorted to when all he wanted was an acceptable shot; one that wound up somewhere where he could find it. But on this highly charged occasion, even the auto pilot would not click in. Jeff's swing was shorter, and noticeably quicker than anything he had exhibited on the practice tee. The resultant drive was a medium-trajectory, bending hook that was destined from the start for the left rough and trees. Rather than posing in good follow-through position, as he did to follow the flight of a well-struck tee shot, Jeff's body language signaled his displeasure with the poor drive. He began to stride forward, off the tee and down the first fairway almost immediately upon completing his swing, not bothering to reach down to retrieve his tee. The crowd reacted to the flight of Jeff's drive with a smattering of respectful but unenthusiastic applause.

Having noted carefully where Jeff's tee ball appeared to have entered the trees, Sand Wedge hustled along to catch up, reaching out for the 3-wood Jeff held out behind him at arm's length as he marched along.

CHAPTER 4

As Quentin Farley was calling out Jeff Taylor's name and list of past accomplishments to the steadily growing number of spectators clustered around the first tee, PGA Tour Commissioner Sid Watterson was in his office within the PGA Tour headquarters building, which was tastefully located in the tall, north Florida pines, 200 feet or so behind the first green Jeff would soon be approaching. Watterson was seated at his desk, sipping a cup of tea and reading the *USA Today* account of yesterday's press conference regarding the planned "International Golf Championship Series." Finishing the article, Watterson sighed and rubbed his eyes lightly with the middle knuckles of his index fingers. He was envisioning the difficult process that probably lay ahead, dealing with what appeared to be the most formidable challenge yet to the PGA Tour's control of professional golf. It was a form of control that the Commissioner sincerely believed, and continually reminded the media, and often the players themselves, was in place to protect the players' own long term interests, allowing them to retain a say in policy decisions affecting their sport, and livelihood.

It was this quality, the fact that the game was largely controlled by the players themselves, that Watterson believed distinguished golf positively, when compared to other professional sports. The owner versus player, management versus labor conflicts that plagued football, basketball and baseball simply didn't apply to golf. And the game was prospering because of it. During Watterson's tenure, television rights fee revenues had continued the dramatic increases that had begun in the 80's when the Tour had been run, some thought autocratically, by Watterson's predecessor. Sponsorship revenue supporting Tour events, as well as spectator attendance, had also continued to climb. It seemed as though corporate America, and Americans themselves were increasingly attracted to the game of professional golf and the athletes who played it.

Watterson had come to the Tour from Washington D.C., where he had been a successful lawyer and lobbyist. He had been the prime mover, and careful coordinator of successful lobbying efforts intended to ensure that the tax code loophole closing reforms of the mid-80's did not negatively impact corporate dollars invested in golf for sponsorships and pro-am participation. The eagerness of Big Business to invest in the Tour was a principal lynchpin of golf's success, and Watterson's efforts had done much to preserve that.

When, soon after the settlement of agonizingly long and expensive litigation stemming from the Tour's attempt to ban so-called square-groove clubs, the Policy Board had offered Sid the Commissioner's job, he had considered it a dream come true. To him, it was a one-of-a-kind opportunity to apply his professional talents to the sport he loved and respected so much. And so far, most thought he was handling the position very well. Through his guidance the Tour was sustaining its popularity and success, in many ways a more daunting challenge than creating success in the first place.

"Patty," Sid called to his administrative assistant, "hold all my calls, and check with Nick and Mary, and make sure we're on for nine, here in my office." Watterson was referring to a meeting he had scheduled late yesterday afternoon for this morning, with Nick Standly, the Tour's Director of Communications and Mary Goldblume, the organization's General Counsel. The Commissioner wanted to carefully review with them the agenda for this evening's player meeting which, in addition to the inevitable critique of the

TPC course conditions, always the first priority at any player meeting, would focus on the proposed "world tour" and what the PGA Tour's official position should be toward it.

Watterson was worried. He had successfully fended off an ill-conceived world tour proposal shortly after being selected PGA Tour Commissioner four years ago. It wasn't that he was against the world tour concept, but he wanted it to be implemented in a thoughtful way, a way that didn't play havoc with the existing PGA Tour and foreign Tour events, sponsors and institutions that had brought professional golf so far in the last 20 or so years. The current proposal, like the previous one, in his judgment would ultimately do the sport serious long-term harm, for the sake of achieving some dubious short-term benefits for the world tour promoters, and a select few of the players.

"They'll be here," Patty called, having confirmed the nine o'clock meeting with the communications and legal departments' administrative people.

Sid got up from his desk, and walked across the spacious office to the wall-length window on the other side of his mahogany conference table. The window offered an expansive view of the first green, where the Tour's crown jewel event was in progress. Watterson was particularly perturbed with the timing of the previous day's press conference. The Commissioner knew full well that the "International Golf Championship Series" promoters, Nori Shumitami and the giant Japanese marketing conglomerate Shiatsu,kk, had selected Players Championship week for their announcement, as a personal slap in the face, and in attempts to detract media attention from the Players Championship.

Gazing through the window, Watterson noticed Jeff Taylor entering the front left greenside bunker, to play what was probably his third shot to the par-4 first hole. Although publicly neutral in his feelings about all Tour members, privately, Watterson liked and respected Taylor above nearly all other current players. "Hole it Jeff," Sid whispered, as he watched him begin to execute the sand shot. Digging his shoes into the sand as he prepared to play, Jeff looked up to the pin and simultaneously waggled the sand wedge, in the fluid and unmistakable fashion of a golf professional, who knows exactly what he is doing. While the Commissioner continued looking on, Jeff executed the stroke deftly. The ball lofted smoothly from the sand, and landed softly, three feet to the left and slightly above the hole. It then released slowly down the slope, rolling to within six inches of the cup. The gallery surrounding the first green applauded enthusiastically.

"Attaway Jeff," Sid whispered. Continuing to look out at the action around the first green, Commissioner Watterson noticed that Jeff and his partner, it looked in the distance to be Trent Blalock, were playing a twosome, rather than a threesome, which is standard for the first two rounds of a Tour event. Slipping a first-round pairing sheet from the breast pocket of his suit jacket, Watterson located Jeff's name alongside the 8:34 starting time and saw that Elroy Robertson should have been in the group with Jeff and Trent. Picking up his two-way tournament radio from the conference table at his side, Commissioner Watterson depressed the "send" button and attempted to contact Tournament Director David Frisch: "David Frisch, this is Sid. Do you know anything about Elroy Robertson withdrawing from the 8:34 group, over?"

Frisch, who was sitting in his PGA TOUR RULES golf cart within a stand of pine trees between the second green and third tee, quickly reached for his radio to respond to the Commissioner's inquiry. "Yes Commissioner," Frisch responded, "his manager advised us of the withdrawal just a minute or two before they were scheduled to go off; said Elroy hurt his back on the practice tee, over."

"Why wasn't an alternate put in?" the Commissioner asked, dispensing with the military-like, two-way radio "overs," as his concern for what was appearing to be a possibly mishandled situation heightened.

"It's my understanding that there wasn't time and no alternates were immediately available," Frisch responded, tensing as he sensed Sid's mounting displeasure. PGA Tour policies and procedures are designed to ensure a full field of players. It is one of the responsibilities of the rules staff to have alternate players available, to substitute in the event of late withdrawals, including last-minute ones such as had apparently occurred with Robertson.

Watterson made no immediate response to Frisch's explanation, intending to emphasize his concern over the situation to his Tournament Director, and allow him to hang uncomfortably for a moment.

"All right," the Commissioner finally said. "But I want a complete write-up on what happened, before you go home tonight."

"Yes sir," Frisch responded, wondering why the Commissioner seemed to be so upset over something that to Frisch was not a big deal.

Watterson pitched the leather-encased radio back onto the nearby conference table. He knew that one of his biggest critics among the players, P. T. Weathersby, was on the alternate list for the Players. It would be just his luck, the Commissioner thought darkly, that it was Weathersby who would have gotten into the field if the Robertson withdrawal had been better handled. Now, chances were, Weathersby would not get to play, find out about the administrative glitch, and make his unwelcome presence vocally known at this evening's player meeting. Due to the world tour issue, the situation at the players' meeting was sensitive and unpredictable enough already, the Commissioner brooded, without the specter of P.T. Weathersby's ire being unnecessarily brought into the equation.

"Commissioner," Patty said, standing in the doorway and mercifully interrupting Watterson's racing thoughts, "Nick and Mary are here for your nine o'clock."

"OK, tell them to come on in," Watterson replied over his shoulder, as he continued to watch play on the first green. Tommy Asaki, playing in the group behind Jeff, had just chipped in from the back collar for an apparent birdie-3, producing from the early morning gallery a medium level birdie cheer which was clearly audible, even within the Commissioner's office.

Chapter 5

"Good morning, Sid," Nick Standly and Mary Goldblume each said, as they entered the Commissioner's office.

"What makes you say so?" Sid responded, as he continued to stare out of the office window, uncharacteristically allowing his words to reveal his apprehensive mood. Usually, and *always* on public occasions, Commissioner Watterson projected the ultimate in terms of calm, cool "collectedness." The tenser a situation became, the more quietly and deliberately he spoke, almost always to great effect. Watterson believed strongly in out-preparing his opponents on business matters, and it was the preparation process for tonight's meeting he wanted to undertake with his two most trusted staff persons.

Sid's unexpectedly negative remark left Nick and Mary nervously glancing at each other, wondering what, if anything, they could say to get the meeting going positively.

"I'm sorry," Sid said, noting the looks of concern on his people's faces as he turned around to face them. "Let's sit at the conference table," he continued, gesturing to the three places at the table nearest to where he was standing. "Might as well watch some golf while we sort through this Shumitami thing."

Indicating her lawyer-like approach to all things, as the three were seating themselves around the conference table, Mary said, "Commissioner, do you really see this as a Shumitami thing?" Her analytical style was always to figure who the decision-maker in a situation was before even attempting to craft an appropriate strategy to deal with the issues.

"It seems to me," she continued, "that we have one set of concerns if this thing is in fact driven by Shumitami and Japanese business interests, and a whole other kettle of fish if some of our name players are heavily committed. My take is that, at a minimum, Norm Thompson is in it big time, and Shumitami is more or less just along for the ride, knowing the Japanese' limitless appetite for professional golf."

"You got at least the Japanese appetite part right, Mary," Standly added. "An NBC guy was telling me just last night that there is a bill pending in the Japanese parliament to make February 18 a national holiday, to commemorate Isao Aoki's victory in the Hawaiian Open, back in '83 I think it was." Aoki's win, where he miraculously holed a 100-yard wedge shot for an eagle on the 18th hole to claim a 1-shot victory over a stunned Jack Renner, was still the only Regular PGA Tour victory to date by a Japanese player.

"That's a good point Mary," Sid said. "Just who are we up against here? Have you two seen the *USA Today* article? I just read it, and I got the impression that this was Shumitami's baby and that he was just trying to get the blessing from Thompson and some of the other name players for credibility purposes."

"Well, if that's the case," Mary interjected, "the drill for us, it seems to me, is to drive home the control issue. You know, who do you guys want running the game, yourselves or a bunch of Japanese industrialists?"

"I like that," the Commissioner responded. "We have to make this thing be seen as a business issue, not a competition issue. We've got to look our guys in the eyes and say hey, these guys want to take over your lives, throw some big-time, probably short-term money at a few of you, and to hell with the other players, the volunteers, the local charities, our existing tournaments and sponsors... In other words, to hell with all of the things that have gotten us to where we are.

"What's the basic format they're proposing, anyway?"

"As I understand it from the press release," Nick responded, "the deal would be a series of 36-hole events, approximately one per month, with the finale, mega-event played during the week between the NFL conference championships and the Super Bowl. They want eligibility limited to the Sony top 20 plus Major champions from the last 10 years, not otherwise eligible."

"Including Players Champions," Sid asked, evidencing his relentless pursuit of the official elevation of the Players to "Major" status?

"No," Nick said, knowing that this additional twist to the story would make the Commissioner even more unhappy. "But

Shumitami did say that they were open to considering other event champions, and did mention the Sun City thing in South Africa and the Memorial."

The reference to Sun City pushed the Commissioner's sense of frustration even further. As most people involved in golf for any length of time knew full well, the Sun City event had been started in the mid 80's as a purely artificial, big prize money driven, off-season event in South Africa, at a time when the rest of the sports world refused to have anything to do with the country, due to its apartheid racial policies. Watterson rocked far back in his chair, a mannerism he often employed when in deep thought, and one the staff sometimes worried would eventually result in his tipping over and rendering himself para or quadriplegic. As if to confirm the intensity of the contemplative process he was engaged in, Sid dabbed the back of his right hand lightly against his brow. He seemed to be at a loss for words. The three sat in an uncomfortable silence.

After several more excruciatingly conversationless moments, punctuated only by Sid's occasional sighs, tongue clucks and mostly inaudible muttering, the Commissioner seemed to recollect himself and resumed the verbal exchange with his staff.

"Has the esteemed Shumitami 'san' heard, do you suppose, that we've got the strongest field in the history of golf playing outside that window this week for $6,000,000?" Sid inquired. The sarcasm palpably, and again uncharacteristically dripped from his words.

Shumitami had mentioned at the press conference, in response to direct questions about the status of Players Champions in the proposed International Golf Championship Series that in his view you can't buy an event's status as a Major, and he felt the Commissioner's obvious attempts to do so in the case of the Players Championship were actually very sad and certainly not good for the game. Standly knew this, but elected not to apprise Sid of these further details, not wanting to send the Commissioner even further afield of the measured, unemotional strategy Standly knew was imperative in handling this matter.

"Sons of bitches," Sid muttered, reacting bitterly to the additional insults it was now clear the new proposal contained, including the hardball attempts toward further dilution of the Players' status among premier professional golf events. "Sorry, Mary," he added, apologizing for his inappropriate profanity.

"That's quite all right Commissioner," Mary responded. "They taught us all about sons of bitches in law school."

"What time does Thompson play?" Sid asked, thinking it might be a good idea to talk with him before tonight's meeting.

"He's off number one at 1:28 with Keystone and Ruiz," Nick answered. "One of the feature groupings for the ESPN afternoon coverage."

"Should we try to get him up here, or should I go down there and try to talk to him?" the Commissioner asked.

There was silence as the lawyer and the communications professional thought Watterson's question through, from their sometimes differing perspectives. Mary was inclined to go along with Sid's idea, being like him, also a great believer in preparation, always seeking to find out what the questions were, as far as possible in advance of the need to state any answers.

Nick's instincts were otherwise. The doomsday scenario that was going through his more emotionally-tuned mind involved Thompson shooting 65, and sitting in the media center commenting not only on his masterful golf game, but how he had managed to keep his mind on golf, even though Commissioner Watterson had spent much of the morning trying to dissuade him from supporting what looked to Thompson to be a great opportunity for the continued good of the game. Nick decided to try to articulate his thoughts.

"I think talking to him before he plays is a bad idea," Nick said, battling the nervous hoarseness that sometimes crept into his voice when he knew he was extemporizing on extremely important and delicate matters. "I can see why you want to get to him before the meeting; but we should at least wait until after he plays. The media will regard him one way if he shoots 65, and another way altogether if he shoots 75. The last thing we need is for him to be leading the Players and making you look bad at the same time."

Another silence fell over the three as Sid and Mary considered Nick's remarks.

"I think Nick's right," Mary finally said. "Anyway, I doubt you'd find out anything that useful in talking with him, particularly when he's getting ready to play."

Silence descended again, as the Commissioner got up and returned to the window, to check out the current developments on the first green. Lenny Johnson had just missed a two-footer and was staring incredulously as his golf ball hung stubbornly on the front lip of the cup. The nervously-stroked ball had traveled the hole's entire circumference, performing a "dreaded 360" as television journalism's clown-prince announcer Gary McCord would say.

"Poor Lenny," the Commissioner chided. "He oughta take that 54-inch putter and put it in the hallway at his house and call it a hat rack." Watterson was very much a purist when it came to golf equipment, and personally believed that much of the radical equipment, which was becoming more and more commonplace on Tour, was detracting from the time-honored traditions and skills upon which he felt, sometimes passionately, the game should remain based.

"OK guys," Sid finally concluded, again insensitive to Mary's feminine presence in the male-dominated world of professional golf business decision making. "I think you're both right. Within these four walls, let's hope Thompson shoots 80."

Returning to his chair at the conference table, the Commissioner sat back down, and the three of them started the tedious process of going over the players' meeting agenda, item by item.

The Rolex "Official Timepiece of the PGA Tour" clock on the Commissioner's office wall pointed to 9:35.

Chapter 6

Jeff Taylor had the honor on the fourth tee, due to his birdie-2 on the third hole. Trent Blalock had parred the third, and was fortunate to have done that. His 5-iron tee shot had over flown the green, leaving him a very difficult lie in the deep, rear bunker. He had somehow extricated the ball to within 10 feet of the hole, and made the ticklish, side-hill putt. Trent felt relieved to have gotten away with one as he watched Jeff contemplating the tee shot he would soon be hitting off the fourth tee.

After the poor tee shot at one, Jeff had managed to settle himself down and begin to recapture the positive concentration he had been building through the early morning. He had played a good recovery shot from the left trees into the left front bunker, and gotten the ball up and down from there, to save par. He had followed the save at one with his first serious overture toward fulfilling the pre-destined 65, by scoring an eagle-3 on the par-5 second, hitting a beautiful 3-wood to the middle of the green and holing a relatively straight-in 20-footer from there. The successful eagle putt had produced a thunderclap-like cheer from the greenside gallery that made Greg Newton back off from the tee shot he was almost ready to hit from the nearby first tee. Starter Earl Schoenberger knew the eruption had come from the hole Jeff was playing. He hoped it meant exactly what it did. Moments later he overheard the hesitating, high-pitched voice of Mrs. Alma Feathers, dutifully reporting her group's scores to central scoring: "Second hole, Blalock 5; Taylor 3." Earl was delighted.

Jeff's solid birdie at the par-3 third, where his 6-iron tee shot had finished less than four feet from the hole, brought his score to 3-under-par, through the third hole. Standard bearer Tommy Lawson had excitedly mounted the red "3" beside Jeff's name on the mini-scoreboard he carried along, as the 8:34 group left the third green and headed for the fourth tee. The spectators following Jeff and Trent, as well as the ones encamped at the next tee could see that something interesting could be happening. Some 10 years ago Jeff had attracted huge galleries all over the country, and was thought by many to have the potential to be the game's next super star. But his popularity suffered an extreme blow when he became the scapegoat for the U.S. team's defeat in the 1989 Ryder Cup Matches. The perception was that he blew the final and pivotal singles match on Sunday, which resulted in Europe winning the Cup for the third consecutive time. Jeff's life in the wake of the Ryder

Cup tragedy had often been pure hell. He had been vilified in the media, often referred to as "Choke Taylor," and had even received death threats. Indeed, since his dramatic Ryder Cup loss, in the late September twilight at the Belfry in England, Jeff's game had never been quite the same. Over the years his popularity with his fellow players and the galleries had been gradually rebuilt. But it was based more in the kind of person he was, and what he had been through, than in what he had accomplished on the golf course since 1989.

His last really respectable performance of recent memory had been last year, right here at the Players. He had held the first-round lead with a brilliant 68, in abominable weather conditions, but had back-pedaled from there, finishing 75-75-77, in a disappointing tie for 58th place.

Waiting for the group ahead to play their approach shots, Jeff and Sand Wedge seemed to be having a low to medium-level disagreement regarding club selection. Sand Wedge was standing by the right-side tee marker, a cigarette between his lips, the Wilson bag strap still across his right shoulder, holding Jeff's 1-iron in his left hand. Jeff was standing in the middle of the tee, staring down the fairway, with his arms folded across his chest. He appeared to be in deep thought. A mild southeast breeze had suddenly kicked up and was blowing back up the fairway, between the tall stands of pine trees that lined both sides of the tee, out to the water hazard that bordered the right side of the fairway and crossed back in front of the green, some 380 yards away. The more experienced spectators could sense that Jeff was debating whether or not to hit his driver.

The long-driving Belcamp was the last to play his approach shot in the group up ahead. His lengthy tee shot had left him only an 80- or 90-yard wedge shot to the green. Jeff continued to watch intently as Gene hit what appeared to be a three-quarter approach shot, launching the ball toward the gallery-encircled target on a relatively low trajectory, under the breeze. The well-played shot hit into the large swale in the center of the green and appeared to curl down the slope, close to the left-rear pin placement. It looked as though Belcamp's aggressive play was about to be rewarded with a birdie.

Jeff turned and walked back between the tee markers and looked over to Sand Wedge who by this time had removed the bag from his shoulder, and was holding it upright by the tee marker, firmly with his right hand. The same cigarette was still between his lips, a nearly one inch ash beginning to curl down as he looked intently into his player's eyes. The caddie still had the 1-iron in his left hand, holding the hosel of the club comfortably between his thumb and index finger. The butt end of the club's black leather grip lightly rested on the smooth, closely-mown Bermuda tee grass. It was clear that Sand Wedge thought that was the club for the shot.

"Let's hit driver," Jeff said, walking a step or two closer to Sand Wedge and reaching into the top section of the bag where the metal "woods" are carried. He tugged off the driver head cover, actually a miniature fur elephant with a "The Hot One" tag hanging from the trunk, pulled out the driver, and returned to the middle of the tee. Flexing his right knee Jeff reached down to tee up his ball. Sand Wedge dutifully put the 1-iron back into the bag, and said "That be the one," insincerely giving affirmation to Jeff's election to hit the driver. "Now make a good swing."

Jeff's hands instinctively assumed their customary overlap grip on the driver and he settled into his standard series of steps, fidgets, waggles and mannerisms that had, more or less, comprised his pre-shot routine since he had started playing the game at age 10, under the sometimes domineering tutelage of his father. He blocked from his mind any memory of the pull-hook he had hit with the driver from this tee yesterday.

At least he tried to. But as Jeff made his downswing to the ball, he felt his right shoulder go past his chin slightly, and he knew from experience that the tee shot was going to start out left of the target, and probably hook some more from there. As nearly always, his instincts accurately foretold the shot's result. The drive, although struck fairly solidly, was left from the start, and, after an agonizingly long, leftward curving flight, finally came down, bounding wildly over the knoll that defined the extreme left side of the fairway. The tee marshall, who had anxiously stepped forward as he watched the flight of Jeff's ball, waved his "Quiet Please" placard frantically, from an upright position, down to the left, attempting to communicate to the forecaddies that Jeff's drive had been hit far left of the fairway, toward the out of bounds.

As Jeff was disconsolately replacing the driver in the bag, Trent said, "You better hit a provisional. I think they're trying to tell us it's out."

That said, Trent began grinding on his own tee shot, selecting a 2-iron and hitting a conservative, low, cut shot into the breeze. His tee ball came to rest safely on the right side of the fairway, leaving him a relatively easy approach shot of approximately 160 yards.

Just as Jeff was preparing to play his provisional ball, this time with the 1-iron, the forecaddie came running excitedly into the middle of the fairway, gesturing emphatically the "safe" sign, like a baseball umpire. The signal meant that Jeff's first ball had somehow stayed in bounds and was in play. Jeff smiled in quiet relief and closed his eyes for a moment in prayer-like meditation. Also relieved, Sand Wedge sighed audibly, eagerly reaching out to Jeff to retrieve the 1-iron and replace it in the bag. Seeing Jeff's good fortune, several people in the gallery clapped their hands approvingly, glad to see one of their favorite players get a good break, preserving, at least for the moment, what appeared to be destined to be a good round.

As Jeff walked down the gentle incline fronting the fourth tee, off to his right he heard a particular voice from the gallery moving with him: "I guess all the luck doesn't have to be bad."

He looked eagerly in the direction of the voice, his eyes instantly finding the unmistakable visage of Sandy Jackson. The wild combination of emotions Jeff had roller-coastered through in the last couple of minutes welled up as he strode in Sandy's direction. He realized that he was delighted, much more so than he expected he would be, to see Sandy again. It had been almost a year.

"Here's looking at you, kid" he said softly as he approached the gallery rope Sandy was standing behind, off alone. Jeff often greeted Sandy this way, and despite the unusualness of the situation, or maybe because of it, he felt some old emotions stirring, as he beheld his former self-proclaimed "number one fan."

Sensing that now was definitely not the time for any sort of reunion, Sandy looked away from Jeff's eyes and said, "Will you for

God's sake start listening a little more to Sand Wedge? You just play, and let him think. He told me, '65 be the number.' Now go make him a prophet."

Jeff found himself speechless in response to Sandy's admonishment. Capable only of another smile and a thankful nod, he strode back into the fairway, crossing over to the left rough, and continuing along, over and beyond the distant knoll, to see where the wayward tee shot had come to rest.

"Why didn't you tell me Sandy was here?" Jeff challenged Sand Wedge as they continued along.

"Why didn't you hit the muthah-fuckin' 1-iron?" the caddie retorted in a heated whisper. "Look at that piss-ant tee shot Blalock hit, and he out there with nothin' more than a damn 7-iron. You hit that damn driver again and we over here needin' a muthah-fuckin' steam shovel... My man," Sand Wedge continued, "just forgets about Sandy and leaves the driver in the bag when I says to. Just play golf and we can make some damn money 'round this place."

Although not a product of much formal education, Sand Wedge was well aware of how much his 10 to 15 percent caddie share of the million dollar plus first prize would add up to, if his player could just somehow play to his full potential for the entire 72 holes.

Jeff silently conceded that Sand Wedge was right, and recognized the extreme need to screw his game-face back on, real tight.

"What have we got from here?" Jeff asked when they reached the point where the forecaddie was indicating Jeff's ball had come to rest. After checking the ball's lie, which appeared to be a "flier," Sand Wedge pulled his copy of the book from the pocket of his caddie bib and was trying to ascertain the point on the fourth hole diagram which corresponded to where Jeff's ball was. Having also slipped the book from his rear pocket, Jeff too was trying to locate his position. After a moment they concluded that the book didn't include any reference to where they were. Jeff had hit it off the map. The shot had been that bad. Putting the book back in his bib pocket, Sand Wedge trotted back up the knoll to its crest, so he could get a feel for how far away the green was. The approach would be a blind one, over the knoll, across the water hazard to the firm, narrow green that was not designed to accept either the length or direction of shot Jeff had left himself. After some fairly hectic computations, Sand Wedge said "I got 177 to the middle, 168 to the far edge of the hazard and we got water in front and all along the left side. You don't even think about playin' toward the pin."

"You got it, Sand Wedge," Jeff responded. "What do you like?"

"Smooth six," Sand Wedge advised. "Worst thing that can happen is we go into the bunker over the right side."

Jeff reached for the 6-iron.

Back at the first tee, the 9:30 threesome had just been cleared to play away.

Chapter 7

The rest of the morning produced the predictable wide variety of heroics, foibles and "who'd a thunk it" kinds of developments that inevitably punctuate Thursday's first-round action in a Major golf championship. Due to the ideal weather conditions, a number of good rounds were unfolding, despite the toughening of the already tough Stadium Course layout Commissioner Watterson had mandated, following last year's -22 winning performance by Jason Knox (69-65-65-67).

The Commissioner believed strongly that even-par, "level," as the British announcers termed it, should be a credible standard in Major championship competition. He had advised the Tour agronomy and field staffs to condition and set up the Stadium Course to offer the players a fair, but severe test of their skills. Accordingly, the TPC's fairways and greens had been rolled and double-cut, lending a green, checkerboard effect to the course, particularly when viewed from the Met Life blimp that chugged along high overhead in the north Florida sky, transmitting glamour shots for the TV coverage that was set to come on the air at noon. Indeed, all parts of the layout had been manicured to a firm, fast and demanding condition, and the thick Bermuda roughs and fringes around the greens had been allowed to become dense and matted. The course was poised to punish errant driving, or tentative putting, and exact a heavy toll for approach shots that missed the green.

Apparently Skip Florine didn't appreciate how tough they had made the Stadium Course play. Emerging from the official scorer's tent after signing his card, he was smiling, joking and apprising anybody interested just how smoothly his 66 had gone. His playing partners, George Fallon and Neil O'Leary had not shared his good fortune, scoring 76 and 78 respectively. They had left Skip to his celebrant antics, and were marching wordlessly along, in the direction of the locker room, and probably a couple of beers. It was clear from O'Leary's body language as he trudged by that he was particularly frustrated. *Florida Times Union* golf writer Tom Schuyler intercepted Fallon and O'Leary about half way between the locker room and the media center, where Schuyler was headed for the upcoming interview with the early first-round leader. In passing, Schuyler asked O'Leary how he liked the way the course had been set up for this year's event. Turning, and making a sweeping gesture with his right arm, as if to emphasize his reference to the entire TPC layout, O'Leary said "You know, what they went and done here?... They ruint a perfectly good swamp." It being clear to Schuyler that O'Leary was not in a mood for further conversation, the writer allowed the comment to drop without any follow up, and continued on toward the media center. Jake Morrison, the Tour's press relations manager spotted Skip and needed a quick word with him. By this time Skip was standing alongside the cart path leading from the 18th green back up to the clubhouse. The player appeared to be explaining, to an admiring, halter-top clad young lady some apparently humorous aspect of his recently-concluded round:

"So, my playing partners, George and Neil don't know what to say. What do you say to somebody that dumb? This guy in the gallery down by nine tee is swearing and arguing with this really nice and kind looking older lady, that George is really a football player, 'cause he's wearing a yellow cap and a green shirt with big ol' Green Bay Packers logos on 'em. So I go up to the guy, and say, 'Sir, the lady's right; he's not a football player. Old George over there is a professional golfer; he just wears clothes that have football team logos on them, you know. He's like a model for NFL logo clothes, understand?'"

Spilling part of the beer she was sipping on her Florida Gators short shorts as she broke up laughing at Skip's story, the girl exclaimed delightedly, "I don't believe it; must have been some FSU dork!"

"Mighta been," Skip agreed, noting that the girl really was attractive. "Hey, maybe I'll see ya later on, down to the Homestead."

"Maybe so," the girl replied. "But here, autograph my shoulder, I forgot my note pad." She handed skip a black, magic marker type pen, continuing to giggle, and sip beer from a Players Championship souvenir cup as she offered up her body for his signature.

Skip laughingly obliged his newly-found fan, noting in the process how nicely shaped and golden-tanned the girl's shoulder was.

Watching the tomfoolery escalate to what looked like could become inappropriate levels, Morrison decided it was high time to get Skip's attention. Jake, like virtually everybody else in golf, liked Skip, but knew his tendency to get a little too carried away in the carnival-like off-course atmosphere of a PGA Tour event.

"Hey Skip," Jake said, reaching out to grasp the player's shoulder and speaking in a fairly assertive tone of voice. "Good round man, hey listen, they'd like to hear about it in the press tent. You're at the top of the board, you know."

Jake's remarks restored Skip's focus to where he was and what he had just done, that being take the early first-round lead in the Players Championship. He winked a "good bye" to the girl and turned to Jake, asking for instructions on where he should go and when. Skip had never been the leader at the Players before. He really didn't know what to do. Pointing to the media center off to the left of the 10th tee, Jake said, "There and now." There was a definite bounce in Skip's step as he moved along toward his date with the press.

As Skip hustled toward the media center, the girl was showing off her autographed shoulder, and wondering where she needed to go to get another beer.

It was high noon at the Players, and things were happening.

CHAPTER 8

As Skip entered the spacious, state-of-the-art media center the Tour had recently added to the sprawling TPC complex, as part of its continuing efforts to elevate the Players Championship to Major golf championship status, he noticed that he had goose bumps. They were due not only to the meat-locker level of the facility's air conditioning, that had been set in anticipation of warmer afternoon temperatures which had not yet materialized, but to the player's sense of excitement as well. Twenty-four year old Skip Florine was, at least for the moment, the center of the golf world's attention. This time two years ago he had been knocking around the Q-School, the Tour's annual torture-test tournament, for players seeking to gain, or regain, Tour eligibility. Skip also had first hand experience with the mini tours, minor league professional golf circuits which had sprung up in Florida and the Carolinas. He had spent many expectant, sometimes desperate weeks and months competing there, as he pursued his dream of playing big-time tournament golf for a living, trying to keep from having to take a day job.

Lucy Tomkins, another member of the Tour's communications staff noticed Skip coming through the doorway, and gestured for him to make his way up to the interview dais, at the front of the room. Members of the working press were either seated at, standing by or milling about their closed circuit TV monitor-equipped work stations. The dominant sounds in the facility came from the nondescript buzz of several conversations going on among the sportswriters and other media types clustered here and there, and the Diamondvision television screen which dominated the left side of the room. The huge TV was tuned to the opening moments of ESPN's early first-round coverage, scheduled for noon to 2 p.m. Additionally, modems hummed and faxes wailed, as the media's initial impressions of what was happening at the Players were transmitted throughout the state, across the nation and around the world. The clickety-clack typewriter press room sounds of yesteryear were nowhere to be heard.

Once Skip was seated and had poured himself a tall cup of Gatorade, Lucy introduced him to the assembled press, many of whom had moved to the seating arrangement located at the front of the room, facing the dais. Lucie announced Skip's hole-by-hole scores and first-round total of 66. In doing so, Lucy read from a photocopy of his scorecard she had been provided by central scoring.

After Lucy had concluded "4-2-4, for a first-round total of 66," Skip took a sip from the Gatorade cup, looked out at his interrogators while adjusting his Top-Flite visor, and said, in the mock country boy dialect he often employed to disguise his own anxiety, "Golly gee, guys... and gals, this is fun. What do you want to know?"

Local writer Tom Schuyler offered the standard opening question: "Great round, Skip, could you tell us a little bit about how it went?"

In response, Skip began to recount each of the 66 strokes that had made up his championship-leading first round. The litany lasted for several minutes, as Skip methodically described the strategies he had employed, the shots he had hit and the results he had obtained on each of the 18 holes. His recall was remarkably detailed, indicating the level of concentration and focus a successful professional golfer devotes to his craft. He described his golf shots in much the way Norman Rockwell might have described the shapes and colors involved in his paintings.

Remembering Neil O'Leary's recent condemnation of the course set up when he had passed by him near the clubhouse, Schuyler followed by asking Florine his impressions of the toughened up Stadium Course.

"I like it," Skip responded. "It's different, you know, 'target golf' on every shot. But the conditioning is perfect, and I'm looking forward to the rest of the week. Just hope the weather stays good, 'cause I've heard this place becomes a real bear when the wind comes up. Got away with hittin' a little ol' 9-iron at seventeen," he continued, referring to the Stadium Course's signature hole, the island-green 17th. "But if the wind comes up and we're hittin' 5's and 6's there on Sunday... could be a different story. You know, when you got it going, you start thinking about that hole at about the 14th, and it don't get any easier from there."

Changing the subject abruptly from Skip's score and his impressions of the golf course, Ned Daily of the *Baltimore Post* asked Skip if he had heard of the new world tour proposal announced yesterday, and if so, what he thought of it.

The question caught Skip off-guard and he turned to Lucy, squinting slightly and shaking his head, hoping to get some direction regarding a response. Lucy leaned over and whispered that the Tour had made no response to the world tour proposal, pending the player meeting scheduled for this evening. Skip recalled for a moment the brief exchange about the meeting he had earlier this morning with Jeff Taylor. He was beginning to see that something big was brewing, but he certainly didn't want to say much of anything until he knew some more about the issues. He'd much rather talk golf.

"I don't know what that's all about," Skip eventually replied. "I think there's a player meeting tonight to talk about it. Until after that, I really don't have any comments to make."

Returning to safer ground, another reporter asked Skip what kind of score he thought it would take to win on Sunday afternoon.

"Gee, I don't know," Skip responded. "It was pretty calm out there this morning, but like I said, if there's wind or they let the greens get firmer, you're going to see some funny zip codes on the scorecards." He knew, for example, that even today, his playing partner, Neil O'Leary, had finished 7-3-7 in posting his ignominious 78. Pausing for a moment and tugging his visor around to a slightly-cockeyed position, while he continued to think about how the weekend might unfold, Skip concluded his answer saying "Tell ya what, I'd take 10-under right now if they'd give it to me, and not even show up. I think that'll be a good number come Sunday afternoon."

The room went quiet, except for the Diamondvision continuing to play along in the background. Mary asked whether there were any more questions for Skip. There were none; so she thanked everyone and wished Skip good luck for the rest of the championship. The press began to filter back to their work stations, returning their attention to their closed-circuit monitors or otherwise continuing to go about their media center routine.

His interest piqued by the reporter's world tour question, Skip asked Lucy "What's the deal with this world tour stuff anyway?"

"Like I said," Lucy answered, "it's on the agenda for the meeting tonight, and I expect the Commissioner will explain his initial reactions, and try to find out what you guys think."

Realizing this was not a subject to be pursued with Lucy, Skip got up from his seat on the dais and said "What I think is that I'm hungry. Where's Commissioner's hospitality during the tournament, same place?"

"Yes," Lucy confirmed, "top floor of the clubhouse."

Skip thanked her for her help and stepped down from the dais, on his way to the clubhouse and some lunch. The 66 had aroused his appetite. And speaking of appetites, he was thinking that he might run back into the girl with the autographed shoulder, somewhere along the way.

CHAPTER 9

After a very promising start followed by the near disaster at the fourth, Jeff's first round at the Players had settled down into workman-like consistency. After escaping the fourth with a bogey, which he knew could have been far worse, he had recorded an uninterrupted series of pars, except for a birdie-4 on the 11th where, after a particularly long and straight drive he had gotten his 3-iron second shot to pin-high position in the right-side bunker, and gotten up and down from there.

Just about the time Skip began recounting his heroics to the media, Jeff stood on the 16th tee, watching Trent Blalock prepare to drive. Like he had been at the fourth, Jeff was 3-under for the day, now, through the 15th. Jeff's name was no longer atop the leader board, but he knew he was still squarely in the hunt. Trent had the honor at the 16th due to his birdie-3 at the par-4 15th. But overall he was having a difficult time, as indicated by the black "7" on Tommy Lawson's scoreboard. It displayed the unpleasant truth for all to see, that Trent was 7-over-par. Even after the birdie at 15, he would have to par the rest of the holes for an embarrassing 79.

Even so, the birdie on the previous hole had apparently buoyed Trent's resolve, and he struck a very solid drive down the middle of the fairway, drawing the ball perfectly toward the left side, around the corner of the dog leg and setting up a very good angle from which to play his second shot. The 16th is a short par-5 and is vulnerable to eagles and birdies if the tee shot is properly placed, as Trent had just done. He acknowledged the appreciative applause of the gallery clustered around the tee with a somewhat lethargic tip to his Maxfli visor as he replaced his driver in the bag. Trent wore the bedraggled expression of an athlete experiencing a tough day, and knew it would take a minor miracle for him to make tomorrow's cut and qualify for a chance at a really good payday on Sunday.

Standing next to Sand Wedge on the right side of the tee after Trent's drive, Jeff was again apparently in the throes of indecision regarding what club he should hit. The hole called for a draw, a right to left curving tee shot such as Trent had just executed. Jeff's more comfortable shot with the driver was a fade, a shot curving slightly from left to right. The dilemma was that such a tee shot would not fit the dog leg left 16th, and would, in all probability run through the fairway, into a stand of palm trees that had been placed there for the expressed purpose of penalizing such a drive. Jeff could hit right-to-left draws with his driver on occasion, but his tendency when attempting to do so was to flatten his swing too much and get too quick, often producing an ugly, duck hook, rather than the long-distance, picturesque draw that was intended. The entire left side of the 16th being bordered by a water hazard and dense woods, there was no room for a hook of any kind.

In a way, the 16th was a microcosm of the type of challenge nearly every hole at the Stadium Course offered. It tempted the player with great rewards, in this case a relatively short and unobstructed opportunity to reach the par-5 green in two, in exchange for a bold and well-placed drive. But at the same time the hole provided severe penalties for the aggressive player who misfired.

After weighing the options and coming to no clear cut conclusions, Jeff decided to turn the matter over to Sand Wedge. Ever since his double salvation at the fourth, where his badly hooked drive had somehow stayed in bounds, and Sandy Jackson had reappeared in his life, with words of wisdom and encouragement no less, Jeff had been repeating to himself, whenever faced with any kind of problematical situation, "Sandy's right, play the shots, let Sand Wedge do the thinking."

Applying the rediscovered lesson once again, "What do you think?" Jeff asked his caddie, fully prepared to hit whatever club Sand Wedge advised.

"I like 3-wood," Sand Wedge answered matter-of-factly, withdrawing the club from its place alongside the driver in the top compartment of the golf bag he had positioned upright at his feet. "You can pinch this one down and turn it all right. Length's not no problem here. Just need to be on the left side. Just make a good swing, and stay behind it."

Jeff accepted the 3-wood and moved over to the left side of the tee. He teed the ball very low and settled into his pre-shot routine. He was committed to what he knew was a high percentage and relatively simple shot. The swing was graceful and seemingly effortless. The club head impacted the ball squarely sending it off like a laser, on a medium-low trajectory, rising to its apex over the middle of the fairway and drawing slightly to the left as it descended, bouncing and rolling into very good position, only 15 yards or so behind where Trent had hit his ball with the driver. The now sizable gallery applauded its approval of Jeff's tee shot as he smilingly returned the 3-wood to Sand Wedge, nodding his appreciation for the gallery's support.

"I play, you think," Jeff said quietly, looking into the caddie's eyes directly for a moment. "I think she may have something there."

"You bet she do," Sand Wedge agreed, and the two of them headed on down the fairway, eager to evaluate whether the well-placed tee shot would present a good opportunity to improve their position in the battle against par.

Jeff's lie in the fairway behind Trent's ball was perfect. Consulting the book, which this time plainly showed the ball's position in the left center of the fairway, Jeff and Sand Wedge figured 221 yards to the opening at the front left of the green, and 236 to the left-center pin position. Jeff was inclined to hit another 3-wood, but Sand Wedge counseled him again to take a more conservative approach.

"I like 1-iron," Sand Wedge said. "Play it low, to the left front, where it hard; it'll bounce right up and release to the pin. Worst you can do is wind up a little short, with a straight little chip, on ups the hill... maybe three, easy four. Lose that 3-wood a little right," Sand Wedge continued, in deference to the water hazard that bordered the right side and approach to the green, "and I be hollering Mayday and we be droppin' a new ball and addin' another shot...Prob'ly come away with six."

Feeling rejuvenated, with a newly found sense of confidence, Jeff's first instinct was to overrule his caddie. The perfect lie of the ball had given him a vivid mental image of a cut 3-wood shot, a type of shot he was almost always comfortable with. In his mind he could envision the shot winding up in the center of the green, leaving him a good chance to duplicate the eagle-3 he had scored at the second. But he caught himself this time and decided to reconsider, remembering again the lesson he had confirmed to Sand Wedge just five minutes earlier, as they were leaving the tee.

"OK," Jeff said. "I play and you think. Hand me the 1-iron, if you please."

Although Jeff attempted the shot Sand Wedge had described, he wasn't as committed to it as he had been to the drive, and he hit the ball a little thin, picking it off the turf, rather than hitting down and through it. Nevertheless, even with the less than perfect execution, the Titleist wound up only about 10 yards short of the green, in very playable position. The worst had happened, but like Sand Wedge had thought and said, it hadn't turned out that bad at all, leaving Jeff a fairly straight uphill chip of around 75 feet. As he strode toward the green, Jeff felt the beginnings of a competitive high building within him. The right juices were flowing through him now and he felt totally at peace with himself, and in love with what he was doing.

Having pulled from the bag the pitching wedge he would use for the chip shot, Jeff told Sand Wedge that he wanted him to tend the flag stick. As the caddie laid the golf bag down and stepped toward the green, Jeff said "Now stay awake up there. I'm going to chip this mother in." As he hustled toward the pin, Sand Wedge luxuriated in how good it felt to have his player saying positive things and expressing confidence again. To Sand Wedge golf was really very simple: If you think you can do it, you can; and if you think you can't do it, you can't. He was liking the way his man was thinking.

Jeff's confidence and inner peace about the shot only grew as he brushed the close-clipped Bermuda grass with his customary three practice strokes. Playing the ball back in his stance toward his right shoe, to take some loft off of the wedge and produce a low, running shot, Jeff knew by the sound at impact that he had caught the ball perfectly on the club face, bumping it low, across the fringe, hitting the green at the precise spot he had selected when lining up the chip moments before. Sand Wedge pulled the pin and watched along with everyone else surrounding the green as the ball tracked straight toward the hole. Jeff had followed through the shot and was holding a classic pose, his hands still on the grip and the club head at about waist level. The shot looked good all the way, and as the ball disappeared into the hole, Jeff finished the follow through of the club forcefully, as if he had taken a full swing, to emphasize his jubilation over his second eagle-3 of the day. Another thunderclap cheer erupted from the gallery.

All of a sudden, Jeff was 5-under-par and only one shot out of the early lead. As they say, the game was on. The confidence and purpose in Jeff's stride as he moved along toward the treacherous island-green 17th were obvious. Sand Wedge had to break into a semi-trot, clubs clanking in the bag, just to keep up.

Chapter 10

"Congratulations, stranger," Lucy whispered excitedly, as Jeff settled into his seat at the media center, also pouring himself, as Skip had, a large cup of Gatorade. The eagerness of her greeting betrayed her special feelings about Jeff as a player, and the pleasure Lucy and nearly everybody else in golf was feeling in seeing him again playing well in a significant, if not Major golf championship. The seating area in front of the dais was packed, despite the fact that it was still early in the first round, and problematical whether Jeff would still be the championship leader at day's end.

"Ladies and gentlemen," Lucy began, "I am delighted to present the first-round leader in the clubhouse of the Players Championship, Jeff Taylor." Looking down to her photocopy of his card, she continued, "Jeff's scores were 4-3-2-5-4-4-4-3-5, out in 34; 4-4-4-3-4-4-3-2-3, in in 31, for a first-round score of 65, 7-under-par. Questions, please."

The usual "how did the round go" question was asked first and Jeff obliged with the standard shot-by-shot review for the next few minutes. He concluded by saying "I started out the day asking my caddie how I could shoot 65. Well, by golly, he told me and we did it. I couldn't be more pleased. This is my favorite tournament on Tour and this is my favorite seat at this tournament. I'd love to be sitting here chatting with you guys, and gals, on Sunday."

"Why is this your favorite tournament," a reporter near the front of the group asked, following up on the comment Jeff had just volunteered.

Kicking himself mentally for having made the comment in the first place, since it invited controversy, Jeff attempted to construct a tactful response. "I guess it's my favorite… among many, many others I enjoy very much, I might add… for both personal and professional reasons," Jeff began. I've been playing here ever since they brought the Tournament Players Championship to Ponte Vedra in 1977. And I lived here in the area, right up in Atlantic Beach for almost 10 years. So naturally, I've made a lot of good friends among the volunteers and the rest of the community, and I look forward to seeing a lot of those folks again each year. And I think the golf course has matured into one of the best we play on Tour each year, certainly one of the best-conditioned. And, of course, the event is special since it's the players' own event. And I'll tell you what, it's a favorite to me particularly this year 'cause I could ride that champion's exemption all the way to the senior tour." Jeff's latter comments were in reference to the 10-year exemption that came with winning the Players. If he had that, his anxious search for a bridge to the senior Tour would be ended.

"So I take it," local writer Tom Schuyler interjected, "that you would like to see the Players recognized as the 'fifth Major.'"

"Sure, I would like to see that," Jeff responded. "But as we all know, 'Major' status is determined by a consensus, not by any one individual or institution, and most certainly not by me."

Shifting the focus of the interview back to the competition at hand, David Thoms of the *Indianapolis News* asked whether Jeff's round had any particular turning point.

"Two big ones," Jeff responded. "One on four and the other on 16. On four, after I jerked the tee shot left over the knoll," (as he had explained in the earlier shot-by-shot description), "I got some very sound advice from an old friend, to just play the shots and let Sand Wedge do the thinking. And then on sixteen I hit the great chip to make eagle and I started to feel really positive and confident. When you feel yourself getting comfortable with those kinds of thoughts, you kind of expect to finish birdie-birdie, and I did. Whatever, I'm just asking my man for a club and then swinging it. I feel more confident about my game than I have for years. Can't wait for tomorrow."

Following up, Thoms asked Jeff what it would mean at this stage of his career to win again.

Jeff sighed audibly upon hearing the question, and took a swig from the cup of Gatorade as he attempted to think through an appropriate response to the question that cut to the quick of the career crisis he was struggling within.

"I'll tell you," he finally said. "It sure would make believing wholeheartedly in myself a lot easier, and that's the key to success in this game, and in life itself, I guess. But tempting as that question is, it's really not relevant to this point in time. I'm happy with what happened out there today and I'm looking forward to going out there and doing it again tomorrow."

"What about the exemption?" another reporter called out. "How important is that to you?" It was obvious the reporters were not inclined to let Jeff brush aside the anxieties they knew must lay somewhere within him, as his competitive fortunes seemed to be languishing in mid-life crisis mediocrity.

Jeff sighed again, appreciating the depth of the question being asked. This time he decided to take it head on. "So you're asking how important a 10-year exemption is to a 43-year old player who hasn't made the top 125 for three years?" he began, pausing again to think further after he had restated the probing question.

"It's obviously very, very important to me at this stage of my career. You know, I was talking a while back with a lawyer friend of mine and the subject of my expiring exempt status came up. The way I explained it to him was that it would be like lawyers who didn't win a big case during the year having to retake the Bar exam to continue practicing law. He said that would be tough, and I assured him that it is. But on the other hand, that's the way it needs to be out here. Eligibility on Tour needs to be linked to proven, and reasonably current competitive ability. Very simply, world-class athletic competition needs to be based on 'survival of the fittest.' So my mission is simple: prove that I'm still one of the fittest. Does the exemption and my need for it produce more personal tension? Of course. Does it produce more anxiety? Only if I let it. A friend of mine helped me understand recently that things are pretty much as we see them. We can appreciate and draw strength from the positives we perceive in a situation, or we can focus on the negatives and become paralyzed with anxiety in the process. Success flows from what I call concentration, fixing your goals in your mind's eye, and blocking out any negative or defeatist thoughts... So boys... and girls... I'm just concentratin' my butt off these days, and lovin' every minute of it."

Jeff paused for a moment, looking out at the reporters who were listening intently to what he was saying. He decided to continue his train of thought. "And also, I'm very fortunate to have had Johnny Simpson, you may know him as 'Sand Wedge,' working as my caddie for the last 15 years. He has a simple philosophy about golf that applies to this championship, to the 10-year exemption, to everything in life really: 'If you believe you can do it, you can; if you don't believe you can do it, you can't. It's just a matter of what you can believe in.' Personally, I believe I can win this championship, and that's what I intend to do."

The philosophical nature of Jeff's rambling response seemed to blunt the rapid-fire nature of the reporters' questions up to that point. Earlier, many of them had taken several notes while he spoke. But now, most simply listened quietly, apparently taken somewhat aback by the depth and conviction of Jeff's remarks. It was as if the group collectively realized that it had forced its way into the player's innermost thoughts, and many of the interlopers seemed to feel uncomfortable there.

"Are you going to the player meeting tonight?" Ned Daily finally asked, changing the direction of the interview and continuing his preoccupation with the world tour story. "And do you think it's distracting for the Commissioner to schedule these meetings in the middle of a tournament?"

Jeff thought twice about responding to what sounded like a dangerous invitation into an essentially political matter, but decided to go ahead and answer.

"If there's any distraction involved," Jeff said, "in my opinion it's because of the timing of the announcement, not the timing of our meeting. I'm sure the Commissioner would rather not be having a player meeting between the first and second rounds of the Players, but I don't see where we have any real choice. Mr. Shumitami's the one who set up the time frame, I'd be interested to know how much he worried about distracting anybody."

"I take it from that that you're against the world tour," Daily continued.

"That remains to be seen," Jeff responded coolly, seeing that he was being invited out onto a very weak branch. "Personally, I don't see any need for a world tour because I think, in essence, we already have one. To me that's what this championship, the Majors, the Ryder and President's Cups and the World Cup are. Taken together those are a world tour and we as players have more than enough opportunity every year to compete head-to-head, on a soundly structured basis that keeps control of the game vested in us, the athletes. I like it that way and I think it has served the fans and everybody else interested in our game very well. But we'll see," Jeff continued, sensing that he had already said too much. "I really don't know exactly what's being proposed and I want to learn some more and hear what Commissioner Watterson has to say tonight. If a world tour is presented in a way that makes sense, hey, everybody has to move forward."

"Why do you think Norm Thompson is so in favor of it?" another reporter from the back of the room called out, failing to mention his name or publication.

"You'll have to ask him," Jeff quickly responded, seeing that this issue could easily begin to eclipse the news value of his or anybody else's 65.

"Any more questions about Jeff's round," Lucy interjected, seeking to steer the interview back toward its intended purpose, discussion of the championship and the day's play.

Her question producing a momentary silence, she took immediate advantage of the opportunity to gracefully end the interview, which showed signs of getting out of hand, by thanking Jeff for his time and wishing him good luck in tomorrow's round. The reporters seemed to accept the closure and began filtering back into the work area of the media center.

"Thanks," Jeff said. "I hope I didn't go too far with that last answer, but I couldn't resist. The whole deal here is control of the game. And I, for one, know who I'm going to back in that race."

"I thought you expressed yourself very well," Lucy responded. "It'll be interesting to see the spin Mr. Thompson puts on things if he's in that chair later this afternoon."

"How's he playing?" Jeff asked as he rose, preparing to leave.

He knew Sand Wedge was waiting for him just outside the media center door.

"Let's see," Lucy said turning to the keypad and computer monitor she had at her work station alongside the interview dais. Clicking a few keys to find the proper information, she said "OK, he's off one at 1:32 and let's see... they've finished one and he is... one over, must have bogeyed."

"Hmmm," Jeff said, surprised to see Thompson off to an apparently shaky start. "Tough course. I gotta go Lucy, Sand Wedge's waiting for me at the door."

"OK, Jeff, play well," Lucy said as Jeff rose and began to make his way for the door, stopping every few steps to shake hands and exchange a few words with the many friends and admirers an athlete has when things are going well.

Jeff located Sand Wedge outside the media center door, holding court with his own collection of youthful interrogators. "You damn right I tells him what to hit," Jeff overheard his caddie telling a couple of souvenir seekers, as he approached from behind.

"Come on Sand Wedge," Jeff called. "Let's get on up to the clubhouse. I'm starved."

Sand Wedge picked up the bag, slinging it across his well worn shoulder, and the two of them began the walk back up to the clubhouse. It was going to take them a while to get there. It seemed like everybody who saw the two coming wanted a handshake, an autograph or at least the chance to wish Jeff well. His stomach was growling, but he was loving it just the same. The walk back from the golf course was just like he had hoped it would be earlier this morning.

When they got to the clubhouse, Jeff told Sand Wedge to go ahead and put the clubs away. Since he played late tomorrow, he wasn't going to practice this afternoon, leaving well enough alone in terms of his golf swing, and allowing himself to savor the eagle-birdie-birdie finish for a few hours.

"What about the 5-iron?" Sand Wedge asked.

"What about it?" Jeff responded. All he remembered at the moment was that he had used the five to "stake" the approach shot at the 18th, setting up his final birdie, and capping the 65.

"You said you wanted it regripped. Said it have too much tape 'neath the grip," Sand Wedge reminded him.

"Oh, that's right," Jeff acknowledged, remembering now that he had told Sand Wedge to have the club regripped as they were walking from the practice range to the first tee earlier that morning.

"Don't touch it," Jeff said, waving farewell as he entered the clubhouse door. "It's perfect. See ya by the green at 12:30."

As he made his way toward Commissioner's Hospitality, Jeff was wondering if Sandy might be up there.

CHAPTER 11

Commissioner's Hospitality, where the players, their families and select PGA Tour-invited VIP's dined and drank during the Players Championship would receive five stars if it were to be rated by the Triple A. In many ways it symbolized just how far the profession of competing in golf tournaments for a living had come, since the "barnstorming" days of the 20's and 30's. In those days the pros were prohibited from even entering the clubhouse, their brand of golf, i.e., playing for prize money, considered by many as the world's second oldest profession.

Now, in utter and complete contrast to the past, at Commissioner's Hospitality, on the top floor of the TPC clubhouse, the players and their guests could dine on tenderloin and sip the finest wine. Or they could drink bottled water and munch on fresh fruits and vegetables, as many of the players in fact did, in keeping with their hyper-competitive professional environment.

When it came to eating and drinking, Jeff was from the "old school." He didn't now and never had abused his body to any great extent, but he wasn't one to shy away from a cheeseburger, or an ice-cold bottle of Michelob. In fact, until Joe Phillips had resurrected his Wilson staff contract last year, Jeff had spent several recent seasons as a member of Team Michelob, using the huge, black and gold Michelob golf bag on Tour, and supporting the brand enthusiastically at any number of corporate outings and related functions. Sand Wedge had been very much against going back with Wilson, because, he said, it would be better to keep all of Jeff's equipment options open. Jeff was pretty sure he knew Sand Wedge's real reason for wanting him to stay with Michelob.

As he entered the aromatic dining and hospitality area, showing his player credential money clip to the elderly security guard at the door, Jeff was in the mood for a drink and walked directly to the bar on the far side of the room. Just as he said "A Michelob please," flashing his patented grin to his friend and TPC bartender Freddy Blake, Jeff felt a firm but friendly grip being applied to his left shoulder. He turned around expectantly to the smiling face of Sid Watterson.

"Great playing Jeff," the Commissioner enthused. "I saw you save par from the bunker on one through my office window, and I sensed you were off to the races."

"Well... Commissioner, thank you," Jeff said, as he accepted the distinctive amber Michelob bottle which Freddy had wrapped neatly in a Players Championship napkin.

"Great round man," Freddy had whispered as he handed Jeff the bottle.

"You got a minute?" Sid continued, as Jeff took a healthy pull at the overdue beer. "I wanted to get your take on the Shumitami deal, and talk over some ideas we've got for the meeting tonight."

Although he really didn't feel like grinding over anything very serious at the moment, Jeff realized that duty called, and, after hurriedly looking about the room for familiar faces, hoping to see one in particular, he said, "Sure Sid, where do you want to go?"

"Over here," the Commissioner said, gesturing to a table in the corner by the massive window overlooking the practice green. As he and Sid approached the table the Commissioner had pointed out, Jeff noticed that two familiar looking members of Sid's senior staff were already seated there, talking and jotting things down on long, yellow note pads. They seemed very busy.

Arriving at the table, Commissioner Watterson began to introduce Jeff to Nick Standly and Mary Goldblume, not knowing for sure whether Jeff had ever met them before. Nick and Mary looked up, and began to rise, each offering a hand in greeting.

"Sit down you two," Jeff said quickly, pre-empting the awkward formalities. "Good to see you again Nick... and Mary," he continued, pausing to look directly into the eyes of each of them individually as he said each name. "Keeping everything under control, and Sid toeing the line are you?"

Nick and Mary laughed nervously and nodded, going along with Jeff's friendly chide toward their boss. Jeff's politeness and easy familiarity visibly relaxed each of them. It was apparent why Jeff's personality and charm had combined over the years to make him a favorite in nearly everyone's book.

"Jeff," the Commissioner began, as soon as they were seated, "we don't want to distract you, to use Ned Daily's word, from your business any more than we have to, so I'll come directly to the point. We'd like for you to speak up tonight at the players meeting when this world tour thing comes up because what you said instinctively in the press tent about it is absolutely right on. We've analyzed Shumitami's press release and talked with everybody who'll talk to us and believe it's nothing but another poorly thought out power grab, by a bunch that doesn't have a clue about what the game is, or how it got to be that way."

Jeff sighed and removed his visor with his right hand, as he ran his left hand through his haircut overdue length auburn hair. It was occurring to him that the dead-last thing he wanted to be doing tonight, as the first-round leader of the Players Championship, was debating golf tournament politics and high finance.

"What's the urgency?" Jeff finally said. "Why can't you just ignore Shumitami and take it up with the Directors at the next Policy Board meeting."

"Because we think we've got an opening," the Commissioner responded, his tone rising to a higher level of insistence. "Nick and Mary think, and I agree, that if this really is a Shumitami-driven proposal, we can kill it before it ever goes anywhere by driving home to the players the control issue. We're pretty sure this is a Japanese TV and corporate marketing based concept; big money put up for 20 to 30 of the name players only, flying in the face of the our schedule, Europe's schedule and everybody else." Sid paused briefly, to let Jeff's thinking catch up. The Commissioner did not want his remarks to appear too highly- charged, or overwhelming to Jeff. "So anyway," he continued, "I called Shumitami, not an hour ago, to tell him that regardless of the merits of what he was trying to do, I resented him announcing it during Players week without even the courtesy of briefing me first. He said that the timing wasn't his idea, and that in fact everything he had said at the press conference had been written out for him in advance by the Shiatsu agency's communications and sports marketing people.

"He actually apologized after I explained why we were so upset. Anyway, I gave him a short course on how we are set up; you know, the roles of the volunteers and charity and everything and how strongly we feel that the game needs to be governed ultimately by the players themselves, et cetera, et cetera, et cetera. Bottom line: Shumitami says they don't want a drawn-out hassle, and that if we can show him, after a fair presentation of what he wants to do, that the players aren't for it, he says he'll fold the tent and move on to other things. I got the impression he's not looking to rock any boats and has probably gotten some bad advice about the level of player support he could expect."

"Wow," Jeff said, trying to digest what the Commissioner had just explained. "That must have been some phone conversation."

"So, I'm going to ask Norm Thompson to state the case in support of the, what do they call it?..."

"International Golf Championship Series," Nick added, seeing that Sid had forgotten the name.

"...At the meeting tonight," Sid continued, "and Jeff, I'd just like for you to listen to what he's got to say, and, if you want to, just say what you think is best for golf long-term. No notes, no slides, just speak your mind." The Commissioner paused again, to let what he was suggesting have time to sink in.

After a couple of silent but thoughtful minutes, Jeff said "OK, fair enough. That's certainly not asking too much." Taking another swig from the Michelob, Jeff added "Now, doesn't anybody want to hear about my 65?"

"I sure would," Nick said.

"Me too," Mary added, as the mood around the table lightened.

"Well, I had a lot of help," Jeff said," thinking about how much Polly's philosophy, Sandy's words and Sand Wedge's advice had contributed to his low score. "But it's sure nice to be back in the hunt."

As the four of them continued to chat, Jeff finished off his Michelob, feeling the guard-lowering effects even one drink invariably had on him, when he imbibed on an empty stomach. He began thinking that maybe he'd have to check back in with his old buddy Freddy.

Knowing that the Commissioner and the staff probably had a million other things to do, Jeff thought it would be an opportune time to excuse himself. Pushing his chair back, he stood and advised that he really did need to get something to eat. In fact, he hadn't completely decided whether to go over to the buffet, or back to the bar.

"I'll be there tonight Sid," Jeff said as he prepared to leave. "And I appreciate the way you've put it. I'll give everything a listen, and put in my two cents, if it seems like it would be helpful to do so, simple as that."

"You got it Jeff," Sid responded. "That's all we're asking."

"Nice to see you Nick, and nice to see you Mary" Jeff said, making eye contact with each of them again, before he turned to walk away. Two steps later he decided in favor of one more trip to see Freddy, thinking he'd earned the right to relax a little, and savor the after glow of his 65, particularly since his second-round starting time was nearly 24 hours away.

"Got any more of those Michelobs?" Jeff asked Freddy as he arrived back at the Commissioner's Hospitality bar.

"For you man, anything," Freddy responded reaching down into the bottom of the giant ice-filled cooler that was generously stocked with Michelobs, Sharps, Cokes and Diet Cokes.

"This one's smokin'" Freddy said, as he wrapped the second ice-cold Michelob with another Players Championship napkin and handed it to Jeff. "You seen Sandy yet, man? I think she's kinda been waiting for you, over there," Freddy said, pointing to a table, off to the far other side of the room.

"No, I haven't," Jeff replied, "not since on the course, but I've been looking for her." He squinted and looked in the direction Freddy had indicated, and located Sandy, sitting with another lady, sipping what appeared to be some sort of frozen drink.

"Thanks man, talk to ya later," Jeff said over his shoulder as he moved in the direction of the table where Sandy and her companion were sitting.

Chapter 12

"They're gonna have to beef up security around here," Jeff said as he arrived at the table where Sandy sat, her back to him, facing the woman seated across from her.

"Well I declare," Sandy said, in the Southern belle accent she playfully lapsed into on occasion, especially after a drink or two. "Sounds just like that little ol' golfer boy I saw out there on that golf course today." Winking at her friend across the table, Sandy proceeded to look back around over her shoulder at Jeff, batting her eyelashes and continuing for a moment the Deep South affectation.

"Why yes, Miss Scarlett," Jeff replied, playing along as he sat down in the chair next to Sandy, leaning over to kiss her firmly on the cheek as he did, "that's me, the fellow who, thanks to you, now just plays, and let's Mr. Sand Wedge do the thinking."

"It shows, on the scoreboard," Sandy said, ending the dixie repartee, which was beginning to sound like a scene in some obscure Tennessee Williams play.

"Jeff, do you know my friend Pam Brewster?" Sandy asked, realizing she had been impolite in not making the introduction sooner.

"No, I don't," Jeff said, rising to his feet and extending his hand. "It's my pleasure Pam," Jeff said, melting her with the patented grin.

"It's wonderful to meet you Jeff," Pam said, accepting his offered handshake. "Sandy's told me so much about you."

"Well, don't believe the bad parts," Jeff replied, returning his eyes to Sandy. Perhaps due to Jeff's one-and-a-half beer, post-65, leader in the clubhouse high, she looked even better than she had this morning out by the fourth tee.

"Gotta run," Pam said, glancing at her wristwatch. "I told Payton I'd meet her over at Sawgrass at two. Call me later on, will you Sandy?"

"Sure," Sandy said. "Say hey to Pat."

"Will do. Nice to meet you, Jeff. Good luck the rest of the way."

"Thanks," Jeff said as Sandy's friend scurried away. "Nice to meet you too."

"Who's Payton?" Jeff asked Sandy, a moment or two later.

"Pam's daughter," Sandy replied. "Rest of us call her Pat."

"Payton's kind of an unusual name, isn't it?" Jeff asked, realizing he was lapsing into irrelevant small-talk.

"Well honey," Sandy said, resuming the southern dialect, "we are after all in Jacksonville, Mayor Jake's bold new city of the South, now aren't we?"

Jeff let Sandy's playful words drop, without immediate response. He looked deeply into her green eyes for a moment and said softly, "God Sandy, you look great. Just like Skip said, absoblankinlutely great." His thoughts raced back to the rainy, unhappy evening a year ago when he had coldly and callously driven her out of his life, claiming neurotically that their relationship was impeding his professional accomplishment. From the perspective of the decidedly healthier mindset he was now practicing, it seemed suddenly crystal clear that his assessment of what Sandy could and should mean to him had been pathetically off target.

"Well, ya know Jeff, I try. But sometimes it's not so easy, ya know? ... Thanks by the way for the Christmas card, I was meaning to send you one too, but I really didn't know what to say."

"Merry Christmas would have been nice," Jeff said, his voice trailing off at the end, as he realized the conversation was now heading toward troubled waters. The silence grew, as Jeff returned to the Michelob and Sandy poked with a red straw at the vestiges of what appeared to have been a frozen margarita, a half hour or so ago.

"Listen, I gotta go too," Sandy said finally, putting her hand around Jeff's wrist and leaning close to kiss his cheek. "I'm on at three down at the Homestead and it's been crazy. You oughtta stop by if you get a chance."

"I will," Jeff said. "But we've got a player meeting tonight that'll probably run kinda late. Are you coming out tomorrow?"

"Wouldn't miss it," Sandy replied as she rose to leave. "You know us groupies... Just love those golfer boys..." Sandy leaned down again, and gave Jeff another kiss on the cheek, her shoulder-length blond hair brushing sensuously across his neck as she pulled away. "Take care Jeff, and play well." It was clear she really didn't want to go, but she did.

Just like he had on the golf course, Jeff found himself speechless as he watched the poetry-in-motion of Sandy walking away. Although 38 years old, Sandy was a dedicated runner, and had retained the slender, girlish figure of a woman in her late 20's. Clad in a pair of white cotton tennis shorts and a polo shirt, she was an attention-grabbing combination of good looks and athletic fitness as she crossed the room toward the door. And Jeff's eyes were not the only ones following her along the way.

After finishing the second Michelob, Jeff realized again that he needed a sandwich, or something, badly. It had been a long and complicated day so far, and showed no signs of simplifying any time soon.

Chapter 13

While Jeff was reuniting with Sandy in Players Hospitality, Sand Wedge was heading his black '89 Mercury Grand Marquis south, down A-1-A toward St. Augustine and the Sunrise Beach Motor Lodge. Like Jeff, Sand Wedge was feeling good about things as he drove along. He had stopped at the Lil' Champ convenience store just south of Sawgrass and treated himself to a quart of Michelob for the drive back to his motel. After a good round he enjoyed unwinding with a cold beer or two and, of course, a couple more Marlboros. He eased down the power windows of the big car and breathed deeply the fragrant, salt air wafting off the Atlantic.

The year was continuing to go pretty well, Sand Wedge thought. His player was showing him things the caddie hadn't seen for nearly 10 years, since back when Jeff was in his prime. The eagle at the 16th was particularly meaningful to Sand Wedge's experienced eye. He reflected on Jeff's prediction of the success of the shot, taking a long pull from the beer, then lighting a fresh cigarette. It was a sure sign, he thought, that Jeff was at least seeing the Zone from time to time, if not enveloping himself completely within it. And the birdie-birdie finish, Sand Wedge continued to reflect, is the stuff of a player who is comfortable with the thought of being the championship leader and, perhaps, the championship winner. The mix of contentment with the first-round score and positive anticipation of what might be in store for the weekend continued as Sand Wedge continued driving south, into St. Augustine, and negotiated the Mercury across the Bridge of the Lions, out onto St. Augustine Beach. The Sunrise was only about a half mile down from the bridge, on the left, across from the Tastee-Freeze.

As Sand Wedge stepped out of his car, the tiredness he felt from the morning's events and excitement suddenly registered on him. Draining the remainder of the beer as he walked to room #18, Sand Wedge looked forward to a quick shower and a good, long nap.

It was around four o'clock when Sand Wedge awoke to a firm knock at his motel room door. The nap had been a deep one and he felt as if he had been drugged, as he slowly came around. The dull ache at the back of his head recalled the Michelob he had imbibed earlier on the way back from the TPC. "Who there," he called out after a moment, sitting upright on the bed and reaching out for the floor with his bare feet.

"Tommy," the voice outside the door came back. "Me and Charlie goin' ova' t' Sea Wall for a beer. You wanna come along too?" Sand Wedge stepped across the small motel room, and opened the door to Tommy Johnson, Wayne Hargrove's caddie. Sand Wedge and Tommy often hung around together at Tour events they were both working.

"M-a-n," Sand Wedge said as he stood in the open doorway stretching and yawning. "I'm fuckin' wasted, man... Time is it, man?"

"'Bout four," Tommy answered. "See where yo' man shot 65. He gonna hold it this time? Or he be on down the road again, like last year?"

"We see now, won't we?" Sand Wedge retorted, miffed a little at Tommy's negative implication. "What Lite man shoot?" Sand Wedge continued, using the caddies' nickname for Hargrove, who had a big Miller Lite Beer endorsement and "Lite" logos on everything: his hat, his shirt, his bag, his umbrella... everything.

"He make seven at 18 for 73. Had the muthah-fuckah 4-under through 16; 17 and 18 eat his ass up. Splash it two time."

"Well," Sand Wedge said slowly, stretching and yawning loudly again, "like the lady say, this be a h-a-r-d game."

"Can be a muthah-fuckah," Tommy agreed. "You gonna come along?"

Sand Wedge pondered Tommy's invitation while he continued to try to wake up. He was hungry and the Sea Wall served a great seafood stew. Maybe, he thought, a little unwinding with Tommy and Charlie, the motel owner, would be a good idea.

"OK, sound good to me, man," Sand Wedge finally said. "But give me five minutes to get it together. I'll meet you guys over there in a little while."

"OK man," Tommy said, and turned to go back to the motel office to pick up Charlie. "See ya ova' there."

The Sea Wall was what you might call a "regular joint." Unknown to most of the tourists who clogged St. Augustine, North America's oldest city, the Sea Wall's clientele consisted mainly of local fishermen and other working-class types. The window-mounted air conditioners hummed loudly to keep the place cool on hot days, and the lights were always low, producing an ideal atmosphere for eating, drinking, telling lies, and, sometimes, a little groping here and there, on late into the evening.

Coming in from the bright, afternoon sunlight, Sand Wedge had difficulty adjusting to the relative darkness inside the Sea Wall. He stood for a moment, just inside the doorway, squinting, trying to locate Tommy and Charlie, who he finally spotted, seated far off in a corner of the restaurant. Approaching the small, Formica-topped table, Sand Wedge began to pick up Tommy's animated conversation. He was, Sand Wedge thought, no doubt relating to Charlie some anecdote about life on the Tour. Charlie loved golf and looked forward each year to Players Championship week, when a few caddies and Players Championship fans would customarily stay at his motel. Charlie seemed never to tire of listening to the caddies recount "war stories." The over-embellishment they typically lent to their tales, and their unique style and vocabulary only added to the richness of the experience.

"You wanna hear about Jimmy Branson?" Sand Wedge overheard Tommy saying, as he arrived at the table. "Lemme tell ya 'bout his young ass."

Noticing Sand Wedge's arrival, Tommy interrupted his story, and he and Charlie chimed an amiable greeting, and motioned for Sand Wedge to sit down. The table was already strewn with beer bottles, saltine cracker packets and small plastic containers of the Sea Wall's locally famous, red-hot cocktail sauce.

"How ya doin'? Sand Wedge," Charlie offered, as Sand Wedge moved around to the empty chair. "Hear Jeff shot lights out!"

"Yeah, yeah, we'll see," Tommy interrupted, seeking to retake control of the conversation. "Everybody know the man can play on Thursday; what nobody know is if'n he can still play come Sat'day and Sunday."

"Kiss my ass, man," Sand Wedge said as he sat down and began looking around for a waitress. He liked Tommy a lot, but the second negative comment about Jeff's chances in a matter of only a few minutes was beginning to rub him the wrong way. "My man be easin' on into the Zone, man, you'll see."

"So you think he's really got it going?" Charlie asked, also a little offended by Tommy's comment. Charlie had followed Jeff's career for over 20 years, and hoped the 65 was an indication that he was truly rediscovering his game, not just an isolated good round, as the opening 68 in last year's Players had apparently been.

"I do," Sand Wedge responded, just as the waitress arrived to take his drink order. He asked for the usual "ice-cold Michelob."

"That would be so great," Charlie continued, "to see him win that thing. I've always loved his golf swing, and that aggressive style he used to have... Charging putts at the hole, never seeming to worry a bit about having to make the come-back four-footer when he missed... Sand Wedge, when did that all change?"

"Best I can tell," Sand Wedge responded, after thinking for a moment, "it was the Ryder Cup in '89 at the Belfry in England. He was 2-up with three to go in the singles match on Sunday, and missed three straight four-footers to lose the match to O'connor... and the Cup to Europe... Took it real hard."

"I remember," Charlie said. "The press was goddamned brutal."

"Let them muthah-fuckahs make the putts when the heat on!" Tommy added. "Prob'ly pass out on the muthah-fuckin' green."

"The pressure must be unbelievable," Charlie said, the mood of the conversation sobering, despite Tommy's emotional interjections.

"Can be a killer," Sand Wedge said softly, reaching for the beer that had been placed in front of him. "After that," he continued, sighing audibly as he reflected back over the many years since Jeff's Ryder Cup debacle, "I tell ya, the man neva' roll the ball quite the same again... neva' quite the same... always a little hesitation, always a little doubt, maybe fear... It's like I keeps telling him: 'In golf, if you believe you can do it, you can. And if you don't believe you can do it, you can't.' It's the believin' part that so goddamn hard."

"Can be a muthah-fuckah," Tommy added, indicating his sincere, although less articulate agreement to what Sand Wedge had said. "So what make you think it gonna be any different up there this week?"

Sand Wedge took a long drink from the Michelob before answering Tommy's question, and savored the mellowing sensation it was beginning to cast over him. "It in his head... and in his eyes, man. I thinkin' by man done found his way back to the Zone."

Silence descended upon the table for a moment as the three

friends pondered Sand Wedge's introspective remarks.

"So you wanna hear 'bout Jimmy Branson?" Tommy said, looking over to Charlie and seeking to refocus the beer talk on less-heady matters. "Check it out. I loopin' for Jimmy and we playin' Bay Hill, two years ago. And we gets paired up with Ted Saxon, you know, the big muthah-fuckah from Long Island, who Jimmy fuckin' hates...."

The conversation went on, well into the night. Tommy and Sand Wedge were in rare form, and Charlie laughed until he cried, many, many times.

CHAPTER 14

The players meeting had been scheduled for 8:00 Thursday night in the huge central conference room at Tour headquarters, across the hall from the Commissioner's office. The massive conference table accommodated nearly 50 chairs around its perimeter, and 20 or 30 more chairs had been placed around the room, along the side walls.

When Commissioner Watterson entered the room at 8:00 sharp, all of the placces around the table were filled except for two at the end of the table nearest to the doorway to the executive wing. Norm Thompson sat at the opposite end of the table. Jeff had located himself inconspicuously in one of the seats along the wall.

David Frisch, the Tour's Director of Tournament Administration, accompanied Watterson into the meeting room and, after carefully pouring two cups of water from one of the pitchers that had been placed around the table, keeping one and placing the other in front of Sid's place at the table, asked loudly for the meeting to come to order. The medium level conversation buzz wound quickly down, and the room fell silent.

As if on cue, just as the silence threatened to become foreboding, if not intimidating, Skip Florine belched loudly, saying, "Excuse me, Commissioner, but that Sonny's barbecue has gotta be the best in the South."

The iciness that had seemed to suddenly grip the room just a moment before, melted away just as suddenly, as everyone laughed, while shaking their heads at Florine's incredible insolence, or uncanny intuition, not knowing which it really was.

Restoring order, Frisch explained that he was circulating a sign-in sheet, and that it would be appreciated if everyone would sign his name, and *only* his name. Since Tour player regulations mandated the players to attend not less than four player meetings per year, and provided for fairly heavy fines for noncompliance, the danger really wasn't that players in attendance would not sign, it was that the 70 or so that had shown up would somehow become 80 or 90 names, by the time the paper got back around to Frisch. After getting the sign in sheet started around the table, Frisch promptly turned the meeting over to Commissioner Watterson and took his seat, visibly relieved that his duties, were at least temporarily over.

As was his style, following Frisch's segue, the Commissioner said nothing for a few moments. The purr of the air conditioning and the occasional rustle of the sign-in sheet being passed along were the only sounds within the room, as Watterson allowed everyone's attention to focus on him.

"Hey Skip," Sid finally said, in a tone of voice several octaves lower than the one Frisch had employed. "You need to try Barbecue LTD."

"Respectfully, sir," Skip retorted, "I get quite enough LTD at your house, thank you very much." Skip was referring to the "Chairman's Barbecue" and "NBC Night" functions that were conducted annually during Players week, in hospitality tents erected over the expansive pool area and back yard at Sid's sprawling, stucco and tile mansion, located adjacent to the ninth fairway on the Valley Course at the TPC. For some reason, and to the bewilderment of many who annually attended both functions, every year they were each catered by Barbecue LTD, a local Jacksonville Beach barbecue-joint, with the exact same Jim-Bob fare: chopped barbecue, potato salad, cole slaw and baked beans. The repetitiveness and uncharacteristic low rent nature of the menu had become something of a private joke among the players, staff and golf industry "regulars" who, nevertheless, looked forward to attending each year.

Sid and Skip's back and forth stimulated more laughs, and further relaxed the atmosphere, which had been Sid's precise intent.

Focusing now on the serious business at hand, Sid took a sip of water and began to proceed with the agenda. "I know many of you are here primarily to hear more about the Shumitami world tour proposal. With that in mind, hopefully we can plow through the other agenda items expeditiously, and leave enough time for everybody to be heard."

"Item number one," Sid continued. "Stadium Course set up and conditioning... Anybody have any comments?"

"Yes sir," Terry Hilton immediately boomed from his position at the far end of the table, next to Thompson. "Who set the pin on 10? Does it make sense to anybody to cut the hole 10 feet up hill from a collection bunker that hasn't been mowed for six months? I fly a 9-iron back there, perfect. It hits short of the pin, bounces 20 feet in the air and releases into the garbage. I got no shot."

"Yeah, a lot of the pin placements were weird," Lawson Bates added. "What about six? I've never seen it over there where they had it today."

"Six green was rebuilt after last year," Frisch stated loudly, to overcome the murmuring and various head-shaking and hand-gesturing side-bar complaining sessions, that had sprung up around the table. "That's why the placement there looked different; and Terry's right, the placement on 10 probably shouldn't have been used in view of the condition of the collection bunker. It won't be back there again."

"What about the greens," Hilton continued, apparently mollified to some extent by Frisch's admission of error regarding the number 10 pin placement. "Are they going to get any water? If they don't and it don't rain, it's gonna be like trying to stop iron shots on a hockey rink."

"The weather service is saying rain Friday night and maybe Saturday, so we're planning on givin' 'em 30 minutes tonight and see how it goes," Frisch responded. "We may syringe tomorrow afternoon, if it gets real hot, but it's not supposed to." Frisch was used to the contentiousness of these sessions, particularly when they concerned one of the TPC facilities owned by the Tour.

The Tour had made an investment decision back in the 70's to begin to build ownership interests in several of the facilities hosting Tour events. It was a decision which remained controversial among the players, even now. As a general rule they felt much more latitude to criticize, sometimes brutally, courses owned or operated directly by the Tour. Even Jeff was on record as a Stadium Course critic, having remarked in 1982, after a disappointing 76 in the third round, that the course called for a type of shot he didn't have, namely, stopping a 6-iron shot on the hood of a Buick.

Commissioner Watterson sat silently, reviewing his notes on the world tour matter, as the criticism and spleen venting continued regarding the Stadium Course. The players were behind closed doors, and the agitation, whether legitimate or in fact due to the complaining player's poor play and high score, was healthy in Sid's view, so long as it stopped short of a palace revolt. It was *public* criticisms that the Commissioner had little tolerance for. He had been advised during the afternoon of Neil O'Leary's swamp remarks, which had somehow worked themselves into part of the questioning of the leaders that had gone on in the media center. He made a mental note to ask Mary Goldblume tomorrow to have one of her people investigate what Neil had actually said, and to whom. The probability was that the Commissioner would levy a $500 fine for "conduct unbecoming a professional."

The gripe session regarding the Stadium Course continued for about half an hour. The gist of the comments seemed to be that the firm and fast condition of the course, while not unfair yet, could indeed become so, if it stayed dry, or if any serious wind came up. The next two agenda items, the appointment of a player committee to review a change in the Tour's autograph signing policy, being recommended by the Policy Board, and the selection of the next player meeting date were handled summarily in a matter of a few minutes. The time had come to discuss the world tour.

"This next item is obviously very important," Sid started out. "I've asked Norm Thompson to advise us how he sees Shumitami's proposal, since he has made no secret of his strong support for it. Like all of you, I will be very interested and open-minded about what Norm has to say. But before that," Sid continued, his words coming more deliberately, and his tone of voice growing ever so slightly softer, "I'd like to take a moment to give each of you my perspective." Before going on, Sid allowed the room to go quiet again.

"Like most of you around this table," Sid began, "I developed a deep and abiding respect for the Tour long before I ever even thought of becoming involved with it professionally. I grew up fascinated by many of the players whose pictures you see around the walls of this room, and lining the hallways of this building. Fascinated not only by their skills on the golf course, but also by their characters, and the character of the game of golf. It is this latter thing that is, in my view, of utmost importance tonight. The good reputation golf has developed over the years must be preserved. To me, it is a precious asset held in trust by you the players, and by us as a professional staff, doing our best to advance your business interests as professional golfers.

"Precious few understand," the Commissioner continued, "the formula, if you will, that makes golf unique, and uniquely successful among all professional sports. It involves much, much more, and bear with me now, than you guys shooting 65. Our success is predicated on two fundamentals: structure and discipline. These two qualities are the foundation on which your opportunities as professional athletes rest. The structure, hammered out by a couple of lawyers in Palm Beach in 1968, allows professional golf to be governed by the athletes themselves. Think about that for a minute." Sid paused again for effect, hoping the depth of what he was trying to say was getting through. You could have heard a very small pin drop on the gleaming oak table.

"Look at other sports. Are they run by the athletes?... Hell no they aren't! Look at auto racing. Most of the top drivers can't even race in the Indy 500 because the car owners can't get along with the speedway operators. That would be like you guys being told you couldn't play in The Masters, because Augusta National wasn't getting along with the PGA... Could not happen... Could not happen," he repeated for emphasis, and allowing again a thoughtful pause.

"Why couldn't it happen?" he asked rhetorically. "Because you guys govern your own sport. You guys make the policy decisions; that's why they called it the Policy Board. Back before '68, the players didn't decide tournament policy matters. Other people did, and they weren't necessarily bad people. But they weren't the ones who had to make the four-footers to keep feeding their families. That's what caused the split between the tournament players and the PGA. Your predecessors wanted to take control of their own livelihood. And they got it! Good God fellas, don't you see how important an accomplishment that was?

"If you don't like what I'm doing, you can take action. You can fire my ass in a New York minute. I hope you don't, but from a structure standpoint, you have the governing authority necessary to do it. What are you going do about Mr. Shumitami if you get upset with him? As I understand it, what he's proposing is like the old CBS Golf Classic all over again, only a thousand times worse. Not only does Shumitami want TV to take control of golf, like CBS was trying to do in the 70's, he wants his TV events to become the competitive standards of the game, the "Majors" of tomorrow, if you will. If this kind of concept goes forward, they won't ask your grandson if he ever won the Players or the Masters. They'll ask him if he ever won the Sony Invitational, a 36-hole TV show played on New Year's Eve to get good Nielsons.

"Guys, those are your roots," the Commissioner continued, looking around over his shoulder and gesturing toward the large, frame-lighted oil paintings on the wall behind him of Ben Hogan, Arnold Palmer and Jack Nicklaus, the legendary players of the 50's, 60's and 70's who contributed so directly to golf's transformation into a popular spectator sport.

"How do you think they'd feel about turning the game over to Mr. Shumitami and a Japanese ad agency... at any price?" Sid paused to take another drink of water. He was tiring as his impassioned remarks were draining away his emotional energy.

After a few more moments, he began again, his voice dropping another quarter octave. "My problem with every world tour proposal I've seen so far is that they are being advanced by outsiders who don't have a clue about where golf came from, or is, as a game, and a profession. And most importantly, how we got here. There's far more involved than big corporate dollars and television rights fees. If we don't protect our structure, and our discipline, we do not only a disservice to ourselves, but also to the generations of players who preceded us, and the ones that'll be coming along in a few years, when we're sitting around with the wife, waiting for 4:30 to come, so we can go out for an early-bird dinner."

With that, Sid paused again and looked searchingly around the table into the eyes of several of the players, most of whom were deep in thought about what he had said. Satisfied that he had communicated what he had wanted to, he finally directed his eyes to Norm Thompson at the end of the table.

"What am I missing Norm?" Sid asked, turning the floor over to him.

Thompson was caught off guard. He had expected more of a question and answer presentation from the Commissioner, allowing him to make his points about the world tour within what he envisioned would become a groundswell of support from his fellow players. He now realized he had unwittingly agreed to be drawn into a one-on-one debate with a master debater. Watterson had in fact attended Northwestern University on a debate team scholarship in the mid 60's.

As if at least to buy a little thinking time, Norm rose to his feet and then reached down to straighten various nondescript papers and brochures he had on the table in front of him. Showing a little oratorical skill of his own, after he appeared to have collected his thoughts, Norm began.

"What have you missed Sid? I'll tell you what you've missed, you and Skip. You've missed Woody's." Norm was referring to another well known Jacksonville Beach barbecue joint. "Their barbecue's 10 times better than Sonny's or LTD." Norm's comment brought another laugh, including one from Sid, and again relaxed the mood in the conference room, which had grown ever more serious as Sid had spoken his piece.

"Have you missed anything regarding the world tour, Commissioner?" Thompson continued, refocusing on the serious matters at hand. "Well, I don't know; you usually don't miss much. And I'd be the first to admit that many of the points you make are good ones. Rather than what you've missed, all I know is what I know about the world tour, which is that it's the best opportunity for us I've seen come along in a long time. When I see players cashing in, in other sports for more money in a one year contract than we can make in a lifetime of winning on Tour, week in and week out, year in and year out, I for one, begin to wonder, hey, why not us too? And that's how I see the world tour, an annual series for the best of the best, playing for money they've earned the chance to play for, by winning Majors and becoming the pre-eminent names in the game. These guys are talking about a hundred million a year in prize money from the get go. I'm not ashamed to say I want to play for it and I think anybody that passes is a fool." With that, Norm sat back down, hoping he had gotten a ball of support for the world tour rolling.

The group sat in uncomfortable silence as no one rose to the support of either Norm or the Commissioner. The air conditioning purred along, accompanied only be intermittent coughs and throat clearings. Nobody was stepping up to the plate.

The Commissioner had just decided he needed to respond to Norm when the distinctive drawl of P.T. Weathersby piped up from the rear of the room. Weathersby's eyes, manner and speech smacked of an afternoon spent in players' hospitality, or some other location where the libations flowed freely.

"Commissioner... sir," the sarcasm was obvious in the insincerely respectful reference, "and distinguished guests and neighbors... Mr. Shumitanya or Shutusaki, or Nagasaki... whatever his name is, ain't lookin' for me on his world tour. I shot my wad in the spotlight years ago... But in my hum-ble opinion," (Weathersby said "humble" like it was two words, pausing to belch quietly to himself between syllables), "all this b.s. about '68 and the founding fathers and control of the game is, with all due respect Mr. Commissioner, *sir*, just that, b.s. You're right all right that this's about control; but its not about control by us. It's about control by you, Sid. You and the suits up here control golf and you know it. I wouldn't know Mr.... whatever, from the guy sitting next to me last night at the goddamned sushi bar, but he couldn't want to control things more than you do. I'm with Norm, get it while you goddamned can. Sid, if you don't want the Japanese guy around to challenge your kingdom, fine, but don't dress up what you're really all about in all this philosophical bullshit."

With that, Weathersby headed for the door, muttering to himself as he left. There was little doubt about where he was going.

As the conference room door banged shut after Weathersby's exit, Skip began to sing faintly and playfully "For he's a jolly good fellow, for he's a jolly good fellow," attempting once again to stir the heaviness that had descended back upon the group.

"Excuse me Skip," Jeff said, rising to speak. "But if you don't mind I'd like to say something... You know, P.T. makes a good point," Jeff started out.

Totally surprised by such a remark from the Tour's albeit aging "All-American boy," despite the growing lateness of the hour, everyone in the room, especially Sid, immediately seemed to perk up, looking questioningly in Jeff's direction. *Where the hell is he coming from?* they all appeared to be wondering in unison.

"Not in attacking Sid, of course," Jeff continued. "That's personal and doesn't deserve further comment. But who does run the Tour?"... Jeff paused for effect.

"Come on guys... Think... That's a very fair question that we should all be focusing on... Is it the players?... Or is it Sid and his people, the suits, as P.T. lovingly refers to them?" Jeff paused again for a few moments between each question, challenging his audience to think these fundamental matters through.

"It seems to me," Jeff continued, "that the Tour is run by whoever we, as players, let do it. If we want to take an active part in governing, we can... That's the beauty of what those lawyers in Palm Beach put together back in '68. Of course, if we don't want the bother, we can abdicate everything to Sid and the staff. I think, if we tried, we could all name an organization or two around the game that have opted to do that. Listen, guys, I don't know Mr. Shumitami from Adam. For all I know he's the best, most well-meaning man on earth. And his world tour deal may be the greatest thing since sliced bread. Norm may be precisely right in that. All I know is that Mr. Shumitami's deal won't work long term, unless it is coordinated into the fabric of the existing Tour family. And I use that term advisedly, meaning that it is developed with respect for existing event dates, for current sponsors, for the volunteers and for the local charities, and everything else. If he wants to make his proposal through the Policy Board, so it can be evaluated within the framework of how we do business, consistent with the structure and disciplines that have worked pretty damned well for us so far, great, and I'm sure Sid and the Board would give it a fair shake. But to announce it out of the blue, with no regard for the Players Championship or anything else, in my opinion, that's way out of control, at least out of our control, and I for one think it's a damned bad direction to go."

After a few moments of a now more restless silence as many of the players began to notice the lateness of the hour, Norm Thompson asked, "Hey Jeff, how do you think you would have felt about this back in the days when you would have been eligible to play... back before the '89 Ryder Cup?" Everyone in the room shuddered at the confrontational nature of Norm's question.

Jeff immediately stood back up to respond. "You just don't get it, do you Norm," Jeff said. "It must have been way over your head, but what Sid was trying to say, and really said very well, is that the Arnold Palmers and the Ben Hogans realized the need to act always in the game's long-term interests. Thirty years ago they could have turned the Tour over to an agency, and got a fortune every week, just to show up. But they didn't, because they recognized their duty to the future of the game, to preserve the structure, to preserve the disciplines, to preserve the players' control over their own destiny, so the opportunity in golf would continue to grow for everybody, not just for you guys winning Majors, but also for the other guys, the ones that only think they can win Majors, guys like me, and Skip, and a lot of the others around this room.

"Is the Players a Major Jeff?" Skip asked, throwing in his usual off-beat interjection.

"Good question Skip," Jeff said. "But, you know, under our structure, at least we have a say in whether it is, or is not, or ever becomes a Major. It's really up to us. I wonder sometimes why we don't just say it is. But that's a whole new issue, and it's way too late to get into that tonight. But I'll tell you one thing, I don't want it up to Mr. Shumitami to decide what's a Major."

The room fell silent again. The only sounds were from Norm Thompson, rustling papers, as he disconsolately crammed them into the briefcase he had opened before him, concealing the bottom half of his face. It was clear he wasn't a happy camper.

"Well guys," Commissioner Watterson said, "I think this has been a worthwhile session, but I do think it would be appropriate to take a straw poll on where we're at on this Shumitami thing. People are going to ask about it tomorrow, and if we don't have any answers, it'll just become a bigger and bigger distraction from our golf tournament, and I don't see how that helps anybody in this room."

"Commissioner," Jeff said, "I move that we send Shumitami a well-worded letter, saying while we are receptive to all ideas that make sense to improve the game, we believe any such proposals need to be submitted through the Policy Board to ensure proper integration of any new events into the existing Tour and international Tours' schedules, commitments, etc."

"Anybody second that?" Sid asked.

"Second," was said almost in unison by about a third of the players, there being apparently a consensus that Jeff's motion reflected pretty much everybody's feelings, except for Thompson's, of course.

"All in favor?" Sid asked, and about three fourths of the right hands in the room were raised. "Opposed?" he continued. No hands came up. Norm had already left the room, seeing that his point of view had garnered no support.

"Well... thanks guys, I think you're taking the right course. The door's not locked, but at least now maybe they'll knock before they try to come in. It's late, so we need to be winding this up. Anything else anybody wants to say?"

This time the silence was sweet to everyone's ears. The meeting was adjourned.

The huge Rolex on the conference room wall said 9:45.

Chapter 15

After the meeting broke up, most of the players headed quickly for the exits from the Tour headquarters building. Those with early second-round starting times were particularly eager to get back to their hotel rooms, to get some rest and regain their competitive focus, in anticipation of the challenges the next morning would offer. The results of the second round would determine who stayed around for the weekend, and a substantial piece of the six million-dollar purse.

Although Jeff's starting time was well after noon, he too had decided to call it a night and head off to his hotel, the Sea Turtle Inn, a somewhat less than first rate beach-front hotel up in Atlantic Beach, where he usually stayed during Championship week, mostly for sentimental reasons. The frenzy his Championship-leading round had propelled him into, and the stress of the player meeting had combined to leave him feeling worn out, despite the nap he had taken back at the hotel after lunch.

But just as he had clicked the unlock button on his courtesy car key ring, Jeff heard Skip's familiar voice calling out from behind.

"Hey, Jeff, wait up." Jeff turned to face his young colleague as Skip approached the side of Jeff's car. "Let's head on up to the Homestead for a beer," Skip said. "There's a lady up there who had me autograph her shoulder after my round today, and I've got the idea she'll be wanting me to autograph her butt too, after a couple of margaritas."

"Nah man," Jeff replied, chuckling and shaking his head at Skip's graphic exuberance. "I'm beat. I'm going to ease on back to the Sea Turtle and hit the hay."

"One nightcap at the Sea Turtle bar then," Skip implored. It was looking like he had something on his mind that he really needed to talk Jeff about, and Jeff relented.

"OK, but I really don't want to make a night of it. I haven't gotten it to seven for a long time," Jeff explained, referring to his opening round 65. "And I'm damned sure not going to screw it up trolling with you up and down the beach."

"It's nothing like that, man," Skip said. "I just want your advice on something that I got to thinking about during the meeting. One drink, that's all, and I'm buying."

"That goes without saying," Jeff said as he stepped into the car. "Follow me up there. It's straight up A-1-A to Atlantic, and hang a right. You can't miss it."

As he drove along, Jeff wondered what it could be that made Skip want to buy him a nightcap at the Sea Turtle, rather than go to the Homestead and chase whatever scrumptious young thing he had apparently charmed earlier in the day. *Autograph her butt?* Jeff thought. He had signed his share of autographs over the years. He remembered in particular a lady in Dallas that had offered him a pair of silk panties to sign, but he had never signed any part of an actual body, at least not that he could recall. *It just keeps getting crazier and crazier out here,* he thought as he cruised up A-1-A, groping in the dark at the unfamiliar radio control buttons, attempting to tune in 96.1 FM, his favorite Jacksonville easy listening station.

As he sat at the stop light at the Beach Boulevard intersection, the music on the car radio changed to *The Lady in Red.* Feeling a warmth pass over him, Jeff reached over and turned the volume of the music up higher. It was one of his all-time favorite songs, and one that always made him think of Sandy. As the music played on, Jeff's thoughts wandered back to a very late evening years ago, soon after they had met, when they had danced slowly in the dark to the music of the song, on Sandy's deck overlooking the ocean. Befitting the lyrics, Sandy, who was pleasantly high after a glass or two of champagne, wore red pumps during the dance, but nothing else. Waiting for the light to turn green, Jeff suddenly felt overwhelmed with loneliness and realized that if he lived to be 100, he would think of Sandy and that night whenever he heard *The Lady in Red*.

Arriving at the Sea Turtle, Jeff steered the car into the "Reserved for Jeff Taylor" parking spot that had been marked in the space immediately to the right of the hotel entrance. Exiting and locking the car, Jeff stepped into the modest lobby, to wait for Skip.

"Didn't know I was in the presence of royalty," Skip said as he opened the lobby door, moments later. "Us mere mortals have to find a place to park way out there in the lot somewhere, doncha know."

"I'm a big tipper," Jeff shrugged, trying to de-emphasize the star treatment the Sea Turtle staff and management annually showered upon him when he stayed there during The Players. "The bar's back around to the right."

Arriving in the lounge, Jeff and Skip went over to a table far in the corner, by the window overlooking the now-deserted beach. A waitress soon arrived and, not noting that they were anybody special, took their drink orders matter-of-factly. Jeff ordered a Michelob and Skip ordered a rum and Diet Coke.

"So what's up, Mr. 66?" Jeff opened, hoping to get whatever it was on Skip's mind taken care of in fairly short order.

Uncharacteristically, Skip didn't respond for a moment. He covered his face with his hands and rocked back in his chair, obviously in deep thought about what he would say next.

"I'm scared," Skip finally said. "As I was sitting there in the room tonight, listening to Sid... and you... and Norm, too... talking about the Tour, and what it means, and where we've come from, and all... I don't know, somehow it dawned on me, finally I guess, just where I am and what I'm doing. I'm one freaking shot out of the lead in a Major championship. All of the sudden, I found myself thinking, you're in the inner sanctum now Florine, don't freakin' blow it... Jeff, I've never had that kind of thought before in my life. I'm not sure how to handle it."

"Wow," Jeff said after a moment, "welcome to life. You finally realize where you are, how much you want to stay there, and how precarious a perch it is, am I basically right?"

"I guess that's it," Skip responded. Just then the waitress arrived with the drinks.

"That'll be five dollars," she said. Just as Skip was reaching for his PGA Tour money clip, Jeff said, "I think we'll be running a tab." He sensed the apparent depth of Skip's dilemma, and suspected they might be there for a while.

"You got it," the waitress said, turning away to serve another table.

Composing himself as he allowed the waitress to move off, out of earshot, Jeff looked across the table into Skip's eyes, noting a look of apprehension that contrasted remarkably with the easy-going appearance Skip ordinarily projected.

"Concentration," Jeff finally said. "Concentration and unrelenting attention to detail are what it's all about. That's the stuff of genius. And although most people probably wouldn't agree, genius is what you and I need to make it to the top out here. Only the very best surgeons 'break par' when they perform surgery; only the very best lawyers 'break par' when they try a case. When it comes to our 'game,' our profession, to even survive, we have to 'break par' almost every day. I don't ordinarily say it to others, because it sounds pretentious, at best, but what you and I are called upon to do, if we want to really succeed out here, is perform genius."

"Hot diggity... thanks man, that sure makes me feel a lot better," Skip replied sarcastically, reeling at the unexpected profundity of Jeff's remarks. "I thought all we had to do was drive it in the fairway, hit it on the green, and make the putt. You know, like they said in that movie."

"That's right," Jeff said. "But doing that requires an ironclad combination of physical and mental skills. That combination is what I call 'concentration,' and to be able to practice it, day in and day out, for the stakes we're after, requires genius. You and I both know that there are a million guys who can play. That guy up there at the bar wearing the Callaway visor can probably drive it 250. But there aren't many who can play when the real heat's on, like we have to, if we want to be able to afford to eat. That's what requires what I'm calling 'concentration.'"

Jeff's further expounding seemed only to perplex Skip more. "Man, you're blowing me away," Skip said as he downed his drink and began looking around the lounge for the waitress. "All I'm saying is that for the first time tonight, at the meeting, I found myself thinking, wow, this really is the real deal, and I'm near the top of the leader board... Hope I don't blow it. That's not me, man. Every other time I can remember shooting 66, I've thought OK, tomorrow's gonna be 65. Isn't that the way you've always thought?"

"That's the way I've always *tried* to think, but it hasn't always worked out that way. It all gets back to 'concentration.' Envisioning success... and I mean latching onto it mentally like a goddamned pit bull latches onto a mailman's leg... Envisioning success, results in success. It doesn't make you capable of what you can't physically do, understand." Jeff paused for a moment to let Skip catch up with what he was trying to get across.

"I couldn't get up and run a four-minute mile," he continued, "just because I envisioned it, no matter how intently. But concentration is the key to everything, especially golf, at the level we play it. Without it, we can't even do what we can do, if you see what I mean. Take Hogan, for example. They say he never pulled the trigger on a shot until he had a vivid, riveted mental image of the result he wanted, emblazoned in his mind. That's concentration. Everything else is blocked out. Everything. That's why he quit playing. He got to the point where he couldn't get the putter in motion because he couldn't picture the stroke he needed and the result he wanted; he couldn't muster the mental image required to go with the physical act of stroking the putter. He never yipped 'em, like I began to do, when I was really struggling last year. He just quit putting altogether. When he lost the power to concentrate over a putt, he quit."

"Holy moly Jeff, I'm not talking about quittin'. I'm just asking you how you stop worrying about shooting a high score when you're leading, and think instead about shooting another low score. You know, I don't want to shoot 80 tomorrow; I want to shoot another 66; but all of a sudden I find myself thinking about the 80 rather than the 66. What the hell do I do?"

Just then, the waitress arrived back at the table and Skip indicated a couple of quick circles in the air with his index finger while continuing to stare at Jeff. His intent was to request another round. The waitress nodded her understanding of Skip's gesture, and moved away, back toward the bar.

The two friends sat in silence for a moment, Jeff finishing his Michelob and Skip poking at the remains of the ice in his glass with a straw.

"What you do," Jeff began, "is to develop a discipline to achieve 'concentration.' In other words, work at developing a way of thinking only about success and the things which lead to success. It's a process that gets harder and harder as you get older, and experience more... good and bad. Bad experiences, if not dealt with, turn into scars, which can impair this concentration process, sometimes forever. Your scary realization tonight is just a nick, not even a scratch. But you need to deal with it right away, and never let it become a scar."

"So, how do I do that?" Skip asked, as the second round of drinks arrived.

"It's amazingly simple, and almost impossibly hard at the same time. You believe in yourself and decide whether you want to succeed or fail. Whatever decision you make, it will come true, provided, of course, you define success within the bounds of what you are physically capable of accomplishing."

"Well then, buddy boy," Skip declared after taking a long pull at his second drink, "I guess you and the rest of the guys are plum out of luck this week, 'cause I just decided to believe in myself and succeed by winning this thing on Sunday."

Jeff laughed at Skip's comment, which mercifully lightened the tone of the conversation, and looked off, out the window to the waves rolling into the Sea Turtle dock. All of a sudden he began to think that maybe he should call Sandy tonight.

"So you're saying that that's it?" Skip asked. "Just believe in myself and decide I'm going to win? Come on Jeff, anybody can do that; it's gotta be harder than that."

"Not really," Jeff replied, resuming his gaze into Skip's eyes. "But with all due respect, my friend, you still aren't quite getting it. Remember, I said your definition of success has to be something within your ability to deliver. You can't just win Sunday by somehow defining that as success. All you can do is play your best on each and every shot. That would be your success. Whether you win or lose is not yours to control. You have to understand that."

Realizing now that Jeff's advice was more complex than what he first thought caused Skip to become silent and begin some introspection of his own. "I think I see what you're saying," he finally said. "It's simple, but it's hard, too. You believe in yourself, but you mess up anyway, so what do you do the next time?"

"You believe in yourself and decide to succeed," Jeff answered.

"And if you mess up again?"

"You believe in yourself and decide to succeed," Jeff repeated.

The two grew silent again as they each thought about the process they were discussing, and how it impacted their lives, particularly in light of the hyper-competitive career choice they had each made, many years before.

"Prob'ly don't get no easier as you get older now do it," Skip summarized, intending with his country-boy dialect to return the conversation to a lighter level. "You know, you done gave me a headache."

"Me too," Jeff said, rising from his chair and yawning. "Listen, I enjoyed the chat, but us old guys need the shut-eye. Why don't you get on down to the Homestead and sign some more autographs? That'll help your concentration. And if you see Sandy, ask her if she's listened to *The Lady in Red* lately."

"OK man," Skip said as Jeff walked away, "see ya tomorrow." Skip wondered for a moment what the *Lady in Red* thing was all about as he looked around for the waitress. He wanted to pay the check and get on over to the Homestead.

CHAPTER 16

Jeff awoke Friday morning to the gentle, purring-like ring of the telephone in his ocean-front room. He read the numbers on the luminescent face of the radio alarm clock on the night stand: 8:11, and wondered who could be calling. Since he didn't play until the afternoon, he hadn't left a wake-up call. He waited for the phone to finish its third purr, then reached out for the handle, and placed it to his ear.

"Hello," he said brightly, trying, as he usually did when receiving phone calls in bed in the morning, to hide his sleepyheadedness, and sound chipper, like he had been up for hours.

"Hey Jeff, it's Sandy. Hope I didn't wake you."

"Don't be silly," Jeff said. "You know me, I've been up for hours... walked the beach... had breakfast, the works."

"Yeah, right," Sandy responded. Sandy did know Jeff all right, right down to his sleeping habits. She knew he was not an early riser, except when he had to be, because of an early starting time.

"Listen, I'm sorry to call so early, but I just got back from my morning run and I've got a million things to get done before going down to the tournament, and I wanted to ask if you'd come over for dinner tonight." She paused for a moment, knowing that her invitation might come as a surprise, perhaps an unwelcome one. "I know it's probably stupid to ask, but you've got to eat somewhere, and I'd really like to catch up a little, you know?"

"Sure, that'd be great," Jeff said, sitting up in the bed as he realized, with a mixture of excitement and trepidation, that without a moment's hesitation his instincts were to go along with what looked to be an overture on Sandy's part to rekindle their relationship; a relationship he thought they had both conceded had come to an end a year ago, on that rainy Sunday night in St. Augustine.

"It's set then, 'bout eight o'clock; don't bring a thing."

"Count me in," Jeff confirmed, resisting a temptation to ask her to drop by the Sea Turtle on the way to wherever she was going now. He knew that Sandy's house was no more than a mile up the beach from the hotel, and he had a lustful image of her standing by the phone in her skimpy running clothes.

"One other thing," Sandy continued. "Is there any way you could arrange a badge for Pam? She only had a day ticket yesterday and would really like to come back out today."

"Not a problem," Jeff said. I'll call Vicki at the Tour and have

her leave something at will call. What's Pam's last name?
"Brewster, B-R-E-W-S-T-E-R."
"Got it," Jeff said. "Tell her to ask at will call. It'll be under her name."
"Thanks Jeff, see ya later, and play well."
"I will Sandy, and thanks. Bye-bye."

Jeff wondered what he was getting into as he hung up the phone. All he knew for sure was that from the first time he saw Sandy yesterday by the side of the fourth tee, it had become clear to him that he hadn't gotten over her. Suddenly he thought of Polly and wondered what she would have to say about Sandy and his re-emerging feelings for her. Jeff remembered Polly's remark about the phony-baloney lying behind rather than in front of his eyes and wondered how that applied to Sandy. He sensed he was on the threshold of a better and healthier appreciation of who Sandy really was and what their relationship could be.

Jeff couldn't have gone back to sleep if he would have wanted to. He got up and walked over to the window, pulling the heavy hotel curtains apart and revealing his favorite beach in the world, Atlantic Beach. Since the ocean was at low tide, the beach was wide and flat. Looking off to the south toward the Jacksonville Beach pier, he could see a few joggers and beach bicyclists putting in the miles. The sun was already well into its climb from the ocean, and the skies were crystal clear. *God, I love this place,* Jeff thought as he looked out.

Jeff had lived in Atlantic Beach for 10 years before his divorce from Cheryl in 1991. "We grew apart," is how he put it, whenever asked why he and Cheryl had parted. Cheryl still lived in Ponte Vedra, not two miles from the Stadium Course. He still spoke to her from time to time, but Cheryl's new husband wasn't keen on such ongoing contacts, so it had been a while since Jeff had talked to her. He had seen her briefly at last year's Players, but nothing since then.

Maybe I'll take the grand tour this morning, Jeff thought, referring to his annual hour or so of meandering in his Buick courtesy car around the old neighborhood. Maybe he'd even stop in Silver's for a cup of decaf and see if any of the regulars were around.

It was 8:30. He had four hours to kill before meeting Sand Wedge. He was looking forward to revisiting some fond memories in the remaining quiet time before beginning again the process of preparing to compete, this time in the second round of the Players.

Turning from the window and walking back toward the bathroom, Jeff noticed that a *Florida Times Union* had been slid beneath the hotel room door. *This should be interesting,* he thought, as he bent down to pick up the paper. He tossed it on the bed, preferring to save it for reading after he had showered and dressed. Maybe he'd take it across the street to Silver's or the Dune Dog, and read it over a leisurely cup of decaf and a large tomato juice.

God, I feel good, he thought. If Jeff could be anywhere, doing anything at this moment, it would be right here, getting ready to spend the morning in Atlantic Beach, the afternoon competing in the Players Championship and the evening having dinner at Sandy Jackson's beach-front condominium. For the moment, all was right with Jeff Taylor's world. He thought briefly again of Polly, thanking her anew for her counsel, and knowing she would approve highly of his current state of mind.

CHAPTER 17

Coming out the unpretentious Sea Turtle lobby door, Jeff immediately noticed the breeziness and warmth of this North Florida Friday morning. The navy blue, TPC logo-crested sweater vest he had decided to wear would be coming off, probably well before noon. Jeff remembered the comment David Frisch had made at last night's meeting about the possibility of syringing the greens, that is hosing them with water briefly during play to ensure that the delicate, closely-cut bent grass didn't die out, if the afternoon proved to be hot and dry. As he crossed the Sea Turtle parking lot in route to Silver's Drugstore, the *Times Union* folded neatly and carried in his right hand, Jeff thought about how the abnormally warm weather might affect play. He could already tell the afternoon was going to be hot and muggy. Looking back over his shoulder to the flags that flew high atop the hotel, he noticed that they were billowing in what appeared already to be a brisk southwesterly wind.

Arriving at the intersection of Atlantic Boulevard and Ocean Avenue, the heart of "downtown" Atlantic Beach, Jeff walked diagonally from the northeast corner to the southwest corner, indifferent to the DON'T WALK sign that flashed irrelevantly in the typically sparse mid-morning traffic. As he walked along, Jeff was laboring to dismiss the anxious thoughts he was having about the more difficult playing conditions he was likely to encounter this afternoon.

Silver's Drugstore is the unlikeliest of places to house a good restaurant. From the street it looks like a typical beach front drugstore. The stock displayed and advertised in its windows was a predictable blend of pharmaceuticals and tourist-oriented beach items: Bayer Aspirin, 36 count, $1.99; inflatable rafts 3 for $10. But back at the rear of the drugstore was one of the locals' favorite breakfast and lunch spots. To the uninitiated, the cafe area was little more than a motley collection of Formica-topped tables and kitchen chairs. But the residents knew that the coffee was rich and hot, and the omelets were clearly the best at the beach, if not the best in all of Jacksonville.

"Well look who's here," Dot Silver said, as she looked up from the newspaper, over her rhinestone studded reading glasses. "If it isn't the local hero." Dot was occupying her usual hostess position, standing behind the glass-topped counter that separates the drugstore area from the restaurant, beside the ancient cash register that still suited her cash only, thank you, sales policy.

"A table by the window please," Jeff said, flashing Friday's first edition of his infectious grin.

"No windows in here young man," Dot said, clasping his arm as she led Jeff to a table in the rear, where she knew he preferred to sit. "Just good food and low prices. I see you've got your press clippings there. Whatcha think of those headlines?"

"You know Dot, I haven't even looked yet, I just had to get over here to see you first," Jeff said, as he sat down at one of the small tables and unfolded the *Times Union.*

"DEJA VU: TAYLOR LEADS PLAYERS" read the local paper's headline. "Wow," Jeff exclaimed softly, whistling as he scanned the brief front page story about the Players' first day results, that concluded with "Please see section C for details."

"Just wish it was Monday," Jeff said as he looked up at Dot, smiling pleasantly again.

"Well, honey, you just hang in there, and know that we're all pulling for ya, real hard. What'll ya have, two over easy with grits?"

"No, not this morning Dot. Just some decaf and an extra large tomato juice. Watching the waistline you know."

"That all?" Dot inquired, wondering how anybody, let alone an active young man like Jeff, could get by on such a skimpy breakfast.

"That'll do it today," Jeff replied, flipping by the front page and local news sections of the paper, and withdrawing the sports section. Dot returned to the kitchen to get the decaf and turn in Jeff's order, such as it was.

Of course, Players Championship news dominated the local paper's sports section. The interior headline read: "TAYLOR GRABS ONE-SHOT LEAD." The lead story was under Tom Schuyler's by-line and recounted what had been a full day of good scores, which were being attributed not only to the players' good play, but also to the pleasant and nearly windless weather conditions. A picture of the Sea Turtle's billowing flags popped momentarily into Jeff's mind; he knew this afternoon in all probability would not offer up such a user friendly golf course.

"What's that Yogi Berra supposedly said?" Schuyler's story began. "'It's deja vu all over again?' Well, that's what it was yesterday in the first round of the Players Championship, as the Stadium Course yielded up flocks of birdies in beautiful and benign weather conditions. Recalling the glory of his first-round performance last year in the wind and rain, local favorite Jeff Taylor fashioned a splendid eagle-birdie-birdie finish to post a scintillating 65, taking a 1-shot first-round lead over the laid-back Skip Florine, and a 2-shot lead over five other players bunched with opening 67's."

Jeff was continuing to read Schuyler's story when Dot returned with the decaf and tomato juice. She had put the tomato juice in a hawg-size, 32-ounce plastic tumbler, the type usually reserved for the iced tea served in copious amounts to the parched summertime lunch crowd.

"You sure you don't want something more?" she implored. "Good Lord, you'll faint from hunger out there in the middle of the fairway and they'll blame it on me for not serving you a better breakfast."

"Nah, this'll do fine Dot," Jeff said as he smiled again and winked at his hostess' apparent consternation. "But I'll leave a note in my locker saying that Dot Silver told me I should have eaten something more, just in case."

"Well, all right, but lemme know if you want something else." With that, Dot left Jeff to his newspaper, just like she would have left Doc Thomas or Mayor Smith or any of the other locals. That was another thing Jeff liked about having breakfast at Silver's.

It was getting close to 9:30 by the time Jeff had finished the paper. The workday breakfast crowd had long since disappeared, and Jeff was alone in the restaurant. Not even Dot was any place to be found. Jeff smiled to himself at this further example of the attractive, small-town lifestyle that Silver's, the Sea Turtle, the solitary traffic light and so many other aspects of Atlantic Beach represented to him. Dot was presumably off running an errand somewhere, or taking a mid-morning break down at the beach. She trusted Jeff to pay his bill, and not steal the store blind as he left. Jeff placed a $10 bill halfway under the jar of peppermint candies on the counter by the cash register and walked on back across to his courtesy car, parked in its honorary position to the right of the Sea Turtle's lobby door.

It was a good time for his annual tour of the old neighborhood.

CHAPTER 18

Turning right as he exited the Sea Turtle parking lot onto Ocean Avenue, Jeff eased the red Buick Riviera he had been assigned for championship week northward, parallel to the beach, 200 yards or so off to his right. This took him through the older section of the beach town, on along to where the avenue curved to the left by the Atlantic Beach Town Hall. The houses were mostly small, but with few exceptions, very well maintained. This part of Atlantic Beach had sprung up in the 50's and 60's, essentially as a blue collar and military retirement community. Many of the houses were actually cottages, and displayed the quaint characteristics of lower-income beachside property, like substantial size boats wedged into smallish driveways, and tiny guest apartments built over the garages.

Jeff continued northward, on by the solitary tennis court that had been installed behind the Town Hall years ago, at the height of the tennis boom back in the 70's, no doubt. Jeff acknowledged as he drove along, that despite having lived in this vicinity for nearly 10 years, he had never actually seen anyone using the court.

Continuing up Ocean, the houses became larger and more modern. The street names changed from simple numbers: Fourth, Fifth, Sixth, and so on, to trendier, upscale, "beachy" names, like Sea Oats Drive, Mariner's Way and Egret Terrace, selected by developers during the housing explosion of the 80's. Sandy's place was at the end of Egret Terrace, on the beach.

Jeff's own address had fallen victim to the upscale revolution, the name of his street being changed from 18th Street to Sea Spray Way, between the time he bought the house in 1981, then under construction, and closed some three months later.

Turning left off of Ocean onto Sea Spray, Jeff now proceeded westward approximately one quarter of a mile to the entrance into the Selva Marina development, an upscale community where every effort had been expended to preserve the live oaks, palms, sawgrass and other "ocean jungle" foliage indigenous to the area. Atlantic Beach and Jacksonville, which is 18 miles due west on the St. Johns river, lie in the middle of a thirty-mile wide belt of latitude, where hardwood oak trees and softwood palms grow side by side.

Jeff's former residence was on the corner of Sea Spray and North Sherry Drive, back from the street, within a generous stand of oaks and palms. The tree-preservation policies of the Selva Marina building covenants were in plain view at Jeff's old house. One of the 50-foot live oaks on the property actually grew through the back breezeway leading from the garage to the kitchen and family room door, the tree's four-foot wide trunk rising up and through holes in the deck flooring and roof made to accommodate it. Jeff remembered the story his builder had told him at the closing about how he was in the process of removing the tree, when Mayor Smith himself had pulled up in front of the construction site, tires screeching, and yelling "You can't cut down that tree! You can't cut down that tree!" as he jumped out of his car and hurried across the lot. Regaining his breath, the mayor had patiently explained that no oak tree over two feet in trunk diameter could be removed without the express approval of the Atlantic Beach historical preservation committee, of which Mayor Smith was the chair. Rather than invest in the time and red tape, the builder had elected to build the breezeway around the tree. Mayor Smith was happy with the decision. So was Jeff. The tree had been quite a conversation piece over the years.

Jeff turned slowly northward, onto North Sherry and came to a stop, leaning across the front seat of the Buick to get a better view of the leaded-glass and oak wood, double front doors, and large great-room windows that dominated the front side of the house. For the one hundredth time, at least, he wished he had never sold it after the divorce and moved to South Florida.

The 10 years or so Jeff had spent in Atlantic Beach were the best ones of his life. Although he traveled extensively playing the Tour, he always looked forward to flying back into "Jax" and unwinding with Cheryl at the beach at the end of the street, or downtown at Ragtime, or Slider's, or any number of other places in the area. In melancholy or sentimental moments over a drink or two, Jeff often claimed a desire to give up the hustle and bustle of the Tour, and retire in Atlantic Beach, eventually running for mayor, only, of course, after Mayor Smith was ready to retire. As he was gazing at the old house, quietly reminiscing, he thought, *You know, if I can somehow win this thing Sunday, I could do that.* He knew that he wouldn't. But it was comforting to think about it anyway. He realized he was fortunate to have such strong feelings about a place it had been his good fortune to come to know.

Again Jeff noted that his perception of things could be either positive or negative. Like Polly had told him, it was truly up to him to decide. "Your daily happiness decision" she had called it. Not so long ago, he often brooded about having left Atlantic Beach, indulging himself in self pity about the disappointments he had experienced since moving to South Florida. Now he found himself drawing strength from his pleasant memories, thankful for the good times he had spent in Atlantic Beach, and focused on the possibility there could be many more of them to come.

Jeff's nostalgia fix almost complete, he continued to ease the Buick northward up North Sherry Drive. His speed fluctuated between six and eight miles per hour, which were pretty much the maximum speeds you could do in a full-size car, the road twisting crazily in and out of the oaks and palms. Selva Marina got no through traffic. If you didn't know precisely where you were going, particularly after dark, chances were, you wouldn't get there. The only real downside the dense and twisted layout of the area had caused Jeff and Cheryl over the years was that they couldn't order home delivery pizza with any real expectation that the delivery person would actually show up. They thought that was a reasonable price to pay for the quiet, away-from-it-all environment they enjoyed.

Glancing at the Buick's digital clock, Jeff noted that it was getting on toward 11 o'clock. Looking outside, he also noted that the palms were swaying liberally, in what was even now becoming a pretty stout wind. He needed to be thinking about getting on down to the TPC. Meandering the car back out onto Ocean, he decided to go back to the Sea Turtle to change clothes. He wanted to put on some lighter weight cotton pants, and he sure wasn't going to need the sweater.

The time had arrived for Jeff to begin putting his game-face on for the second round of the Players Championship.

Chapter 19

It was shortly before noon when Jeff arrived at the TPC. Following the signs to Contestant Parking, he navigated through the hectic spectator traffic which indicated that the second-round gallery turnout would be huge. The players' Buick courtesy cars were exempt from the long lines and traffic jams that befell the general public. Seeing one, with the PGA Tour logo on the door and the lime-green, Contestant parking pass hanging behind the windshield, the burly, sunglasses-clad Florida State Highway patrolmen controlling traffic around the grounds would spring into action. One of them would put out his left hand to stop everything else in sight. Then, briskly pumping his right arm and blowing his whistle if necessary, he would direct the player out around the mere mortals, to wherever it appeared he wanted to go. Jeff parked in the roped-off lot reserved for the players, not more than 50 feet from the stairway leading up to the huge TPC locker room.

As he arrived at his locker, Jeff noticed a pink "post it" slip placed just below the brass nameplate on the locker door. "Jeff, please give me a call, when you've got a few minutes to talk about last night's meeting. Best of luck, Sid" the note read.

"Come on Sid, what now," Jeff muttered softly, as he wadded up the slip of paper. Due perhaps to his anxiety in preparing to re-enter his profession's ultra-competitive pressure chamber, Jeff, perhaps unnecessarily, assumed Sid's message foretold some further request to become involved again in business matters. He was glad to do what he had done last night, but enough was enough. As far as he was concerned the current order of business was shooting another good score. He wasn't inclined to grind anymore with Sid and the staff about the world tour, or anything else. What could there possibly be that couldn't wait until Monday? He decided not to even think about calling Sid until after his round, if then.

Remembering the warmth of the weather, Jeff took three new Wilson golf gloves from the dozen pack that had been placed in his locker earlier in the week. The hot weather and perspiration would probably require two or even three gloves to be used during the course of today's round. Like yesterday, he worked one of the new gloves methodically onto his left hand, checking the fit again by pinching the palm. "Show time."

And like yesterday, he emptied the pockets of his khaki pants, placing the contents on the top shelf of the locker, except for the two ball-marker sixpence coins, which he returned to his right front pocket. Then he took the bright orange book from the locker shelf and slipped it into his left rear pocket, along with the crisp envelopes containing the other new golf gloves. Thinking of the sixpence coins for a moment, Jeff remembered the night three years ago when Sandy had given them to him. She told him that she had brought the coins with her from England for luck when she had come to the States back in 1980, at age 19, to attend Indiana University on an athletic scholarship. While at Indiana she had studied business and finance, and captained IU's Big Ten champion women's track team during her senior year. If the coins could help Jeff to more success on the greens, Sandy had said, they would be serving their highest purpose.

"Show time," he repeated, trying to shake himself from his musings.

As usual, Sand Wedge was precisely where he was supposed to be, seated atop the golf bag, alongside the practice green. He extinguished his cigarette as he saw Jeff approach, placing the ashless butt into the pocket of his caddie bib, and reached into the bag to withdraw the Zebra putter that had performed so creditably yesterday. Sand Wedge had already opened a fresh sleeve of Titleist 3's and marked them with three black dots within the dimple immediately below the 3. This would ensure the ability to identify Jeff's ball in play, if necessary in a difficult or unusual circumstance. For example, in an unplayable lie situation, before taking relief a player must be able to identify his ball. This meant that Jeff and Sand Wedge would have to establish to a rules official's satisfaction that a ball was Jeff's Titleist 3, not just a Titleist 3.

Nodding to Sand Wedge, as the concentration building for the challenge at hand began to etch its way onto Jeff's face, he accepted the putter and the three balls, and walked onto the practice green.

As usual, to begin his pre-round preparation Jeff dropped the three balls a few feet away from one of the practice cups near the side of the green. Employing the cross-handed grip on the putter handle he had used so effectively on a number of important short putts yesterday, he stroked the first ball firmly into the center of the cup. The click of the balata ball against the face of putter felt solid and precise. As Jeff positioned the second ball with the head of the putter, preparing to execute a second practice putt identical to the first, he felt himself rock slightly in the now freshly-blowing wind, and noticed that it was whipping his pant legs as he stood over the ball. He widened his stance slightly, to better anchor his body as he stroked the ball. Nevertheless, the ball bounced slightly as it left the face of the putter, and curled under the left edge of the cup, lipping out gently and stopping directly behind the hole, an inch or so away. As if to erase from history the second putt's undesired result, Jeff immediately reached out with the putter head and pulled the second ball back into position in the middle of his stance. He repeated the cross-handed stroke, making sure to accelerate the head of the putter as he stroked the ball toward the hole. The contact on the ball was another solid and satisfying click this time, and the ball disappeared into the cup. By now, Sand Wedge, the white towel draped over his shoulder, had assumed his position on the practice green behind the target hole, watching his player's technique as preparations for the second round began in earnest. "That right," he said. "Release the putter through the ball... That right."

Jeff continued for several minutes to hit practice putts of varying lengths. He and Sand Wedge were trying particularly hard to note the effects on the roll and pace of the ball the wind appeared to have. The practice green was growing dryer, harder and crustier by the minute in the warm and windblown conditions. A downhill, downwind putt of 20 feet had to be just barely touched to stop anywhere close to the target hole. Just as Jeff had attempted such a putt, stroking one of the Titleists toward the hole Sand Wedge stood behind, some 20 feet down the green, Jeff heard Norm Thompson's voice from behind, "Jeff, excuse me, but could I talk with you for just a minute?"

Not bothering to watch the result of the putt he had just hit, Jeff turned around to face the player with whom he had shared the nasty exchange at last night's meeting.

"I want to apologize Jeff, for what I said last night. It was uncalled for, and I regret it."

Looking into Norm's eyes as he spoke, Jeff could see that Norm was speaking with great sincerity. "Don't worry about it Norm," Jeff said. "It was an emotional moment for all of us. I think we were all very near, if not a little bit over the edge. Everybody except for Florine, of course."

"Isn't he something," Norm agreed. "He's either the coolest cucumber or the most clueless fool we've got out here. I don't really know which."

"I think he means well," Jeff observed. "I'll tell you what, I wouldn't mind borrowing his putting stroke for a couple of years."

"You through playing already?" Jeff asked, remembering that Norm had an early starting time today, and must have come over directly from the ninth green, where he had finished.

"Yeah," Norm responded, "shot 74. I'm in at plus one overall. Probably be playing the weekend, but no great shakes, my high stuff's no good when it blows. That's probably why I've never won in Florida."

"Pretty rough out there?" Jeff asked, looking to the swaying pine trees, which told the story well enough.

"Yeah, but not too bad, the rules guys set the pins and tees pretty fair. They apparently knew we were gonna have a lot of wind. Listen, I know you're off 10 pretty soon, I just wanted to apologize and get us back on the same page. You and Sid both made me do some thinking last night, and I want you to know that I respect where you're coming from. Maybe it does make the most sense for the world tour ideas to be run through the policy board before they're announced to the press."

"I sure think so," Jeff said, relieved that what he thought might be another difficult conversation, was resolving on such an upbeat and positive basis.

"Good luck and play well, Jeff," Norm said, extending his right hand for a handshake that he hoped would bring complete closure to the anger and frustration of the previous evening. Jeff gladly clasped Norm's offered hand, and then returned to the business of preparing to face a windy and fast Stadium Course.

He and Sand Wedge were due on the 10th tee in about 45 minutes.

Chapter 20

The 10th hole on the Stadium Course, where Jeff and Trent Blalock were to begin their second round, is one of the most difficult driving holes on the entire course. From the back of the championship tee, the fairway appears as a narrow shelf, angled from right to left, bordered with dense trees on the right and a deep, unkept waste area and more dense trees, all along the left. The tee is back in a chute, with spectator mounds on the right and behind, producing something of an amphitheater effect, although nothing so dramatic as the first tee.

Nevertheless, as Jeff waited for his second round to begin, he was within the throes of his usual first-tee anxiety.

Due perhaps to the fact that he had shot 80 yesterday, and would need divine intervention to make this evening's cut, Trent, on the other hand, appeared to be the epitome of calm as the two players awaited the starter's introduction. He stood silently between the tee markers, holding a Callaway Big Bertha driver by his side, with his right hand placed about two thirds of the way down the shaft. Trent held the club with the face turned upwards, and every minute or so, he would bounce his golf ball off the driver, sending the ball three or four feet up in the air and over his left shoulder. Trent would complete each act of the routine by catching the ball behind his back, with his left hand cupped backwards. Anybody watching Blalock's nonchalant demonstration of dexterity and coordination was probably wondering how in the heck he could have ever shot 80.

A few moments after the Belcamp, Swisher and Hartsfield group ahead of Jeff and Trent had played their second shots and were walking toward the 10th green, volunteer starter Nelson Headley moved to the center of the tee, raising a small megaphone to his lips.

"Ladies and gentlemen, introducing the 1:38 starting time, from Brownsville, Texas, currently at 8-over-par, please welcome Trent Blalock." The gallery, which covered the mounds around the tee, and extended two or three deep, all the way down the right side of the fairway, applauded appreciatively, their respect for Trent's skills undiminished by his unimpressive first-round score. But most of them were not here to see Trent play anyway.

"And from West Palm Beach, Florida... but formerly, and *really* from Atlantic Beach" Headley continued, adding the local reference to great effect with the excited and festive crowd, "the first-round leader of the Players Championship, with a score of 7-under-par 65, ladies and gentlemen, please welcome Jeff Taylor."

The reception of the crowd to Jeff's introduction was enthusiastic. Jeff managed a smile and tipped his visor as he moved to the left side of the tee to tee up his ball. If he threw up, he thought, at least it would be among friends. Engaging his "auto pilot" swing more successfully than he had on the first tee yesterday, he managed to strike a playable, if not spectacular drive down the right center of the fairway. The 10th was playing down-wind, so its usual severity from the tee was missing anyway. Jeff had done what he had to do: get the ball safely in play. He felt a pleasant wave of confidence flow over him as he handed the 3-wood to Sand Wedge and prepared to watch Trent's drive. Trent gave notice immediately that he wasn't leaving anything in the bag, crushing a high, drawing drive down the right side, turning it right to left, back into the center of the fairway, perfect. The two players and their caddies strode off, much of the huge gallery moving with them.

Looking up to the now bleached-out blue, but still clear skies, as he and Sand Wedge walked down the 10th fairway, Jeff noted that the Met Life blimp and its chugging buzz were nowhere to be found, grounded, no doubt, due to the high-wind conditions. *No TV glamour shots today,* Jeff thought. The chamber of commerce and Mayor Smith would not be happy. The media coverage of the

Players Championship had literally put the Jacksonville beaches on the map as a tourist destination, particularly a golf-tourist destination, in the late 70's and 80's. In competition with Pinehurst, North Carolina and Palm Beach County, Florida, little Ponte Vedra, home of the TPC and the PGA Tour, boldly claimed itself the Golf Capital of the World. Jeff thought the boasting was a little pretentious. But what the hey, he loved the place anyway.

Sand Wedge arrived alongside Jeff's ball first, laying the golf bag on the fairway about five yards to the right of the ball's position, and then hurriedly began stepping off measurements from various landmarks indicated in the book. Jeff had withdrawn the book from his back pocket for what appeared to be a more pensive consultation, leaving the ambitious pacing and measuring to Sand Wedge.

His computations completed, Sand Wedge advised Jeff that he had "157 to the center, 164 to the pin, garbage front left." In addition to giving the distances, Sand Wedge was saying don't be short and left. Jeff recalled last night's criticism of yesterday's front-left pin placement, which, at least on Terry Hilton's "perfect" shot, cruelly and unfairly fed into the garbage Sand Wedge was advising him to be sure to avoid. David Frisch had been a man of his word. Today the pin placement was back-right, all but taking the garbage out of play.

"What do you like," Jeff asked, tossing up into the breeze a few blades of the closely-mown Bermuda grass he had reached down and plucked moments before, to get a better sense of the strength and precise direction of the wind that would undoubtedly affect the flight and spin of the Titleist 3 on his next shot. Jeff was determined to continue the "let Sand Wedge do the thinking" strategy that had served him so well in route to yesterday's 65.

Sand Wedge apparently wasn't sure. He reached down and plucked some blades of grass of his own, and tossed them up into the breeze, as Jeff had done. Still unsatisfied, the caddie looked off in the direction of the tall pine trees to the left of the green. They didn't seem to be registering the degree of wind that seemed apparent out in the fairway.

"Little eight," Sand Wedge finally said. "Take off just a little; don't wanna get it up too high."

Jeff thought for a moment... "OK, little eight it is," he said, assuming his stance and rotating his shoulders back and forth a few times in the manner he would do when executing the shot. The shoulder routine was an exercise Jeff often did, particularly early in the round, to ensure looseness in his arms and upper body. After three or four repetitions of his clubless swing, Jeff paused and looked up questioningly in Sand Wedge's direction. Sand Wedge was standing quietly, a new cigarette dangling from his lips, looking toward the green, as if expecting to watch Jeff's shot as it approached the target.

"Hell-o-o," Jeff said. "Hey, wake up; I'm gonna hit eight, but you need to bring it to me first."

Panic registered in Sand Wedge's eyes as he realized his oversight. He hustled over to the bag and withdrew the 8-iron, wiping the black leather grip with his shoulder-draped towel, and brought it quickly over to Jeff's position.

"Sorry boss," Sand Wedge muttered as he handed Jeff the club.

"It's OK man, relax," Jeff said, smiling as he accepted the iron. "Good God, you'd think this was a Major or something."

"Million dollars be very Major," the caddie responded quietly. "Now make a good swing."

Jeff struck the shot confidently, seemingly effortlessly. The ball flew on a medium, controlled trajectory into the middle of the green, and released after impacting the firm, wind-dried surface, rolling all the way to the back, some 25 feet to the left of the pin. The shot had been better than the result, and demonstrated to Jeff and Sand Wedge the firmness of the greens, and the difficulty of the wind conditions they would likely be having to cope with all day.

"Dancing," Jeff said, with some disappointment, as he handed the 8-iron back to Sand Wedge, noting that although the results of the shot weren't as good as he probably deserved, he was nevertheless on the green with a reasonable birdie putt opportunity. "I will need a putter though," he continued, not able to resist the temptation to kid Sand Wedge just a little more about his previous absent-mindedness. Sand Wedge took it with good humor. He liked this attitude his player seemed all of a sudden to be showing, acting self-assured and confident, like he believed he could win.

Like Sand Wedge had told Jeff a thousand times before, "You're good enough to win, if you believe you can win, it's the believing part that takes some work."

Chapter 21

As the afternoon wore on, the increasingly difficult playing conditions wreaked more and more havoc on the players' scores, and kept the electronic leader boards around the Stadium Course flashing, blinking and changing, in nearly constant flux. Benefiting from his early second-round starting time, which had allowed him to avoid at least some of the wind, Rocky Stillwell had somehow managed a 69, to go with his opening 68 and tie Jeff for the mid second-round lead, at -7.

But most everybody else, especially those among the Friday afternoon starters, was going backwards, as the dry and fast course conditions, combined with the blustery, southwest wind, allowed the Stadium Course to exact its paybacks for Thursday's relative generosity. Skip Florine, for example, had fallen all the way from -6 to even-par, having bogeyed the 10th and 11th, his first two holes of the day, and then, lost all four wheels off his game at once, at the diabolical, island-green par-3 17th. As if to make his light-hearted comments about the hole in the media center Thursday into some sort of grim, self-fulfilling prophecy, he had missed the 17th green short and to the right with his 6-iron from the tee, and then over flown the green with his sand wedge pitch from the drop zone. He had somehow gotten his second pitch from the drop zone on the putting surface, but could do no better than two-putt from there, scoring a horrendous quadruple bogey-7. Skip had trudged to the 18th tee with a gait that was the antithesis of his exuberant stride to the media center just 24 hours ago. Sadly, the normally ebullient young player had learned first hand that golf's vicissitudes, from euphoric joy to utter despair, know no bounds.

While the players labored through the afternoon, the spectators spectated, socialized and partied. Friday afternoon at the Players had, over the years, become much more than just a sporting event. It had become a happening, the place to be and be seen in Jacksonville in late March. In fact, the Players was threatening the annual Florida-Georgia college football game in the Gator Bowl for billing as the world's largest outdoor cocktail party. The warm temperatures and volatile scoring only added to the supercharged atmosphere.

Amid all the grinding and muttering of the players, and the crescendo-building hoopla of the gallery, rules official David Frisch sat on his golf cart, in his preferred position, between two green and three tee. He was very tired from the 18-hour day he had put in Thursday and looked forward to the end of play today. After the second round, the field would be cut to the 70 lowest scores and ties, probably reducing by more than half the number of players to be dealt with in Saturday's third round. Although well concealed by the PGA Tour visor and state trooper like, mirror-lensed sunglasses, if the truth be known, David's eyes were closed along about 3:00 when his two-way radio cleared, indicating that someone was trying to contact him. Startled, David leaned forward and picked the radio up, from the compartment to the left of the golf cart's steering wheel. He quickly turned the volume knob down, so the forthcoming voice would not disturb Thad Grigsby, who at +4 for the championship was on the projected cut line, and in the process of grinding over a difficult putt to save par at the par-5 second.

"David Frisch, this is Peter Grimes, come in please, over." The faintness of the radio volume contrasted with the apparent urgency in Grimes' voice.

"Peter Grimes," David spoke softly into his radio, already putting the cart slowly in motion, in search of a new location, away from the gallery and out of earshot of the players. "This is David, what have you got, over."

"Well David, you're not going to believe this one. But I think we had a rules committee volunteer just blow an unplayable ruling over here at the 10th."

"What'd he do?" David asked, beginning a slow burn. He had been absolutely against the current policy of inviting golf industry dignitaries to the Players to perform as rules officials. Let 'em come, David felt, but don't put them in a position to screw up a critical ruling. He wanted all rulings made by his staff, period.

"Looks like he improperly granted the player relief," Grimes responded. "Apparently the player claimed his ball had stuck in the top of a palm tree. He was given a drop without having to retrieve the ball and identify it as his. Got it up and down for five. Coulda' been seven or more if ruled correctly as a lost ball."

"Who's the player?" Frisch asked, hoping it was somebody on his way to 82 and the Jax airport five minutes after he changed shoes in the locker room.

"Arlen Baker-Charles, 5-under through 10, way up on the leader board."

"Shit," Frisch said into the radio, placing the heel of his left hand to his forehead, as he tried to figure out what to do next. "Please tell me this didn't get on the air," he continued, thinking it would be bad enough to unravel the mess if it was an essentially unnoticed screw-up, but utter hell if it had been shown on the air, or even taped.

"ESPN showed it wall-to-wall," Grimes advised.

"Dammit... Goddammit," Frisch intoned, knowing his afternoon, and evening, and probably the entire weekend were now committed to sorting out the sordid details, and explaining how it could have happened and what it meant, to the players, to the media... and to Sid.

Speak of the devil. David's radio cleared again.

"David Frisch, this is Sid, what in the hell is going on down there?"

"Commissioner, I'm on my way over to 10 right now to talk to Peter Grimes. He just reported it to me two seconds ago," David responded, his cart now at full speed, heading around the northwest corner of the clubhouse, toward the 10th hole.

"See me when you've got a full report."

"Yes sir," David responded, clicking off the radio and slamming it down on the seat beside him. As he continued driving out to 10, Frisch vowed this would be his last Players Championship. At least the last one he would oversee as Tournament Director. Frisch was a 61-year-old retired Navy Captain, with now over 20 years experience handling rules and tournament administration at Tour events. In the frustration of the moment, he was thinking that he no longer needed or wanted the grief that would inevitably be involved in dealing with the mess he had been dispatched to investigate. He was wondering why he hadn't taken early retirement last year, when it had been so graciously and generously offered.

CHAPTER 22

Jeff's first thought about the 17th came as he and Sand Wedge were sizing up his iron shot into the 15th green. The direction of the approach shot there, and the tee shot he would have to hit at seventeen were similar. The thought was not a pleasant one. The most difficult wind angle for Jeff, and most golfers, to play is when the wind is quartering and against from the left, that is, coming from between 10 and 11 o'clock, if noon is the line of the target. In such situations, the slightest mis-hit on the ball results in a shot pushed far to the right, and usually well short of the target. At seventeen, short and right is an area populated by alligators, large mouth bass, and Skip Florine's golf ball, among many thousands of others.

Arriving at seventeen tee, Jeff had maintained his -7 position and was tied for the lead with Rocky Stillwell, who was in the clubhouse, out of harm's way, at least until tomorrow. Jeff had bogeyed 12 and 13, but bounced back nicely with birdies at fourteen and sixteen. Looking at the island green from the front of the tee as the threesome up ahead putted out, Jeff resolutely acknowledged the architectural brilliance of the design. It was really an easy hole under most conditions, but also as gut-wrenching as they come in conditions like these, and situations like his. As he walked back to Sand Wedge, who was positioned with the Wilson bag upright, alongside the right-side tee marker, he secretly wished Trent had the honor. Jeff would love to see what the swirling wind did to Trent's ball, before he had to play. But Jeff knew he would have to hit first, and club selection was going to be a high-stakes guess.

Joining his caddie beside the bag, Jeff stole Sand Wedge a wry smile and asked the usual question, "What do you like?"

Sand Wedge already had the club in his left hand. "We got 130 to the front, 139 to the middle and 147 to the back; two-club wind, quarterin', at ya. Hit the 6, smooth; don' wanna get it too high."

Jeff turned his gaze back toward the green and walked out into the middle of the tee. He was trying to see if he could detect any pattern to the swirling wind, which threatened to blow off his visor, forcing him to tug it even lower and tighter onto his head as he continued to study the situation. He thought Sand Wedge's advice to hit the 6-iron was probably right; he was just trying to commit himself to the club, and the type of shot he would have to execute.

Returning to the bag, Jeff nodded to Sand Wedge and reached out for the six. The caddie toweled off the grip one more time and handed his player the club.

Jeff elected to tee his ball on the extreme right side of the tee, causing Sand Wedge to have to move the bag back a few feet, to be clearly out of the way. The shot he had conceived in his mind was a knock-down draw, working the ball on a lower trajectory, back into the wind, so it would push the ball down, not off-line, toward the alligators. As he progressed through his pre-shot routine, he anticipated the flow of confidence and inner peace he had been experiencing over so many shots since the wedge chip-in yesterday, at the 16th. But it didn't come. He clicked on the auto pilot and made his swing.

Jeff knew by the position of his right shoulder at impact that he'd gone over the top of the shot slightly. In doing so he had in essence turned his 6-iron into a 5-and-1/2-iron, sending the ball off slightly left of the intended line, and drawing. The shot's fate depended on whether the wind held the ball up, or the Titleist bore on through it, winding up long and left, and just as wet, as short and right. Having finished the follow through, Jeff anxiously followed the flight of the ball, still maintaining his grip on the club, but holding it straight out to his right side, leaning his body to the right also, as if his body English might impart some magical, counter-balancing physics, which would pull the ball down to a safe landing, on the far left side of the green.

"Push it wind, push it wind," Sand Wedge urged," his cigarette clenched between his front teeth as he talked, and anxiously squinted, following the precarious flight of the ball.

Whatever the causes... the forces of nature, the collective will of the onlookers, or divine intervention, disaster was avoided. The wind finally seemed to grab the descending ball and pushed it down safely, onto the extreme left rear edge of the green, no more than a foot from the railroad ties that formed the perimeter between the putting surface and the surrounding water hazard. The reaction from the gallery was a strange combination of cheers, and sighs of relief. For effect, Jeff clutched his chest and feigned two or three "rubber-legged" steps as he walked back to hand the 6-iron to Sand Wedge. The gallery around the tee laughed at Jeff's theatrics, delighted that their hero had escaped disaster. Jeff winked at the caddie and turned to watch Trent face the challenge he had just survived.

On the way to seventeen green the sense of confidence Jeff had waited for in vain over his tee shot began to return. Something was going on, and he was liking it. He was hitting the ball well, getting clubbed perfectly by a well-prepared and motivated caddie, and getting some good breaks along the way. He felt himself easing into the Zone he had so frequently operated within instinctively as a younger player; that delicate, yet awesomely powerful level of self-assured concentration which compels success, like the North Pole compels the needle of a compass.

In his mind, Jeff saw the long birdie putt at seventeen go into the hole, several moments before it actually did. Jeff acknowledged the resounding birdie roar of the thousands assembled on the spectator mounds and in the hospitality tents along the left side of seventeen with a contented clasp of his right thumb and forefinger to the brim of his visor.

Winking once again to Sand Wedge as they left the green and proceeded across to the 18th tee, Jeff had reassumed sole possession of the lead of the Players Championship, and he seemed to be wearing the mantle very comfortably.

Sand Wedge didn't say anything as he marched along at his player's side. He knew the Zone when he saw it, and also knew this was a good time to be quiet and let his man do his thing.

Chapter 23

Jeff played the last 10 holes of his second round with the calm assurance of a professional who is comfortable in what he's doing. His serenity and focus were often in vivid contrast to the ever-mounting unpredictability of the conditions, as the swirling winds continued to blow, and the festiveness of the gallery continued to rise. As Jeff approached the ninth green, his final hole for the day, shadows cast by the tall pines along the left side of the fairway marbled the crusty, very firm and now lightning-fast green.

Jeff had played his 3-iron second shot on the long par-5 into excellent position on the right side of the fairway, some 45 yards from the center of the green. The faithful throngs who had followed him most, if not all of the afternoon, lined the spectator mounds along the right side of the fairway, a vantage point which allowed them to watch not only Jeff and Trent's play on the ninth, but also players finishing on the 18th, on the other side of the long, narrow lake that separates the Stadium Course's ninth and 18th holes.

After consulting the book briefly, Sand Wedge advised that it was 37 yards to the front of the green, 46 to the pin. He emphasized the "to the pin" yardage, indicating that playing for the pin was his recommendation, although since the Zone-entering transformation he had noticed in Jeff at the 17th, Sand Wedge had been soft-pedaling his advice, deferring to Jeff's instincts to conceive and then execute the shots he continued to demonstrate complete confidence in making.

Despite the treacherous, late-afternoon conditions, Jeff had managed to add three more birdies to his round after the unbelievable one at 17. He had faltered only once, with a bogey at one, when his approach putt, a wicked downhill, side-hiller had gotten away from him, sliding down the slick putting surface some 12 feet past the cup. It had been his first three-putt green of the Championship. True to his newly found, rock-solid form however, Jeff had come right back with a birdie at the second, holing a 15-footer. The Titleist had rolled straight toward and then into the hole, as if the ball were traveling on tiny rails. So, as he continued to contemplate the approach to nine, Jeff was an impressive 3-under for the day, and -10 overall.

Commissioner Watterson had inconspicuously joined the gallery lining the right-side mounds overlooking the ninth green, and, while delighted, along with most everyone else, by Jeff's masterful play, was also wondering what on earth it would take to make even-par a Championship-leading score. Reviewing the master scoreboard off to his right, however, Sid quickly dismissed the thought, noting that despite yesterday's lights-out scoring, only a handful of the field remained under par after 36 holes, and it looked like +5 would be good enough to make the cut. The Stadium Course was offering the desired Major challenge.

Reaching into the bag, which Sand Wedge held upright, two or three yards to the right of the ball, Jeff selected a 9-iron. Sand Wedge was a little surprised by Jeff's club selection, since he saw the shot as a good opportunity to fly a lob wedge in to about 10 feet short of the pin, allowing it to release on up to the hole, due to the extreme firmness of the green. As Jeff settled into his routine over the ball, it became clear to the caddie that his player had another type of shot in mind. Playing the ball back in his stance, toward his right foot, and positioning the grip of the club well forward of his address position, Jeff had decided upon a bump and run shot, reminiscent of the type of approach that was so popular in Britain, before the modern era of irrigated fairways and greens. Sid, the onlooking golf tradition purist that he was, was about to see a shot that he would love.

Executing the stroke once again with the seemingly effortless style he had displayed on nearly every shot all day, Jeff struck the ball crisply, sending it from the face of the club on a low trajectory, bouncing first some five yards short of the green, then onto the front of the green and running on along toward the hole. The reaction of the gallery to the shot began to build as the ball bounced onto the green. The expectant voices surged louder and louder, as the Titleist continued to roll on, across the shade-covered, lightning-quick bent grass. The crowd's reaction mushroomed toward a thunderous cheer, but was then punctuated at the end by a collective sigh of disappointment, as the ball caught the left edge of the hole, threatening to disappear beside the hard leaning pin, only to gently lip out and come to rest, no more than six inches to the right of the cup.

Jeff had begun walking toward the green as he watched the shot release toward the pin, breaking into a trot as he "chased" the ball to the hole, and fell to his knees in anguished disbelief, when the ball flirted with the cup, but spun out. On his knees, amid the noisy reaction of the crowd, while the ESPN broadcasters attempted to describe the dramatic scene to the television audience, it began to register pleasantly on Jeff where he was, and what he was doing. Rising to his feet, he appreciatively doffed his visor and scanned the admiring crowd. Sand Wedge had handed him the putter so he could finish his ball into the hole and make way for Trent, who was still waiting to play his third shot from the green-side bunker. Jeff had just shot the best 68 of his life.

Returning the putter to Sand Wedge as they left the green, and headed with the now extremely wind-blown Mrs. Alma Feathers toward the scoring tent, Jeff finally began to sense how dead- tired and drained, both physically and emotionally, he was.

"My man," Sand Wedge said approvingly as they walked along. "My man." He wasn't inclined to say anything more. Knowing about the Zone, the caddie just wanted his player to stay there for two more days, no questions asked, no explanations needed.

"Sand Wedge, that's what you call golfin' your ball," Jeff said resolutely as they walked along, acknowledging the well wishes of the excited fans who lined the gallery ropes leading to the scoring tent behind the 18th green.

"My man," Sand Wedge nodded, smiling in full agreement. "My man."

Chapter 24

If they removed the bar stools, and covered up the beer taps and liquor bottles in the long, but extremely narrow area off to the left of the entranceway to the Homestead Restaurant, the last thing you would guess it to be is a cocktail lounge. But that's what it is. And between 5 p.m. and midnight on any Friday or Saturday night, or any night during Players Championship week, it is the place to be for the upscale golf crowd of Jax Beach and Ponte Vedra. The tarnished Maximum Occupancy sign by the cash register behind the bar said 24, but during the establishment's rather extended happy hours, the head count was typically closer to 50 or 60, which made for very cramped conditions. Body contact among the patrons was not reserved for consensual situations. It came with the territory. According to local opinion, you could get more cheap feels in one trip from the Homestead Bar to the restroom and back, than the average FSU freshman got in an entire semester.

The Homestead's food menu is down-home country fare: fried chicken and fish, served family style, along with biscuits you could use to break out a window, and oceans of red eye gravy. But for the denizens of the Homestead's architecturally unique bar, the restaurant's food is not the thing. The attraction is the tradition of the place, and, for some, the relative likelihood of getting lucky.

Needless to say, at 5:50 on Friday afternoon, the television in the teeming Homestead bar was tuned to ESPN's late second-round coverage of the Players, taking place at the Stadium Course, some five miles across the marsh, as the egret flies. The crescendo that erupted from the revelers as Jeff's approach at nine nearly went in the hole caused ripples in the gravy boats, all the way to the back of the restaurant.

A large, matted and framed color picture of Jeff accepting the World Series of Golf trophy from Deane Beman, another local hero, adorned the limited wall space above the bar, and there was little doubt who the imbibing patrons favored for this year's Championship title. The inscription on the picture had been penned by Jeff right at the bar around midnight three years ago: "To Sandy and the gang at the Homestead - if your tee time is before 9:00, stay away from the upside-down margaritas."

The drink Jeff's inscription referred to was a curious local concoction that involved the drinker, usually at least two sheets to the wind already, turning around and leaning his or her head back over the bar. The bartender, usually Sandy, then would proceed to pour the margarita ingredients, tequila and triple sec, directly into the customer's open mouth.

Legend had it that veteran Tour player Barry Reel had supposedly gulped six of them on a missed-the-cut Friday evening in 1983, chasing each with an ice-cold Heineken. No one knows for sure what happened to him the rest of the night. Supposedly, he was next seen by the first foursome playing the Jax Beach Municipal Course Saturday morning, sleeping in his underwear in the bunker alongside the second green. Barry's debacle was merely one chapter in the many volumes of rich and earthy Homestead lore.

Skip Florine, who, by posting his second-round 84 had established a new Players Championship record, lowest first-round score ever to miss the cut, looked intent upon following in Barry's footsteps. Sitting at the end of the bar, his attention shifting between the TV and the girl to his right, the one whose shoulder he had autographed some 30 hours before, Skip had a shot glass of Jack Daniels and a green bottle of Heineken in front of him, bearing witness to his night's mission: drink too much and hope for "luck."

"Go in the *hole*," Skip exhorted as he glanced to the TV screen to see Jeff's ninth-hole bump and run shot rolling toward the cup. "God *damn*," he continued, rising to his feet as Jeff's ball lipped out of the hole.

"He's such a great guy... such a great guy," Skip repeated, turning from the TV to gaze admiringly again at the beautifully- shouldered Rebecca Prentiss.

"Never met him," Rebecca replied. "But I know my mom used to have a crush on him; made Daddy mad sometimes. He used to live up in Atlantic Beach, you know. Moved away a few years ago when he and his wife got divorced... You like Jeff a lot do you?"

Rebecca asked, interested by Skip's extreme animation when he had reacted to Jeff's near-miss.

"I surely do," Skip responded... "Far as I'm concerned, people like Jeff are what it's all about. Works hard on his own thing, but always has time for the other guy, always takes the other guy's point of view into account... I first met him about two years ago, playing a practice round at the AT&T, he called it 'the Crosby,' in Monterrey. We were playing Pebble Beach and I wanted to get some practice playing out of the bunkers... So I finish putting out at one and go over to the bunker and drop a couple of balls, and then blast 'em out onto the green. Jeff looked at me kinda funny, but didn't say anything... There were about 50 or so people standing around the green watching us play... We go on over and drive off of two, and as we're walking on down the fairway, old Sand Wedge walking along, smokin' as always, Jeff comes over to me, just as nice as he can be and says 'Skip, you know you really shouldn't do what you did back there. It gave those folks watching us around the green the wrong impression. You know, this is their course, and they can't just go throwin' balls in the bunkers, and hittin' practice shots out of 'em. So we shouldn't either. 'But how am I gonna find out how the sand in the bunkers on the course plays then I ask, it's totally different from the stuff in the bunkers in the practice area...' He looked me in the eye, flashing that grin of his and said, 'Well then, if you want to practice from the bunkers on the course, hit your approach shot, or your drive into 'em on purpose. Then everybody's happy, you get your practice and you don't offend anybody in the process.' Just to illustrate his point, on two he hit into the front bunker on purpose, and then blasted out, into the hole. 'God I love it out here' he said as we walked to number three tee. 'Skip,' he said, 'you're gonna love it too.'"

"Wow," Rebecca responded, noting the obvious respect Skip had for Jeff. "Hey, I've got an idea. Why don't you stay the weekend and we'll go out there and root old local hero home a winner."

"I've checked out of the hotel already," Skip replied, nevertheless warming to the idea. He didn't really need to be on "down the road" to New Orleans until Tuesday.

"Not a problem," Rebecca replied, sending a shudder of titillation through Skip's travel and hotel room-weary bones.

"And I'm already booked on the 10:30 flight to New Orleans," Skip continued, referring to the Delta flight scheduled to leave Jax later that night, loaded with Tour players who had missed the Players cut.

"Not a problem," Rebecca said again, repeating the exact intonation of the words she had just used, as if she were some kind of live and foxy Chatty Kathy doll. She reached into her purse and produced a miniature cell phone. "Call Delta and change it, the number's 735-6600." Being a Delta stewardess, Rebecca knew the number by heart.

Skip shuddered again, twice this time, and accepted the phone, keying in the numbers Rebecca had said.

"Hello, this is Skip Florine, and I have a reservation on the 10:30 flight to New Orleans"... He waited as the agent verified the information... "And I'd like to change that to Monday night, same flight"... He waited again as the agent checked out the availability of the new flight... "Super good, see y'all Monday night."

Leaning over close to Rebecca and admiring the still autographed shoulder with a whole new level of appreciation, Skip handed her back the phone and said, "We got a deal."

With that, Rebecca challenged him to an upside-down margarita, winking and saying, "Your starting time tomorrow's not gonna be 'til way after nine."

CHAPTER 25

Commissioner Watterson came into the scoring tent while Jeff and Trent were reviewing and signing their cards. Trent had carded a respectable 72 in the second round, but it was not going to be enough to overcome the hole he had dug for himself with yesterday's 80. He was +8 for the Championship, and accordingly, down the road to New Orleans.

Jeff's situation was the opposite. He was expected shortly at the media center, as the second-round leader. Sid wanted to tell him so personally. Jeff's second-round 68 having been added and re-added, reviewed and re-reviewed, he signed the scorecard on the line beside "Contestant," and turned it in, making it official that Jeff Taylor had a 4-shot lead, at a score of -11 after two rounds of the Players Championship.

As Jeff prepared to stand up to leave the tent, he felt the same grip on his left shoulder he had felt yesterday at Commissioner's Hospitality. He turned around to Sid's beaming face.

"Congratulations, Jeff," Sid said. "That's unbelievably great playing. Obviously, the media want to see you in the press tent; OK if I chauffeur you over there on my golf cart?"

"Sure," Jeff replied with his usual smile, then feeling a twinge of dread, remembering the note Sid had placed on his locker, and the reasons why he chose to ignore it. Jeff really had no time, energy or interest in any further discussions about the world tour issue, or any of the other business issues Sid was constantly managing. Jeff knew he was squarely within one of the greatest competitive and professional opportunities of his career and he was not about to be side-tracked into anything else; not now, not tomorrow and not Sunday. He hoped he wouldn't have to be so blunt with Sid. But he would be, if Sid started grinding again about the world tour, or other Tour business.

The atmosphere Jeff and Sid stepped into outside the scoring tent was festive, bordering on tumultuous. It was now getting on toward 6:30 and the record crowd was bringing the concept of TGIF to a new level. Gallery ropes separated Sid and the Commissioner from the crowd as they walked the few steps to where Sid's "PGA TOUR RULES" cart was parked, and autograph seekers and well-wishers of all ages, shapes and sizes strained against the yellow cord, desperately offering a cap, or a program, or a piece of paper for Jeff to sign. Three college-age girls, wearing identical "Delta Gamma" midriff tee-shirts were calling to Jeff and waving an impromptu sign they had made, using notebook paper and lipstick: "Jeff Taylor, give us your shirt."

Acknowledging the bedlam and smiling at Sid as they prepared to get into the cart, Jeff said, "Florida-Georgia game's gonna have go some to top this."

"Yeah, I guess so," Sid said, his face registering some disdain as he looked around at the commotion. He seemed concerned that the carnival atmosphere was approaching a level of bravado inappropriate to the dignified image he and the rest of the Tour staff labored so hard to maintain at all Tour events. The "personality" Sid idealized for the Players Championship was a tricky thing to capture. He didn't want the event to emulate the tradition-enslaved stuffiness of The Masters or the U.S. Open. But on the other hand, he didn't want to see it assume the ribald, Mardi Gras-like characteristics of NFL football or NASCAR. He wanted people to have fun at the Players; but he also wanted an environment that maintained its dignity, and respect for the game and the players' profession.

As they rode slowly toward the media center, in some places, where they blended with the pedestrian traffic, literally inching forward, the Commissioner said, "Jeff, I really appreciate what you said and did last night. Your take on things absolutely turned the tide, and postured us just right on this whole world tour thing. I had Mary and Nick prepare a letter this morning, along the lines your motion last night suggested, and we sent it out to Shumitami's people... I guess it was about 9:30, 10:00 o'clock maybe. Miraculously, and I use that term advisedly, because resolution of these types of issues expeditiously, even rationally, has not been my frequent experience in the four years I've had this job, his people faxed a response back to our office, just before noon. It indicated that while they continue to believe a world tour concept is needed and would be good for golf, they recognize the need to integrate the concept into the existing Tour schedules and commitments, and therefore plan to pursue implementation by requesting the opportunity to present their concept to our Board, the PGA, the European Tour, the USGA and the R&A for input, before any further steps are taken."

"Great," Jeff responded. "That's all you really wanted, isn't it?"

"Well, it's pretty damned good. Let's put it that way. Of course, I'd have preferred for them to just go away altogether. But at least this should put the media attention back on our Championship, and sets the agenda for a dialog, rather than the 'Screw you, here we come' approach they indicated in their press conference Wednesday."

"Any down side?" Jeff asked, his curiosity piqued, notwithstanding his vow of 10 minutes ago, to steer far and wide of any involvement in business matters for the rest of the weekend, at least.

"Mary's a little concerned about the idea of all the governing bodies coming together to evaluate things. Says it could be viewed as a conspiracy, you know an antitrust thing. You know lawyers: institutionalized paranoia. But I'm sure we can work around that. So we'll see."

They had finally arrived at the media center door. "So anyway," Sid said, as they entered the building, "I just wanted to personally express the staff's appreciation for your interest and support. Play well the rest of the way. But hey, take it easy on our golf course, will you?" With that, the Commissioner waved farewell and walked off to join a group of reporters who were motioning for him to come over.

Looking up to the front of the room, Jeff saw Lucy Tomkins gesturing for him to come forward to the interview area. It was the first time Jeff had been in the media center on two consecutive days for a long time.

Arriving at the dais, Jeff was greeted by Lucy as if he were her eldest brother returning home from the war. "Welcome back, stranger no more," she gushed. "Pour yourself some Gatorade and take a seat. I'll do the introduction."

Jeff sat down in the interview chair, filling the cup while preparing to answer the types of questions sportswriters ask to aging athletes who, for whatever reasons, have returned to the spotlight of their sport.

Lucy made the introduction: "Ladies and gentlemen I would like to introduce Jeff Taylor, the second-round Players Championship leader with a 36-hole total of 133, 11 under par. Jeff's scorecard today was as follows." Like yesterday, Lucy proceeded to read Jeff's hole-by-hole scores, ending with his second-round score of 68 and then calling for questions. Also like yesterday, Tom Schuyler asked the mandatory overview question and Jeff began to systematically recount his round, shot-by-shot. He did so without elaboration until he got to describing his near-disaster at seventeen. After recounting the details of the problematical 6-iron tee shot, that somehow found its way onto the extreme left rear of the green, he got philosophical for a moment, talking about the surge of confidence he felt as he was walking to seventeen green and how it seemed to envelope him for the rest of the round. After that, he reverted to the robot-like descriptions of his play, winding up with the bump and run at the ninth that had nearly gone in.

Picking up on Jeff's confidence theme, Tom Schuyler asked "Do you feel confident about tomorrow, and what's your game-plan for playing with a 4-shot lead?"

"I feel very confident about tomorrow," Jeff responded. "And very fortunate to be four shots out in front. This place really feels like home to me and I can't think of anything I'd rather be doing tomorrow than teeing off last in the third round of this Championship."

"What about Shumitami's letter today to the Commissioner? How do you feel about that?" Roy Thomas of the Miami Herald asked.

"I understand it's encouraging," Jeff said. "But I haven't read it and don't plan to until Monday, at the soonest. With all due respect to Mr. Shumitami, I'm kinda busy right now, trying to win a golf tournament."

"But we heard you were very vocal at last night's player meeting," Thomas continued.

"That was last night, in a business meeting," Jeff responded, his tone and manner becoming impatient. "Tonight, we're at the golf course, and that's where my attention is staying for the rest of the weekend. The Commissioner and his people are ready, willing and able to deal with Mr. Shumitami and I wish all of them well. But I'm here to play golf. And that's what I plan to do."

The assembled press seeing, and accepting that Jeff wasn't going to be led into any kind of debate or further discussion of the world tour matter, the questions returned to the fair game of how Jeff had played, how he found the course conditions, and so on. Jeff did his usual diplomatic best to answer everything, peppering his responses with occasional humor and personal anecdotes, demonstrating the charm and personality that had made him a media favorite for over 20 years.

Noting that it was getting to be 7:00, time to be ending the interview, Lucy spoke up as Jeff finished his remarks on what he thought the winning score on Sunday would be. "My score" is what he first said in response to the question, before going into some more detail, to fairly answer what was being asked.

"Anything further, ladies and gentlemen," Lucy said. It was her way of saying that it was getting late and time to be winding things up.

"One more question Jeff," Tom Schuyler said. "How do you feel about the blown ruling affecting Arlen Baker-Charles?"

"Don't know anything about it," Jeff responded.

"Well ESPN showed it for all to see," Schuyler continued, while Lucy wished she had a lever she could pull to drop Schuyler through a trap door in the floor. "And it's obvious Baker-Charles was given unplayable lie relief without first having to identify the ball. They say it should have been ruled a lost ball and a stroke and distance penalty. The way it turned out, he saved bogey and is in at 5-under.

"That's a screwy deal then," Jeff said shaking his head and looking over to Lucy for guidance. "I'll obviously defer to David Frisch and the rules staff on that one."

"The official wasn't one of David's guys though," Schuyler continued, refusing to let the matter drop.

Lucy took over. "Tom, look, the rules staff is looking into the whole thing and they'll do whatever the Rules of Golf provide for. But come on, that's not a matter for Jeff or any of the other players."

"Not unless Baker-Charles wins," Schuyler concluded, turning to walk back to his work station.

"I guess we know his story for tonight," Jeff said light-heartedly, restoring a more relaxed mood for the hangers-on who remained in the interview area.

"Thank you Jeff," Lucy said, ending the interview session. "And the best of luck tomorrow."

It was nearly dark when Jeff emerged from the TPC clubhouse and walked down the stairs leading to the parking lot and the red

Riviera. It had been a memorable day and Jeff wondered with equal parts of anticipation and hesitancy what the night and the reunion dinner at Sandy's would be like.

CHAPTER 26

Turning right again, out of the Sea Turtle parking lot, onto Ocean Avenue, this time on his way to Sandy's and the dinner she had invited him to some 12 hours ago, Jeff eased the red Riviera along the same route he had traveled this morning, on the nostalgia tour of his old neighborhood. The narrow streets of the beach town were dark now, except for the pools of luminescence at the intersections he drove through. After passing the old Town Hall, Jeff began looking for Egret Terrace, where he would turn right, and continue on past the PRIVATE DRIVE NO OUTLET sign, down to the beach and Sandy's condominium in the Egret's Landing development. Jeff lowered the windows on the Riviera as he drove slowly along, drinking in the welcome and relaxing sound of the ocean waves rushing up to the shore, as they did at the end of a windy day.

Pulling into the Egret's Landing parking lot, Jeff turned to the left and proceeded to the north end of the building, where Sandy's end-unit apartment was located. Her fully-restored, British racing green TR-6 was parked in front of number 6334.   Jeff steered the Riviera into the adjacent Guest parking spot, and, noting the time on the Riviera's digital clock, 7:59, turned off the engine. For some reason, the headlights on the car stayed on after he turned off the ignition, spoiling, he thought, the stealth Jeff was trying to employ in approaching Sandy's residence. He still wasn't sure acceptance of her invitation had been such a good idea, and he had planned to sit in the dark car for a moment or two, for a final self-debate on whether or not to go in. Fearing the Riviera's modern features, he now remembered the car had a sentry system, which kept the headlights on for 30 seconds or so after the engine was shut off, had blown his cover, Jeff dispensed with any final indecision, got out of the car and proceeded to walk up the cedar entranceway to Sandy's house. As he walked, he dismissed any second thoughts about his decision to come, and allowed the positive instincts he had felt this morning upon hearing Sandy's voice over the phone take back over. Pressing the door bell, he was now sure, was the right thing to do.

After his second push on the faintly illuminated door bell button, Jeff heard Sandy's voice, coming, it sounded, from somewhere back in the house: "Come in Jeff, it's open."

Realizing Sandy was probably still in the bathroom, "preening," to use her term. Jeff turned the doorknob and let himself into the front hallway which separated the parlor off to the left from the country kitchen and great-room area, off to the right.

"Hello-o" he called, shutting the door behind him. "Are you decent?"

"Not yet," Sandy called back, stepping partially out of the bathroom into the hallway, and looking back toward Jeff as she busily blow-dried her blond hair. "Give me five minutes," she said loudly, to be heard over the whir of the dryer, ... "And pour us a glass of wine, why don't you. There's an open bottle of Black Opal in the fridge." Black Opal was one of their favorite Australian Chardonnays. Jeff had not known Sandy back in the 80's, when his greater financial success on Tour had allowed him to indulge in more expensive tastes, such as the French champagne he and Cheryl had often enjoyed, to celebrate his homecomings, back before the divorce.

Jeff couldn't help but notice that Sandy wasn't dressed when she stepped out into the hallway. Glimpsing her body momentarily, sent a wave of desire through him, and his thoughts racing back to the intimate times of their relationship, when he would often bring a glass of wine to her in the bathroom, as she finalized her always-effective beautification process, in preparation for going out. One of Sandy's many charming personality traits was her uninhibited attitude about her body. Probably because she kept herself in such good shape, she often felt no need to wear clothing while she primped in front of the bathroom mirror, or lounged around the bedroom, reading or watching TV. On many such occasions she would engage Jeff in conversation, or occupy herself with whatever she was doing, oblivious to her stunning nakedness.

As he walked across into the kitchen, it struck Jeff again how much he had missed the closeness of their relationship, and how wrong he had been to turn Sandy away as his career unraveled a year ago.

Pouring the two glasses of Black Opal into the wine glasses Sandy had placed on the counter, Jeff decided it would be prudent under the circumstance to put Sandy's glass in the refrigerator, rather than deliver it to her in the bathroom. Taking his glass with him, he decided to go out on the cedar deck that overlooked the beach, and the boiling waves rushing up to the shore.

The high winds of the afternoon had subsided somewhat, and a scallop moon was rising over the Atlantic. The temperature was still balmy for late March, but the humidity was relatively low, at least for Florida. The picturesque scene was a soothing respite within what had been another jam-packed day.

Standing by the railing at the end of the deck, looking out over the ocean, Jeff entered another "zone." The one reserved for people basking in the afterglow of accomplishment, while at the same time confidently anticipating their next opportunity. He smiled inwardly as he recognized that he really was looking forward to tomorrow's third round. He wasn't fidgety, preoccupied or anxious, wondering if he'd be able to hang on under the pressure, and not blow it. He was looking forward to doing just exactly what he was capable of, and now deeply believed he could do: win the Players Championship.

"Here's to you, Polly" Jeff said softly, lifting his glass to toast in absentia the unlikely friend and mentor he had happened across in Orlando last fall.

Jeff's eyes drank in the full panorama of the view, from the Jax Beach pier lights stretching out into the sea, down past the Sea Turtle to the south, to the blinking red lights which marked the jetties at the mouth of the St. Johns river, to the north, up in Mayport.

"Sixpence for your thoughts," Sandy said as she joined Jeff out on the deck, closing the sliding-glass door behind her. She wore a pair of black silk running shorts and a loose-fitting, "Indiana University" tee shirt.

"They're worth more than that tonight, my dear," Jeff replied, as he turned to face his hostess for the evening. "Here's looking at you kid," he continued, restating the opening line he had used yesterday on the golf course. On their first date, Jeff, who was a big Humphrey Bogart fan, had taken Sandy to see a special showing of *Casablanca* at the Neptune Beach art theater. Over the years, the movie had become one of their favorites. They had often spent quiet nights together, watching the classic film, sometimes reciting the lines of the script, which both had nearly memorized.

Jeff walked over and clinked glasses with Sandy and sipped at the Black Opal, as he continued looking into her green eyes.

"You golfer boys," Sandy sighed, her return of Jeff's stare belying the impersonality of her remark. "I do declare," she continued, averting her eyes to the horizon, and adopting again the Southern belle accent she had employed yesterday afternoon, to mask the apprehension she felt then, as she did now. Jeff and Sandy were both struggling with the deeply-mixed emotions each other's presence brought on. An uncomfortable silence descended as they looked at each other and smiled... and nodded, as if agreeing to some unstated proposition.

"What a round of golf Jeff," Sandy finally said, knowing the topic of Jeff's golf was usually good for some lively talk, when he was playing well, that is.

"I'm pleased," Jeff responded, understating the obvious. "Things just feel right all of a sudden. I'm not really sure what it is, but I'm going with it, and it's more peaceful now than it's been out there for years... and years. But tell me about you," he continued. "How've things been with you? I just can't tell you how great you look and how happy it makes me to be here. After St. Augustine, I wondered if I'd ever see you again. I thought the 'no card' at Christmas time pretty well sealed it."

"You might not have," Sandy said, somewhat to Jeff's surprise, "if you hadn't hit that horrendous drive on four yesterday. It was so stupid, and I could see you weren't listening to Sand Wedge. I just had to say something... And then when you came over to me, and took the time to be sweet, right in the middle of everything you must have been going through. Well, what can I say?"

"You don't have to say anything," Jeff said, reaching out his arms and encircling Sandy's waist. Sandy started to step back, but just as quickly relented, cupping her wine glass between her hands and leaning forward, her cheek pressing into Jeff's shoulder. "Here's looking at you kid," Jeff repeated softly, stroking Sandy's hair with his free hand, and kissing her lightly around the eyes, which were now moist with emotion. It had been a long, hard year apart for both of them. They stood together quietly for several minutes, looking intermittently at each other, and the beauty of the surrounding view. It was one of those times when silence is, by far, the best possible means of communication.

CHAPTER 27

The only bad thing about leading a Tour event after 36 holes is having to play in the last pairing on "moving day," the players' term for Saturday's third round. It was a procedure dictated by television, to ensure that the leaders were on camera during the hours of the broadcast, scheduled today on NBC from 2:30 to 6:00. So Jeff had the dubious honor of a 1:52 starting time, when the wind would probably be at its most robust, and the firm Stadium Course greens would be at their quickest, and most "spiked up" by the rest of the field who had gone before. Ironically, the best third-round playing conditions were reserved for the bottom end of the field, the players just making the cut.

Saturday is called moving day by the players because for almost everyone still competing, a good round on Saturday moves them into position to win, while a bad round moves them out.

The weather had stabilized appreciably from yesterday, with the wind laying down quite a bit, and shifting around to come out of the northwest, bringing with it just a hint of the South- Georgia paper mill smell that had dominated Jacksonville so intrusively, back in the pre-EPA days of the 40's and 50's. "What's that smell?" the Yankee tourists out on the Jax Beach boardwalk would say. "Georgia-Pacific," the Crackers would answer. Jeff had grown actually to like the paper mill smell, in small doses. It reminded him of the good times back in Atlantic Beach, and high pressure weather systems that brought along the northwesterly breezes, blue skies and cooler temperatures. It was the suffocating, southwest winds, like yesterday's, and their usual high humidity that he really didn't like.

Jeff was paired with Rocky Stillwell who, playing early on Friday had managed a 69 to go with his opening 68 on Thursday. Stillwell was one of the Tour's more flamboyant young players, known for his prodigious driving distance. The veteran handicappers were somewhat surprised at Stillwell's mastery of the Stadium Course's sometimes severe accuracy requirements. Stillwell's length was not matched by his consistency, and little of the "smart money" was on him to be there at the end, come Sunday afternoon. Privately, the handicappers were also a little surprised at Jeff's position. No one was expressing any dubiousness over Jeff's chances, out of respect for his past accomplishments and because he was so well-liked. But many, such as Sid, who knew the game and its pressures well, were secretly wondering if Jeff could hold it together. It had been almost 10 years since he had last won, at the World Series in Akron, and it is common knowledge on Tour that the winner's circle gets harder and harder to enter, the longer a player is away from it.

But at noontime in the media center, the story of the moment wasn't Jeff, Rocky Stillwell, the weather or anything concerning the upcoming third round. The story was the fallout from the Baker-Charles ruling in the second round. Neither the electronic media nor the print media was inclined to let the controversy drop. ESPN's 11:00 a.m. SportsCenter Saturday morning had shown the tape of the flubbed ruling in its excruciating entirety, some seven uninterrupted and embarrassing minutes for the Tour. *The Florida Times Union* was typical of the print coverage. "Blown Ruling Threatens Players" was the sports section banner headline the local paper decided to print. When pressed, in the media center late Friday evening to explain, now for at least the hundredth time, how this could have happened, Tournament Director David Frisch had lost it, explaining, now in exasperation, "OK, what do you guys want me to say? It was an ignorant, stupid, committee ruling. What do you want us to do? Hang the guy in effigy?"

"But what if Baker-Charles wins?" the press insisted.

"If he wins... he wins," Frisch had replied wearily. "I guess you could call it rub of the green."

Now, a new, and even juicier twist on the fiasco was circulating through the rumor mill. Supposedly, the committee official was insisting that his ruling was proper, and was threatening the media, Frisch and the Tour with defamation litigation. The official's position was that a spectator had corroborated Baker-Charles' claim about his ball lodging in the palm tree, and that the corroboration was sufficient identification of Baker-Charles' ball to justify relief.

The only problems with the official's theory were (i) USGA Rules of Golf Decision 28(b)-91, which ruled on a nearly identical set of facts, that spectator corroboration was not sufficient identification to justify unplayable lie relief, and (ii) that after the conclusion of play, a local teenager from the gallery had scaled the palm tree, all 40 feet of it, and retrieved the ball. It was a ProStaff 1, most certainly not Baker-Charles' Maxfli 7.

The hands of the three-sided Rolex moved on toward 1:52. Chatting with fellow competitor Rocky Stillwell and starter Earl Schoenberger on the first tee, Jeff retained his foundation of confidence and inner peace. But as usual, he couldn't have spit, even if he would have wanted to, and could have puked, though he sure hoped he wouldn't, even though he was among friends, a whole lot of friends.

Chapter 28

An almost eerie silence enveloped the first tee amphitheater as Jeff teed up his Titleist 3 near the right-side tee marker. Stepping back from the ball, he took a couple of ultra slow-motion practice swings with his driver as he looked down the narrow fairway, bordered on the right with a water hazard and a mounded waste area. Warmth, confidence and good feelings were coming to him, but slowly, and hadn't quite yet arrived. He stepped to the ball and clicked on the fail-safe auto pilot, envisioning a basic, non-spectacular drive landing somewhere on the fairway, or even in the waste area, but nothing left. Like he had seen on Thursday, left was dead. His repetitive series of pre-shot movements and waggles dialed in, Jeff made his swing, catching the ball just a hair off center, a tiny fraction toward the heel of the club face. The sound of the shot was solid enough, and the flight pattern of the drive was acceptable, although not what Jeff had intended. The ball landed on the right side of the fairway, bouncing and skipping from left to right, coming to rest in the medium Bermuda rough, alongside the right-side waste area. The gallery applauded respectfully, although not enthusiastically, knowing Jeff's tee shot had not been his best. They could see that the pressure of the situation was registering on their man. The first hole was almost always the toughest one all day for the leader, no matter who he was. Jeff acknowledged the gallery's applause with a customary tug on his brand-new visor, and stepped over to Sand Wedge's side to replace the driver in the bag, winking pleasantly at his caddie as he did so. He and Sand Wedge then watched quietly, along with everybody else, as Rocky prepared to crank what in all likelihood would be the longest tee shot launched from the first tee all day. Rocky disappointed no one.

As he and Sand Wedge walked down number one fairway, Jeff noticed Sandy and her friend, Pam, walking along, just outside the ropes, among the legions that appeared to be intent on following Jeff and the long-hitting Rocky all the way around the course. He veered away from Sand Wedge toward Sandy and Pam's position, to get the up close and personal hello out of the way, so he could return to the competitive cocoon he needed to climb into for the next four hours. Making eye contact with Sandy, he winked and then inconspicuously touched his left thumb and index finger to his left earlobe, sign language they had worked out soon after they had first met which meant 'If I wasn't out here doing this, I'd like to be with you.' Sandy signaled back. Jeff then made eye contact with Pam, and winked at her. He had only just met her, fleetingly the other day, but Jeff was a big believer in eye contact. That's the kind of guy he was; he liked to look people in the eye. It was one of the reasons he was so well liked. Pam melted again, as she had Thursday at Commissioner's Hospitality. Jeff veered back to join Sand Wedge, who was approaching the area of Jeff's ball in the right-side rough. The player and the caddie were each flipping through the book, to the page diagramming the first hole as they walked along, immersing themselves back into the business at hand.

Jeff's mediocre tee shot had left him a difficult approach shot on what was a pretty simple hole if the drive was hit well, like Rocky had hit his. Rocky's position was probably 70 yards ahead of Jeff's ball, leaving the young player with no more than a three-quarter sand wedge approach to the right front pin placement. Jeff's ball, on the other hand, was 150 yards from the pin and setting down in the matted Bermuda rough. It would be a hard shot to gauge. If it came out hot, it could easily go over the back of the green, leaving an extremely treacherous downhill, lightning-fast chip or pitch. If the club caught up in the thick Bermuda grass, and the shot came out heavy, it could wind up far short of the green, but the chip from in front would not be so difficult. Jeff decided to play a firm 9-iron, to make sure that even if he caught a flier he wouldn't go too long. Sand Wedge concurred with the strategy, and moved the bag off to the right as he handed Jeff the nine, taking care to towel the grip with the ever-present towel draped across his shoulder. Sand Wedge had taken time to position the towel carefully, so that the red "W" was turned out, in view of the TV cameras, just as Joe Phillips, Wilson's sales representative, had requested, on the practice tee about an hour ago.

The somewhat muffled sound of the impact of the shot indicated that Jeff had indeed caught it heavy, and the ball would have no chance of reaching the green, even with the fast and firm conditions. It landed some 30 yards short of the green, and bounced and rolled only a little, stopping on the up-slope some 20 or so yards short, and probably a good 80 feet away from the hole. Nevertheless, Jeff winked to Sand Wedge as he returned the club to the bag and said "Smartest thing I couda' done." Sand Wedge acknowledged his agreement with a slight nod, "My man." He had a good feeling as walked along at his player's side, toward the first green. Jeff was thinking good. Just like he used to. He had put a positive spin on a marginal result, the essential key to the winning attitude necessary for good golf. Sand Wedge's man was still clearly operating within the awesome force field of the Zone.

Although certainly far short of where he hoped to be with his second shot, Jeff had left himself with a fairly straight, uphill approach, across the closely clipped Bermuda fringe, and then onto the fast, bent-grass green. Jeff elected to play the shot with the putter, and stroked it masterfully. The ball stopped dead on line, no more than 10 inches short of the hole. Jeff marked his ball with one of Sandy's sixpence coins, and stepped to the side of the green to watch Rocky size up the ticklish, down-hill 20-footer he had left himself for birdie. Rocky, who had an amazingly fluid putting stroke for such a brutish long ball hitter, putted his ball expertly down to the hole, leaving it no more than four or five inches to the left, dead even with cup. Replacing his ball on the green in front of the sixpence coin, Jeff stepped back to size the short putt up, sliding the coin back into his front pocket. Looking straight away at the hole, much as he had done from the tee when preparing to drive, he stroked the putter a few times. He was approaching the tiny putt as if it were a much more substantial challenge. Scorekeeper Mrs. Alma Feathers and others in the gallery began to wonder what they were missing. Was there some fiendish obstacle between Jeff's ball and the hole that only his experienced eye could see? Alma began to worry, but she had no reason to. Rocky and Sand Wedge knew exactly what was going on. Jeff was wisely using the tiny putt as a kind of dress rehearsal for the putts of more challenge he would be facing during the course of the round. He was taking the opportunity to go through his careful pre-shot routine, getting the rhythms and tempo set for what was to come. When he made the stroke it was "low and slow," with the putter accelerating nicely "through the ball." The putt tumbled perfectly into the center of the cup. It would have gone in even if the hole were only one millimeter wider than the ball. Jeff winked at Sand Wedge as he handed him the putter and walked placidly to the second tee.

CHAPTER 29

While Jeff, Rocky and the other 72 players who had made Friday's +5 cut were grappling with the Stadium Course, some trying merely to survive, others valiantly making, or seeking to make a move to get into position to win the Championship on Sunday, Commissioner Watterson sat in his office, grim-faced, meeting with David Frisch, Nick Standly and Mary Goldblume. NBC wanted to do a live, five-minute on-air feature with the Commissioner, regarding yesterday's Baker-Charles ruling. Despite Sid's protestations to the network that doing so would only exacerbate an already ugly situation, NBC Sports producer Aaron Fleming insisted that the ruling was a story, and NBC was going to tell it, with, or without the Commissioner's input. Sid knew he had no choice but to participate. It was precisely the last thing he would have chosen to do this Saturday afternoon.

"So what do I say," Sid asked the group, "when they ask me what we're doing about what happened?"

"It seems to me there are two main issues to deal with," Mary said. "First we need to address the rules issue, and second we need to discuss, I guess, the liability issue."

"And the rules issue really needn't be that big of a deal," Nick added. "Calls are blown every day in other sports. Look at the Steelers-Colts playoff game a few years back. Good God, the ref watched the receiver go out of the end zone and then back in and catch the pass that determined who played in the Super Bowl. Come on, compared to everyone else, our rules procedures are... impeccable."

"But in football," Sid pointed out, still unconvinced that the story Nick was suggesting would sell, "the official doesn't have seven minutes to get it right." He was referring to the excruciating, seven-minute film clip of the incident the TV media continued to repeat over the air, fanning the flames of the ugly and distracting story.

Sid's continuing negativity brought an uneasy silence back to the group, as none of the staff people were sure of what exactly to suggest next.

Mary decided to plunge ahead. "Of course, that's true, but let's face it, the rules of golf are pretty darned complicated, and it shouldn't be that incredible that every now and then somebody doesn't get it right. Frankly," Mary continued, "and I'm not trying to criticize you David, if David hadn't gotten frustrated with the media questions, this whole thing would probably have blown over last night."

"Mary, I'm sorry, and maybe you're right," David said. "But Commissioner, I've been afraid of this kind of thing, ever since we decided to make Players Championship rules duty some kind of class reunion for everybody who thinks they ever knew what an out of bounds stake was."

"Understood and noted David," the Commissioner responded, his tone of voice softening and his delivery becoming more deliberate. "But remember next time that a big part of your job is dealing with the press on rules matters... patiently. You know how they are... You just can't lose your cool, and start calling every 'has been' in golf, what did you say? ... 'Ignorant and stupid?' ...You know better than that."

Uneasy silence returned.

"Aren't ignorant and stupid the same thing?" Nick finally asked, trying to break the icy log-jam that was again gripping what was supposed to be a meeting focused on solutions. The group needed to determine a strategy to deal with what had become an exceedingly troublesome matter, one that continued to distract media attention from the Championship, and the 'players, sponsors, volunteers and local charities' themes that are supposed to be dominant, whenever the Tour is involved.

"OK, OK," the Commissioner said. "So what you all are saying is play up the complexity of the rules and say that just like in all sports, every now and then a call is blown, and that's life, the world goes on. OK, I buy it," Sid concluded. "I guess it's all we've got."

"What if you're asked whether the Tour will change the policy regarding inviting industry dignitaries to actually do rules at the Championship," Mary asked, knowing that part of her responsibility was to anticipate questions Sid might be asked, hopefully to keep him from being blind-sided.

"That's easy," Nick said. "That's a matter for the Policy Board, and we'll be working with them to develop an agenda for their next meeting in May at Muirfield."

"Beautiful," Sid added, indicating that he was completely comfortable with that response, should he need to use it.

"What about the liability threats, Mary?" Sid asked, shifting to the second area they needed to deal with.

"We cannot talk about that publicly," Mary responded emphatically. "Certainly not today and not in an impromptu live conversation with NBC. Commissioner, I know it's not your style, but I really recommend a big 'no comment' on any legal liability questions."

"You think he can prove defamation?" Sid asked, somewhat surprised by the degree of concern his counsel seemed to have over what to him seemed like a completely frivolous, almost laughable legal threat.

"I'm not so worried about the so-called defamation case, Commissioner. I agree, that one has major problems, like the fact that truth is a defense. The guy did act incompetently, which is at least pretty darned close to ignorant and stupid. The exposure I'm concerned with is to the players. Like our own Tom Schuyler keeps saying, and writing, over and over again, what if Baker-Charles wins? Somebody's out a mil and 10 years of exempt status. I wouldn't want a jury ascribing a price tag to that."

Frisch choked on the Diet Coke he was drinking when Mary mentioned the word "jury," spilling the contents of the can all over his shirt and pants, and sputtering embarrassingly as he tried to clear his windpipe and regain his cool.

"Relax David," Sid said with some alarm, seeing David's sensational reaction to what Mary had said. "She's a lawyer, for Chrissake. She's paid to think that way."

Growing dead serious again, and looking back at Mary, Sid asked, "You don't think any of our guys would do that do you Mary?"

"No," she responded, "not really. But it happened at the Indianapolis 500 in 1981. The race officials blew a call against Bobby Unser, and a court took the race away from Mario Andretti six months later... not a pretty picture."

"We've got to get this honorary rules officials issue on the agenda for the Policy Board," Sid concluded, beginning to appreciate that otherwise he was playing with fire. "And I agree, no comment, by anybody, on the legal stuff."

With that Sid excused the staff, except for Nick, and the two of them continued preparing for the impending NBC interview, trying to anticipate everywhere the conversation could go.

Chapter 30

Jeff's first confrontation with serious adversity in the third round came at the ninth, the long par-5 hole he had so masterfully birdied at the end of the day yesterday. Today, the hole was playing back into what was becoming an appreciable breeze, and Jeff had blocked his tee shot slightly to the right, producing a high, hanging type of drive of relatively short distance. Like he had on one, Stillwell had thundered his tee ball past Jeff's, a good 70 to 80 yards on down the fairway.

Intent upon moving the ball with his second shot to the general area he had played from yesterday afternoon, just short of the green, Jeff had aggressively selected a 3-wood. He kept the shot low, into the wind as he had planned, but it turned over, hooking from right to left, and skipped into trouble in the waste area guarding the left front approach area to the green. "*Ouch*," Sand Wedge thought as he watched the shot's result. Like at the first, at the ninth, left is dead. The caddie noticed that Jeff's wink this time when handing back the 3-wood, seemed a little forced, more like a twitch.

Through the tough par-3 eighth hole, Jeff had been motoring along beautifully, shaving another stroke from par to go -12 for the Championship. He had birdied the tough fifth, holing a no-brainer 40-footer from all the way across the undulating green. "Sometimes the hole just gets in the way," Jeff had told Sand Wedge, when he had handed him back the Zebra, repeating one of the phrases he had often used in the past, when things were going well, and he was holing putts from everywhere.

When they came to the lie Jeff's ball had found at the ninth however, Sand Wedge knew that Jeff's newly found, impervious attitude was going to be placed to a stern test. The ball had wound up between two exposed roots of the cypress tree that dominated the left-side waste bunker. It looked like it might be unplayable. The caddie laid down the bag and pulled out the book. It was time for some study and imagination, if there was to be any hope of salvaging par, or maybe even bogey.

As could be expected, NBC had descended on Jeff's predicament, like white on rice. The whole saga of his quest to regain Championship winning form, after so many years of struggling in the unfortunate throes of middle-age mediocrity, was the theme line the entire TV production was driving home to the viewers, with typically overstated, and hyped-up drama.

The TV coverage Saturday had opened with footage of the thoroughbred Secretariat, galloping majestically, in slow motion, to the tape at the 1973 Kentucky Derby. That was the same year Jeff had won his first Tour event. The syrupy voice-over intoned: "the great Secretariat most surely will never run to victory again… but what about Jeff Taylor… one of the fabled golfers of Secretariat's era… is Championship form still within his capability?… Stay tuned and see, as NBC Sports proudly presents the 26th edition of the Players Championship, from the Tournament Players Club at Sawgrass, in Ponte Vedra, Florida."

As the pictures from the hand-held NBC television cameras were indicating to viewers around the world, Jeff's ball was located between the two tree roots, which were each exposed nearly three inches above the ground, and ran diagonally across the line from Jeff's ball to the green. His only shot, and it would be a risky one, would be to play back in the direction of the tee. He would somehow have to pitch the ball back onto the fairway, a sufficient distance away from the roots to be clear of the tree for his fourth shot, and somehow get it up and down from there, if Jeff entertained any hope of saving par. Sand Wedge would probably have paid good money for a bogey-6, then and there, if anybody was selling them.

Looking up at Jeff from the book, which he had been studying for some time, and pointing to a drainage grate some 30 yards away, Sand Wedge said, "If you can get it to there, it's 110 to the middle, 107 to the pin."

"What about declaring it unplayable?" Jeff asked, his words being picked up and transmitted live, over the air, by the ambient sound dish the NBC crewman held up like a serving dish, not 10 feet from where Jeff and Sand Wedge were trying to decide the Titleist's future path.

Looking around, Sand Wedge said, "No good, man... Two club lengths don't get you out from 'hind the tree. An' you go back, keepin' the point between, you gonna be in the jungle."

Jeff thought and figured some more about his predicament, coming eventually to the same conclusion that Sand Wedge had: He would have to try the backwards pitch from between the ugly roots. Bending down to pass under the low-hanging branches of the cypress tree, Jeff approached the imprisoned ball carefully, assuming a clubless stance, to begin to get a feel for whether or not what he was considering was actually possible. Re-emerging from under the tree to the side of the fairway, Jeff called Rocky over, to have him watch Jeff play the shot, to ensure that no inadvertent rules violations occurred.

When Rocky was in position, Jeff walked up to Sand Wedge who was now holding the bag upright, three or four yards behind and to the right of the position of the ball, to select the club he intended to use for the shot.

"Cake," Jeff said to Sand Wedge, with another wink, a clearly unforced one this time. "Give me the sand wedge, Sand Wedge."

The four million households watching NBC, and hearing every word Jeff was saying, must have been thinking, *This is either the cockiest, or stupidest golfer of all time.*

Of course, Sand Wedge knew that Jeff was neither of these. It was the Zone again, the caddie realized. Jeff just believed, really believed, he could execute the shot. To virtually everyone else's amazement, and the loud rejoicing of the onlooking gallery, execute the shot he did. The Titleist flew out crisply from between the roots and bounced and rolled into ideal fairway position, within a yard or two of the targeted drainage grate.

"My m-a-a-n," Sand Wedge said, beaming with uncharacteristic animation as he slid the sand wedge back into the bag.

"Great shot, Houdini," Stillwell said as Jeff emerged once again from beneath the cypress tree, to the further delight of the crowd who had witnessed the drama.

Johnny Miller, the NBC announcer who had resumed the over-the-air commentary, which had been suspended while the ambient microphones had transmitted the actual sounds of Jeff's tribulations uninterrupted by announcer explanations, was beside himself. "I can't even begin to tell you how good that was," he said, referring to Jeff's recovery shot. "Something's going on here with Mr. Taylor; he is a man with a mission. I can't recall when I last saw determination like he's displaying out here today."

After the heroics of the "root shot," it really came as no surprise that Jeff got up and down from the drainage grate for par. It didn't surprise Sand Wedge, and certainly not Jeff.

He had seen the 107-yard approach shot stop two feet from the hole in his mind's eye, several moments before it actually did.

Chapter 31

Jeff followed the miraculous par at nine with more solid play on the Stadium Course's back nine. Most of the extremely difficult holes are on the inward side, after the course turns back toward the clubhouse at the 13th. It was not uncommon for players turning the front side at even-par, or better, to nevertheless post mediocre or even poor scores, losing their momentum toward the end, as they encountered the layout's severest tests. But Jeff's game and attitude, as he continued along as the Championship leader, remained clearly up to whatever challenges the course offered. Following solid pars at the 10th, 11th and 12th, Jeff had birdied the 13th, vindicating the bogey he had made there in Friday's second round. In so doing, he had moved his overall score to -13 and was lapping most of the rest of the field. Stillwell, for example, despite his awesome driving and impressive putting skills, had slipped to +2 for the third round, and -5 overall, a distant eight shots off the torrid pace Jeff was setting.

The only player staying close to Jeff was Baker-Charles. Playing two groups ahead of Jeff and Rocky, in front of a sizable gallery of his own, Arlen was lighting it up this moving day, at an even faster pace than Jeff was.

Jeff and Sand Wedge were aware that something spectacular was going on up ahead, from the unmistakable birdie roars that were erupting from time to time, and had watched Baker-Charles' relentless progress against par as it was flashed over the electronic, Coca-Cola sponsored leader boards, located alongside each tee and green. Through the 17th, Jeff and Sand Wedge noted as they reached the green at the 16th, Baker-Charles was a whopping -7 for the day, and -12 for the Championship, just one shot from tying Jeff for the lead.

Having completed the 4:05 on-air session with NBC, basically, he and Nick thought, unscathed, Sid sat watching the TV coverage in Commissioner's Hospitality. The Commissioner was sipping a Diet Coke, and privately hoping, although he liked Arlen personally, that Baker-Charles would make a "snowman," golfer talk for an

8, or worse on the 18th, the hole the TV showed he was about to play. The fact that he, and only he, appeared to be able to match Jeff's incredible level of play, would only serve to highlight further the unpleasantness stemming from yesterday's botched ruling. Indeed, as both Sid and David Frisch had watched Baker-Charles' steady climb up the leader board, from -5 at the start of the round, to -8 at the turn, then to -9,-10 and -11, and now -12 through the 17th, they each felt like people living out their worst nightmare.

Sid's thoughts kept returning to Mary's scary statement about liability. *Could such a horrendous thing really happen?* the Commissioner wondered. He concluded in his own mind that such a development was highly unlikely, and that, in any event, idle worrying about it accomplished nothing. He allowed his full attention to return to the giant Diamondvision monitor in the corner of the room. Maybe Arlen would yank his tee shot off the 18th into the middle of the lake bordering the entire left side. Such things had surely happened before, indeed seven times already today, the NBC announcer was saying as Arlen teed up his ball.

But this was not a day for Baker-Charles drives to wind up in lakes. He creased a beautiful low, boring draw down the right center of the fairway, the ball's flight pattern following the sloping, right to left contour of the demanding finishing hole perfectly. From there, Arlen played a similarly gorgeous 4-iron, low and drawing into the wind. The ball stopped on the green in ideal position, just eight feet below the hole. Given the white- hot game Baker-Charles obviously had dialed in, conversion of the putt was more or less a formality, the ball rolling straight up the slope and into the hole, as they say, "like it had eyes."

Baker-Charles had just tied the Stadium Course record of 64, going to -13 for the Championship, and reducing Jeff's once formidable lead to zero.

Jeff was sitting on his heels, baseball catcher style, lining up his birdie putt at the 17th when the eighth and final birdie roar of the day from Baker-Charles' gallery erupted around the 18th green. He knew exactly what the crowd noise meant: he was now tied for the Players Championship lead with Baker-Charles. In times past, such a development as this, another player taking dead-aim at his leading score, and closing the margin completely, despite his own outstanding play, would have probably unnerved Jeff, and negatively affected his own resolve and concentration.

But not today, not here, not anymore. Jeff's entrenchment in the Zone was unshaken. In response to the cheer at the 18th, Jeff merely looked up to Sand Wedge, who was standing at the hole, tending the pin and also surveying the line of the upcoming putt, and asked calmly, "See anything?" Sand Wedge removed the flag stick, continuing to hold it in his hands, across his knees like some sort of elongated baton, as he also squatted down for a closer look at the line.

"Don't see much," the caddie finally responded. "Look pretty straight to me... Maybe might die a little left at the end... Depend on the speed."

Jeff acknowledged agreement with Sand Wedge's assessment, as he rose and prepared to stroke the putt. He gave it a good roll, but the ball did die-off to the left as it lost speed at the hole, curling across the left front lip of the cup, to the collective, and audible "oooohh" of the thousands looking on.

Jeff felt the reassuring satisfaction of having hit a very good putt, although this one had not gone in. He knew, and accepted without concern that such was an ever-present part of the game of golf. He tapped the par putt in and headed, along with Sand Wedge, toward the demanding 18th tee.

The obvious confidence of the player remained intact as he strode purposefully along. Due to Baker-Charles' sizzling third-round score, his hard-earned lead was gone, but Jeff remained comfortable in the face of the challenge. On the tee, he winked easily again at Sand Wedge as he reached for the driver.

Chapter 32

As the gathering dusk was bringing to a close the activities surrounding the third round, the media center continued to buzz. Two basic stories dominated. The first and foremost of them, much to Sid's dismay, was the controversy that continued to surround Baker-Charles' position as co-leader, in light of the Friday ruling. The second hot topic was whether Jeff could break back through to win a Championship, particularly in light of the long drought he had endured since last winning nearly 10 years ago.

During Arlen's press interview following his course record-tying 64, the player had angrily refused to answer any more questions about the ruling fiasco, saying that while he would be happy to answer any questions about today's or tomorrow's play, he would be damned before he would answer any more "petty and repetitive" questions about what happened yesterday, when, according to Baker-Charles, he had entrusted a rules matter to the supposed expertise of the official, precisely as he was supposed to do.

Indeed, Arlen made a good point. He was bound to follow the directives of the official, even if he suspected that the ruling was going wrong. To have done otherwise would have been to risk penalties to himself for delay of play, perhaps even disqualification. In the player's defense, the confusion surrounding the ruling had at the time presented him with a dilemma of his own, and he resented the ongoing implications that in obeying the official he was somehow taking advantage, or competing unfairly.

Jeff's take on the matter was similar to Arlen's. He had good-naturedly challenged Schuyler to "Get a life, Tom" when the reporter had persisted in questions to him about the ruling. Jeff insisted that the story of the Championship was how the players had played today, and how they might play tomorrow.

The fact of the matter was that everybody except Jeff and Arlen had, on this moving day, moved away from any realistic chance of winning the Championship. The third place scores of Lenny Dreyfuss and Rocky Stillwell were -5, a distant eight shots behind

Jeff and Arlen. Sunday figured to be a two-man competition for the win, with everybody else vying for third through 72nd positions. The press was digging for more drama, in hopes of uncovering something that would translate into interesting copy.

The ultimate hardball question was put to Jeff by Murray Greenstone of the *New York Times*. "If you lose to Baker-Charles," Greenstone had asked, "would you consider legal action?"

"Against who?" Jeff had responded.

"Against... whoever," the reporter had continued.

Instinctively, Jeff had said that he would never pursue litigation as a means to win a golf tournament. "I can't imagine doing such a thing," he had responded. "That's not what our game is all about. If it ever comes to the point that a judge or jury somewhere is deciding who wins the Players Championship," Jeff had concluded, "I hope I'm either long gone, or deaf, dumb and blind, because I sure wouldn't want to see or hear anything about it."

After leaving the media center and making arrangements for meeting Sand Wedge tomorrow around one o'clock, Jeff had done his autograph and glad-handing duties with the spectators that still remained, in the gathering dusk around the walkway and entrance to the players' locker room. He had slipped the Titleist 3 he had used in parring number eighteen into his right rear pocket, and got a kick out of giving it to a young boy who was standing alongside his well-dressed and attractive mother. Absolutely delighted to have the ball, the boy eagerly requested Jeff to sign the photocopy of his third-round scorecard the boy's mother had purchased at the TPC Charities concession.

"Gee, thanks, Mr. Taylor," he had said, "I sure hope you beat that Baker guy tomorrow."

"Now Jimmy," the mother had added, "don't bother Mr. Taylor any more, he has lots of things he has to do."

"No problem ma'am," Jeff had said, as he continued on through the door, flashing Saturday's last on-course edition of the famous Taylor grin, as he looked directly into the mother's eyes.

Chapter 33

It was nearly 7:30 and growing dark as Jeff guided the Riviera onto A-1-A for the 10-mile trip back up the beach to the Sea Turtle. He had arranged with Sandy to meet her in his room around 8:00, to unwind for a while and then maybe see about getting a light dinner at Ragtime, or Slider's, or another of their favorite local restaurants. The restaurant scene, such as it was around the Jacksonville Beaches, "Florida's First Coast," as promoted by the Chamber of Commerce, was one of the things Jeff liked best about the area. With a few exceptions, the cuisine wasn't all that spectacular. But the seafood was always fresh, usually swimming in the Atlantic the night or morning before it was served. And the beach town ambience of many of the local establishments, all the way from Mayport and Atlantic Beach to St. Augustine, was usually friendly, casual, and often times, picture-postcard quaint.

Letting himself into his hotel room, Jeff looked forward to seeing Sandy again and relaxing with her over another glass of Black Opal. He had arranged with room service to have a bottle delivered, on ice, around 7:30. "Hello-o," he said, as the door swung open. In his mind's eye he had pictured Sandy standing on the hotel room's tiny balcony, looking out over the ocean, in a sort of serendipitous continuation of the good karma that had transpired last night at her house.

But there was no Sandy there, on the balcony, or anywhere in the room. He looked off anxiously to the left at the bathroom door, thinking she might be in there. But the bathroom door was open and the bathroom itself was dark. In fact the whole room was dark, the shaft of light from the hallway coming through the open doorway was the only illumination. Surprised and disappointed, Jeff wondered what must have happened. He closed the door behind him, and the room grew completely dark, as he groped along the wall for the light switch. Looking forward into the room as he did so, he noticed the amber message light slowly throbbing on the telephone by the bed. No one but the Championship office, Skip and Sandy knew he was here, so he expected the message was from her and would enlighten him on what must have happened.

Jeff finally found the light switch, and flipped it on, illuminating the room completely. The bottle of wine and ice bucket had indeed been delivered as requested, and were stationed alongside the television set at the foot of the bed. A "Compliments of the Sea Turtle" card was tied around the neck of the bottle. The inside of the card was inscribed, "Best of luck tomorrow, Jeff, and come back anytime" and signed individually by what appeared from the number of scrawly signatures, to be the entire Sea Turtle management and staff. He smiled, appreciating the warmth and sincerity of the gesture, and only wished Sandy was here to share it with him. He decided to open the bottle and pour himself a glass of the Black Opal before he called for the message. Some messages, he knew, were better received with a glass of wine in hand.

Sitting now on the side of the bed, holding the phone receiver in his left hand, and the glass of wine in his right, Jeff awkwardly pressed 2#7, as instructed by the placard next to the phone, to access the hotel phone mail system. While waiting for the access to connect, Jeff acknowledged his surprise that the Sea Turtle actually had such a technologically- advanced service as phone mail. He had expected to actually hear the message read to him by a real person, the night clerk, like in the old days.

After the beep, Sandy's voice came through: "Jeff, I'm sorry to have to change the plans for tonight, but Manny called in sick and I just had to go to the Homestead to help out. I was off last night, as you know. Anyway, I'm so sorry, but I'll be getting off at midnight and I'd love to swing back by your room after that, if it's OK with you. But if you'd rather take a rain check, I'll understand. I know you've got a pretty big day planned tomorrow. Well, let me know, call my home phone, 776-9990 and leave a message. I'll call there and get it later tonight, when I get a minute at this crazy place. Love you."

"Rain check," Jeff thought, smiling to himself as he hung up the phone. "Not a chance."

Replacing the phone handle to its cradle, Jeff took a sip from the wine glass he was holding. He thought for a moment that maybe he would go on over to the Homestead, but on reflection, he decided that wasn't a good idea. The place would be packed, and smoky, and he wouldn't be able to spend any time with Sandy anyway. Besides, he was tired and wanted to remain focused on the positive, even-keel he had going. He decided he would put on the old parka and fisherman hat he always kept in his suitcase, for occasions when he wanted to ensure that he would be unnoticed, and go across the street to Slider's for a light, fresh-fish dinner. Maybe, for old time's sake, he'd stop into Pete's for a beer on the way.

Rising from the bed, Jeff walked across the room to the window and pulled open the heavy curtain. Opening the sliding glass door, he stepped out onto the tiny balcony he had imagined Sandy on as he was driving back from the TPC. Like last night, the scallop moon hung suspended over the Atlantic, close down to the eastern horizon. The ocean was black except for the lights of a few fishing boats clustered here and there some five miles out from shore. The only sound was the rhythmic splash of the listless, two-foot waves breaking against the Sea Turtle pier and then washing up to the beach.

Jeff took another sip of the Black Opal and closed his eyes as he felt a warming glow of contentment pass through him. He felt at peace with himself and the world.

His thoughts returning to Sandy, Jeff began to reflect on the times they had spent together. He had met her at the Players four years ago when she, as a TPC Charities volunteer, had requested him to visit briefly with a wheelchair-bound elderly lady who had always wanted to meet him. He had done so alongside the first tee during the Wednesday practice round, and had become immediately attracted to Sandy in the process. She had a wonderful English accent, athletic good looks and an infectious, positive personality. When Jeff had read in the *Times Union* the next day about how Sandy had won the 30-39 year old division of the TPC Charities 5K run, he had immediately called to congratulate her and, in the process, asked if she might be free for dinner. To his relief and delight, Sandy had accepted, and their rich, but sometimes topsy-turvy relationship had begun.

Jeff had been surprised to learn that Sandy worked as a bartender at the Homestead, but he understood her explanation that it gave her something to do and a place to meet and talk with people. He saw how it rounded out the early retirement lifestyle she had adopted since moving to Atlantic Beach from Long Island, after a financially successful but emotionally and spiritually draining professional career.

Scanning the dark horizon again, Jeff acknowledged that Atlantic Beach was home and Sandy was the woman he loved. He decided to call the number and tell her so. He wanted her in his arms again tonight.

CHAPTER 34

Driving east along Atlantic Boulevard across the Intracoastal Waterway bridge, in the sparse, post-1:00 a.m. traffic, Sandy was preoccupied with mixed emotions. She had been glad to receive Jeff's message that despite the lateness of the hour, he hoped she would come by the Sea Turtle, which she could see up ahead as she crested the bridge. But at the same time, she wondered whether she was allowing her emotions to draw her once again into an ultimately unsatisfactory and futureless relationship, a relationship in which the bad times had outnumbered the good times, and the loneliness and disappointment had outweighed the happiness.

Five years ago, Sandy had left a 12-year marriage because the relationship with her husband had become one made up of these same unbalanced characteristics. Their two-career lifestyle, both Sandy and her husband had been workaholically immersed in the investment banking business in New York, had produced a lot of money during the 80's, but too little of the fundamental things that make married people happy: passion for life and each other, and the time to pursue those passions.

So Sandy had come to north Florida, seeking distance from the grind of the investment profession and the hollowness of a burned out, taken-for-granted marriage. She had met Jeff at the championship four years ago, and had been immediately attracted to him, for all of the obvious reasons and some that were not so obvious. He quickly became one of her most constant patrons at the Homestead, typically sipping a few chardonnays and recounting to her a long list of anecdotes about the fascinating and often hilarious world of professional golf. In addition to coming to Ponte Vedra for the Players each year, Jeff would manage his schedule so as to get back through Jacksonville whenever he was not playing the Tour. The most challenging times for their relationship were the missed-the-cut Friday evening trips he would sometimes route through Jax, often in a dejected mood, sorely in need of support and companionship.

Ironically, what had attracted Sandy to Jeff most, his sensitivity, was what had driven them apart a year ago, during a quiet and unpleasant dinner Sunday night after the championship. Disappointed by his play, and immersed in self-pity, Jeff had proclaimed that maybe their relationship was one of the distractions in his life that was keeping him from succeeding professionally.

That had been enough for Sandy. She had spent too much time already, she thought, trying to prop up Jeff's self esteem and get him refocused on the blessings in his life, rather than what he too often perceived as the "slings and arrows of outrageous fortune," whenever his competitive fortunes took a downward turn. She had simply got up and left the restaurant when these revelations about Jeff's "distractions" had been pronounced, over the rim of a brandy snifter he held close to his lips. She had gotten a cab, and ridden the 25 miles back up the beach from St. Augustine to Atlantic Beach grimly resolved to have nothing further to do with Jeff or his professional and personal anxieties. Sandy had remained committed to her decision until Thursday morning at the fourth tee, where she couldn't repress the desire to speak to him in what appeared to be a moment of crisis.

And that one brief encounter had been enough to undo the resolve she had tried to maintain since the long cab ride home a year ago. There he was again, looking directly into her eyes again, smiling that smile again, and she found herself thinking, maybe, just maybe it might all be worth it. The good times, like last night at her house on the beach, had always been so good.

And she had noticed that Jeff was projecting a calm and relaxed attitude, unlike what she had ever seen from him before.

But Sandy wondered, as she drove along, if she was kidding herself into thinking that somehow a rekindled relationship with Jeff could become something other than an ultimately disappointing and heartbreaking repetition of the past.

The alarm clock on the night stand said 1:13 when Jeff awoke to the sound of Sandy inserting the key into the hotel room door lock. She opened the door slowly, the light spilling in from the hallway and dialing up gradually, as if controlled by some sort of rheostat. Sandy closed the door carefully and quietly behind her, and the room returned to pitch black, except for the numbers on the clock. Jeff could hear her patting the wall along the short hallway leading into the room, as Sandy made her way in the darkness.

"Hell-o-o," Jeff said softly. "Go ahead and turn the light on. The switch's there on your left, by the bathroom door." He remembered groping for it when he had come into the room earlier that evening. But the room remained dark. All Jeff heard were clothes rustling and a coat hanger being removed from the small closet by the door, and then replaced.

"Go back to sleep, and quit worrying about me," Sandy whispered, a few moments later, the proximity of her voice indicating that she had somehow made her way through the dark and to the side of the bed, unscathed. Jeff rolled over and reached out in the direction of the whisper, his arm closing around Sandy's bare hips as he pulled her forward. Laughing, she fell onto the bed and into Jeff's eager embrace.

"Are you sure we should be doing this?" Sandy asked. "Unless I'm misunderstanding what they're saying on ESPN, tomorrow's... no, today's got to be one of the most important days of your life."

"All the more reason for me to be thankful that you're here with me," Jeff responded, increasing slightly the pressure with which he hugged her, and luxuriating in the sensuality of her touch and the erotic familiarity of her smell.

"Why the change?" Sandy asked. "I thought this kind of thing was a... what did you call it... a distraction?"

Jeff realized that Sandy was referring to the ill-conceived remarks he had made last year during their unpleasant Sunday night dinner at Colombia, St. Augustine's touristy Spanish restaurant. His thesis on that dismal occasion, which he developed silently, as he brooded over several tumblers of Courvoisier, was that he needed to rededicate himself totally to his golf game, to regain the competitive skills he felt were eroding, due to the many distractions in his life, including Sandy.

"Maybe I've finally grown up," Jeff said. "I guess I've finally appreciated that family, and friends, and ties to the community are 'what life's about,' as you would say it. I think this week I've realized that Atlantic Beach is home for me, and it's home... and a damned good home, whether I shoot 65, or 85; whether I'm playing the Tour, or giving lessons at the driving range over on Beach Boulevard, or shooting pool at Pete's when I'm 70 years old."

Jeff paused his unexpected stream of consciousness for a moment, and stroked Sandy's hair and slender back, as he continued to explore the thoughts he all of a sudden wanted to express. He smiled inwardly as he realized deeply that his desire for Sandy was complete; physically, emotionally and mentally.

"Until a few months ago," he continued after a moment, "I had it exactly backwards. I somehow had it in my head that all these things were distractions, and that my focus on them, or even any thought about them, was keeping me from performing my best on the golf course, which is, for better or for worse, what I do for a living. That was the unfortunate mindset I visited upon you last year in St. Augustine. I had just shot, what? Whatever, it really doesn't matter. And I needed something... someone to blame. So in a way, I guess I blamed myself, and took it out on you. 'It's all because I spend time thinking about friends, and family, and Sandy, that's why I can't play; I let myself get distracted,' I thought. Well, I'm finally beginning to see that that's just not the way it is. I love it here, and I love you. And I finally understand that these are the assets in my life, not the distractions. Feeling sorry for myself when I shoot 75 is the distraction. No job is a life in and of itself. A job is only a means to a life. You, and what we can have, and do have around here, that's my life. Sure, scores are important, because they're my job. But they're not my life."

Sandy tightened their embrace yet another notch, as if to express her concurrence in Jeff's revelations without the need for further words. She felt like a teacher seeing her favorite but often self-indulgent student finally receive his diploma.

The two drifted along through the night, in the peaceful quiet that envelopes people who realize how wonderful it is to be together, doing what they are doing, exactly where they are.

Chapter 35

Jeff arrived at the Stadium Course just before noon on Sunday morning. The weather was the very best North Florida has to offer. The wind had died back down to an insignificant level, "A mere zephyr," as former CBS golf announcer Ben Wright used to say, and the temperature was around 75. A crystal clear, azure blue sky had replaced the bleached-out, unstable conditions that had dominated on Friday and Saturday. The Met Life blimp buzzed along on its patient, unobtrusive cruising, high above the beautiful, emerald network of fairways and greens below, which was punctuated with glistening lakes and gleaming white sand bunkers.

Due to the continuing dry conditions, the field staff had given the greens and fairways a full hour of water Saturday night. That, combined with the double-cutting and rolling of the course which had been laboriously carried out, commencing with the dawn's first light, left the Stadium Course looking its very best, poised beautifully to continue to test the players' nerves and skills. Everything had been painstakingly set for the culmination of the Championship, "to identify the best player," to use the USGA's explanation of their goal when conditioning a course for Major championship play. By nightfall, the identification process would be complete.

Standing once again in front of his locker, organizing himself for what promised to be the most important round of golf of the many thousands he had played in his life, Jeff was trying to keep his mind from racing ahead to the afternoon's inevitable challenge. He was taking things slowly. He had even avoided the relative intensity of driving back down Third Street, the "main drag" through Neptune Beach and Jax Beach, when coming from the Sea Turtle south to Ponte Vedra and the TPC. Instead, he had driven the 10 miles back down the beach, all the way along the 25 miles per hour-posted beach road, keeping things slow and relaxed, well under control. "T-e-m-p-o," he repeated softly and slowly to himself every few minutes.

More than anything else, Jeff knew this day would test his patience, his ability to make the right decisions, and then execute golf shots one by one, golf shots he believed in, and knew he could make, unhurried and unintimidated by the importance of the moment. As he put on a new Wilson glove, and put the sixpence coins and the book in his pockets, Jeff felt the confidence and inner peace that had so enveloped him at times on Thursday and Friday, and all day long yesterday, begin to settle in. But he wasn't all the way there yet. The game-face was coming on, but the fit was still a little loose. Jeff had to concede to himself that he was human after all, and the stakes that would hang in the balance over the next five hours or so were of awesome significance and importance to the rest of his life. Closing the locker door, Jeff could only mouth "show time" in the faintest of voices, as he slapped his hands together, only meekly. Walking this time over to one of the toilet stalls rather than the lavatory mirror, Jeff flipped the silver clasp of the stall door and stepped inside. Not only did he feel like puking; this time, he did.

Jeff's starting time of 1:52 was a duplication of yesterday's time. Of course, he would be paired with Championship co-leader Arlen Baker-Charles. Actually Baker-Charles would have the honor in the final pairing, by virtue of his being the first to post the -13 score of 203 he and Jeff shared at the close of yesterday's third round. This turn of events actually pleased Jeff, since it would give him the added buffer of seeing how Arlen handled the pressure of the first tee drive, before he himself faced the challenge. Even in the very best of times, the first tee had never been Jeff's favorite place. For him, the initial tee shot was just something to get over with.

Chatting with Quentin Farley and Earl Schoenberger casually while awaiting the appointed hour, both players were apparently working overtime to at least give the impression that this "day at the office" was merely routine. Arlen was trading one-liner jokes with the two championship committee volunteers.

"What do you call 300 Wall Street lawyers at the bottom of the East River?" Arlen asked them, allowing a moment or two for a response, but getting none. "A good start," he had continued, then laughed robustly at his own punch line. Everyone, including the eavesdropping spectators, accepted the cleverness of the worn-out joke, and laughed, even if they'd heard it years before. Jeff laughed too, when he heard the others, but he had tuned out Arlen's words long before. His senses were now fully focused inward, as he tried to settle toward the Zone and a deep-set belief in what he was capable of doing, and now committed to do.

As Quentin was announcing Arlen onto the tee, Jeff quietly handed the driver he had previously drawn out of the golf bag back to Sand Wedge. "I need the 3-wood," he had said to the caddie, failing to look him directly in the eyes. Jeff's club change had not gone unnoticed, and sent a ripple of anticipation through the gallery around the first tee. The electricity in the air as the two players prepared to play away fairly crackled.

Chapter 36

NBC came on the air at 2:00 with its usual melodramatic opening. While a collage of Met Life blimp-provided beauty shots of the TPC and Ponte Vedra Beach swirled across the screen, the emotion laden voice of Dick Enberg set the stage: "The Players Championship... the players themselves call it golf's first 'significant' event of the year... Attracting what many say is the strongest field of all championships, many in the game say it's time to elevate the Players to 'Major' status, placing it among golf's elite championships, The Masters, the U.S. Open, the Open Championship and the PGA... Oh my, Johnny Miller, this promises to be a memorable Players Championship final round indeed..." The NBC announcers then went on to each give their spin on what the key elements of the final round would be. The thrust of the commentary was that Jeff needed to start strongly and Arlen needed to somehow avoid any let down, such as often follows a brilliant, record-tying round like he had recorded yesterday.

The elaborate TV lead-in taking nearly 10 minutes, the first actual play shown to the viewers was tape-delayed shots of Jeff and Arlen approaching the first green. Jeff played first, from just off the left side of the fairway. From there, his line to the right rear pin placement required him to play across the steep-faced left front bunker, keeping the ball to the left of the swale in the center of the green, that from Jeff's angle, would repel the ball into the right front collection bunker. The shot was going to be no bargain, and this was definitely not the way Jeff and Sand Wedge wanted to be starting out the final round.

Sand Wedge placed the distance to carry the bunker at 139. Wind was not a factor, but the lie in the short rough was. It looked to be a flier, from which a solid impact would produce a shooting-type shot that would land hot and release with virtually no back spin, running over the back of the green. From there, it would be nearly impossible to chip or pitch the ball reasonably close to the hole, with any hope of saving par. The firmness of the green, despite last evening's watering, compounded Jeff's dilemma. Baker-Charles looked on from the location of his ball in the center of the fairway, in near- perfect position to approach the green, as Jeff and Sand Wedge continued to study Jeff's situation.

The TV announcers were dramatizing like they smelled blood already. "Just exactly the kind of predicament Jeff didn't want early in the round, Dick," Johnny Miller was saying.

Counting on the flier lie to add distance to the flight of the ball,

Jeff decided to hit a hard 9-iron, hoping he could just barely carry the bunker, landing the ball in the relatively soft fringe, and thereby deaden the release and keep the ball on the green. From a clean lie in the fairway, a 139 yard carry would ordinarily call for an 8-iron.

"Make a good swing now," Sand Wedge said as he shouldered the bag and stepped a few paces away.

Jeff almost pulled it off. His swing felt good and the contact on the Titleist 3 was very solid. But to Sand Wedge's very experienced eye, the shot looked all the way like it was going to wind up a yard or two short. "Fly...Fly," he had urged as the ball soared toward the target. But it was not to be. As usual, Sand Wedge's innate distance finder had been laser-like accurate, the ball landed one yard short of the fringe in the upper face of the steep left-side bunker, and buried, under the lip. Jeff's round had just gotten very ragged, very early. The collective moan from the gallery encircling the first green told the story. Returning the club to Sand Wedge, Jeff had no comment to make, and no winks to wink.

The tape delay coverage turned to Arlen, whose shot was a routine 135-yarder from the center of the fairway. Perhaps himself feeling some of the pressure he was trying so hard to mask on the first tee, Arlen executed a very poor approach, catching the ball heavy and leaving it a good 10 yards short of the green with a long uphill, sidehill chip. The game that was so clearly "on" just a few moments before, appeared to be at least temporarily "off," for both players.

The live TV coverage picked up with a close-up of Jeff's ball buried in the bunker, with no more than one fourth of its surface visible. Only the "eist" part of the name and 50 or so of the surrounding dimples were distinguishable above the surface of the sand. The TV announcers had determined the shot to be "impossible."

The most immediate of the myriad problems the shot presented was that there appeared to be no place to even assume a stance to try to play the ball toward the green. The ball was imbedded in the top of the steep face of the bunker, some four feet above its base. It was possible that Jeff would have to play the shot sideways, off the face of the bunker. It would appear like some strange adaptation of tee-ball, with Jeff swinging the club horizontally like a baseball player.

If he was lucky, he could dislodge the ball, and flop it down onto the floor of the bunker, from where he could play a fairly routine shot. Consulting for a moment with Sand Wedge, they decided that was Jeff's only real choice. He could, of course, claim an unplayable lie, but if he did, he would have to drop the ball in the bunker, with the real possibility of it plugging again. If he could somehow scrape it out, it would hopefully roll to the bottom of the sand, and maybe leave him a good lie from which to play his fourth.

The decision made to attempt the tee-ball shot, Jeff accepted the sand wedge from his caddie, and entered the bunker. He took care to dig his Foot-Joys solidly into the sand, since the swing he would need to make would be a forceful one. He needed for the club to enter the sand just a fraction behind the ball, moving enough of the heavy sand to free the ball from its impacted position. If Jeff contacted the ball directly, he would only bury it even deeper in the face of the bunker, compounding his already serious problem. As necessary, Jeff took a full and powerful swing as the huge gallery collectively held their breaths. Much of the dislodged sand coming straight back into Jeff's face, he did not see the result of his efforts. But the positive reaction of the gallery told him that he had succeeded in moving the ball at least somewhere. He wiped the sand from his face and off the front of his cotton sweater with his free hand, keeping his eyes closed as he reached out to Sand Wedge for a towel.

Looking up finally from the towel, Jeff saw that the Titleist now rested cleanly on the sand at the bottom of the bunker, a condition from which he could play a normal bunker shot. He stepped back out of the sand to regroup, hoping that by doing so he could begin building a confident and uncluttered approach to what he was doing. So far, he had struggled over every shot, preoccupied by potential disasters, rather than focused on the success he knew deep within, his talent and years of experience could deliver.

Standing outside the bunker practicing his normal bunker-shot swings while Arlen played his chip from in front of the green, Jeff felt himself begin to unwind and relax. Arlen's stroke was again not his best. He seemed to scoop at the ball tentatively, hitting a low, running chip that scooted a good 15 feet past the hole. It was clear that Arlen was in the grip of some demons of his own.

The bunker shot Jeff now faced was not unlike the one he had executed expertly from this same position in the first round, leaving the ball within a foot of the hole. A sense of growing calm flowed through him and Jeff's mind set seized upon a shot like Thursday's, as he swung the club on the second bunker shot. The ball arched smoothly out of the sand onto the green, and released on across to the pin, stopping within three feet of the hole. The crowd reacted to the shot with loud applause, sensing that Jeff would escape what looked not five minutes ago like certain disaster, with no worse than a bogey-5.

Arlen's putt never seriously threatened the cup. He had hit it with a tentative, decelerating stroke that pulled the ball to the left from the start. He had tapped in disconsolately for an unimpressive bogey-5.

Jeff, on the other hand, had an opportunity to make a "good" bogey. Although after his second shot Jeff figured to lose two, maybe three shots, if he could convert the three-footer, he would leave the first green still tied for the lead. Psychologically, it would be like making birdie. Replacing the ball on the green and returning the six-pence coin to his pocket, Jeff concentrated on maintaining the warming sense of confidence that had begun to flow with the bunker shot. He breathed deeply, and methodically re-enacted his pre-shot routine, just like he had done here yesterday over the eight-incher. Just like yesterday the backstroke was low and slow, and the head of the putter accelerated through the ball. The Titleist rolled crisply into the heart of the hole, fulfilling once again the image of success Jeff had seen moments before in his mind's eye. The crowd thundered what must have sounded in the parking lot a half-mile away, just like a birdie cheer.

Chapter 37

Commencing with the second hole, Jeff began striking the ball with the same seemingly effortless grace that had characterized his play yesterday. The TV commentators observed repeatedly that his game, his whole manner really, was projecting a sense of calm and assuredness that was truly remarkable, given the intensity and importance of the Championship. His own first-hole jitters beginning to subside, Baker-Charles also began to settle down at the par-5 second. Both players made birdie fours after reaching the green with their second shots, bringing themselves back to even-par for the day, and -13 for the Championship. The leader board by the second green noted that up ahead Rocky Stillwell was making things happen, birdieing numbers two, three, and four consecutively to go -8 for the Championship. If he could post -10 or better, the NBC commentators were saying, he would force either Arlen or Jeff to play at least a decent round to win, not always an easy thing to do, amid the pressures of leading in the late stages of a championship offering over one million dollars and 10 years of exempt status to its winner.

Jeff and Arlen matched pars at the third, fourth and fifth holes and approached the sixth still tied for the Championship lead at -13. But at six, Arlen made his first bad swing since the weak approach at one. He had selected a 1-iron for his tee shot, since the sixth is relatively short and narrow, bordered on the right by dense trees, and on the left by the Stadium Course's customary lateral water hazard and unkept waste area. He apparently lost his commitment to the shot somewhere along the way, and fairly stood straight-up at impact, blocking the shot badly to the right. The club had come completely out of Arlen's hands at the top of his awkward follow through, and slammed down to the tee at his feet as he disgustedly watched the path of the poorly struck ball, deep into the trees on the right. The gallery reacted with uneasy silence... One courageous supporter finally saying, "That's OK Arlen, you can get 'em." Baker-Charles tore open the Velcro closure to his golf glove, beginning angrily to remove it from his left hand, and stalked off the tee back toward the water cooler, leaving it to his caddie to hustle over and retrieve the misbehaving 1-iron.

Comparatively, Jeff's movements in sizing up, preparing for and executing his tee shot at six were a work of exquisite athletic art. Like yesterday and most of Friday, his demeanor personified a professional athlete at peace with himself, and believing in what he was doing. He too had decided to play from the sixth tee with a 1-iron. But unlike Arlen's forced and hurried effort, Jeff's t-e-m-p-o was perfect, like some sort of slow-motion, yet powerful metronome. The clubhead's contact on the ball was square, and the shot rocketed down the center of the fairway, bounding and rolling to rest just short of the sprinkler head 113 yards from the center of the green.

Baker-Charles' problems were worse in fact, than what they appeared to be from the tee. His only available shot from the trees was to punch the ball, back toward the fairway. But even that was problematical, as he would have to send the ball between two substantial pine tree trunks, that stood between his ball and the only way out. Taking a few minutes to survey the situation, but happening upon neither a miracle, nor any more attractive shot possibility, Arlen attempted the "through the goal posts" punch, making sure to keep the club face under control and strike it squarely back into the ball.

But he couldn't pull it off. The ball struck the pine tree trunk to the left squarely and shot back, nearly hitting Arlen in the face. He ducked and the ball shot on past, across the Stadium Course perimeter canal and into the backyard of 6678 Pinehaven Way, in one of the housing developments built around the TPC, out of bounds. Seeing the ball come to rest in the residential back yard, beyond the white stakes, Arlen looked helplessly over to his caddie with the blank, devastated expression of someone who had just witnessed a plane crash. He now lay three, still in jail. A situation not unlike the one the blown ruling had allowed him to escape from at the 10th on Friday, had bitten him back. It was as if the golf gods had decided they had waited long enough to settle the score.

This time, under the rules of golf, Arlen had no options. All he could do was place another ball in the same place behind the two pines and try again. On the second attempt, the ball shot through the opening, but hit another tree before reaching the fairway and dropped straight down. From there Arlen did manage to chip the ball into position in the fairway, taking very little time to do so, the frustration of the entire situation being almost more than he could bear.

Jeff and Sand Wedge were standing patiently by Jeff's ball, calmly reviewing the book while Arlen was self-destructing off to their right. "Um hum," Sand Wedge said somewhat smugly, to no one in particular. "Like the lady say, 'this be a h-a-r-d game.'"

Jeff was saying nothing. He was taking some easy, fluid practice swings with the pitching wedge he would eventually be hitting, visualizing the ball coming down in the middle of the green and stopping near the left rear pin placement. When it was his turn to play, he reproduced in fact what he had already seen in his mind.

As if to finalize Baker-Charles' calamity, Jeff rolled in his birdie putt, pushing his Championship leading score to -14. The best Arlen could salvage was an eight. He walked dejectedly off the green, now five shots out of the lead he had shared on the tee, less than 20 minutes ago.

David Frisch sat on his trusty golf cart to the left of seven tee watching what was transpiring with Baker-Charles through field glasses. Although, like the Commissioner, David also liked Arlen personally, he would have to admit, given the circumstances, it didn't exactly break his heart to see Arlen fall apart. Just at that moment David's radio cleared. He suspected he knew what was coming. "David," the unidentified voice came softly over the radio, "let's thank our lucky stars buddy."

"I just hit my knees and gave praise to the Man, over" was David's response to Sid, as he put his cart in motion, headed for the area between the seventh green and eighth tee.

The rest of the front nine went fairly uneventfully for Jeff, assuming playing Championship golf with over one million dollars and a 10-year exemption at stake could ever be reasonably termed "uneventful." In a way, every breath Jeff drew was eventful. But he was finding the way to stay focused on what he now fervently believed: he was capable of the shots he needed to make to win. His pars at seven, eight and nine were wonderfully methodical, given the circumstances. Jeff made the turn 1-under for the day and -14 for the Championship. With Arlen's demise at six, the only other serious threat to Jeff over the remaining nine, so long, of course, as he kept his own emotions and attitude under control, appeared to be Rocky Stillwell, who was in the midst of the type of round Arlen had played yesterday. After Jeff and Baker-Charles had putted out on nine, there had been a loud cheer erupt from the vicinity of the llth green, across the lake. Moments later, the leader board off to the left of the ninth green recorded the reason for the cheer: Stillwell had just eagled the 1lth and now stood at -11 for the Championship. It was clear that Jeff was going to have to earn whatever he got. The strongest field of players ever assembled wasn't going to roll over and play dead.

CHAPTER 38

As Jeff and Sand Wedge were walking along the 200-300 yard cart path that leads from the ninth green, around the back of the 18th, to the 10th tee, it occurred to Jeff that he hadn't seen Sandy since he had left her this morning at the Sea Turtle. She had said she was going to go home and change and come right out to the course. He suspected however, that she had decided to stay home and watch the final round on TV, in the companionship of a bottle of Black Opal. It had always been difficult for her to follow Jeff's play at the golf course, particularly when he was in contention. It made her nervous, and she was afraid that somehow her nervousness would negatively affect Jeff's score.

Arriving at the 10th tee, Jeff dismissed any more thoughts about Sandy, and refocused his attention on the business at hand, dialing a low, controlled-draw tee shot into his mind's eye. As he and Arlen waited for the players up ahead to clear the landing area, Jeff took a moment to survey the surroundings. The gallery was incredibly big, as all Championship play was now focused on the back nine of the

Stadium Course. Since the last pairing, Jeff and Arlen, had now cleared the ninth green, the grounds crew and volunteers were removing the flag sticks from the cups on the front side, and taking down the gallery ropes bordering the now deserted fairways. The Championship was moving on toward its impending resolution, over the Stadium Course's demanding and unyielding final few holes.

Jeff's drive at the 10th was serviceable, but not spectacular. He had gotten it a little high with a 3-wood and it hung to the right, coming to rest on the extreme right side of the fairway. From there, his angle to the right-center pin placement would not be good. Baker-Charles' drive hooked left dangerously into the left-side waste area. It was clear that Arlen's Waterloo at six had broken his resolve. He had followed the quadruple bogey-8 with two more bogeys, at seven and eight, and now stood at only 7-under for the Championship, 6-over for the day. Given the hugeness of the purse, each shot Arlen was giving back was very expensive indeed. If he could somehow right himself, although his chance to win the Championship was probably gone, he still had a crack at a very good payday.

As Jeff and Sand Wedge stood at the right side of the 10th fairway, studying the book and preparing for the approach shot into the 10th green, another roar erupted, off to their right at the 12th green. It could only mean one thing: Stillwell had birdied again and Jeff's lead had now shrunk to two. "Um um..." Sand Wedge muttered as he looked off in the direction of the 12th, shaking his head. Although he knew his job was Jeff's game, he had had about enough of one guy, then the next guy shooting lights out and coming after his man. "Um um," he repeated, as he continued to gaze over toward 12.

"Hello-o," Jeff finally said to the distracted caddie, having returned the book to his left rear pocket, and decided that the shot called for a 7-iron, played away from the right-side bunker protecting the pin, toward the center of the green. Jeff's voice startled Sand Wedge back into action, and he turned around from his gaze toward the 12th to evaluate the distance and desired line for Jeff's shot to the 10th green. Looking down quickly to his book, which he still had opened to the 10th hole diagram, the caddie said, "I got 160 to the center, 166 to the pin. Don't mess with anything right. Smooth seven to the center."

"Way ahead of ya, my man," Jeff said as he reached over for the seven.

Sand Wedge's assessment of the shot gave Jeff an added measure of assurance as he took his stance and methodically repeated his preshot routine. Jeff's swing was effortless again and the Titleist flew on a beautiful, medium trajectory toward the middle of the green. It hit the firm putting surface solidly and pitched forward twice before the back spin on the ball stopped it abruptly, some 20 feet to the left of the hole. The enthusiastic reception for the shot from the gallery around the green confirmed that it had come to rest in good position. "My man," Sand Wedge said softly as he accepted back the 7-iron and handed Jeff the putter.

As Jeff neared the 10th green, applause from the gallery encircling it, now 15 or 20 rows deep, began to break out sporadically, and then grew steadily as all of the spectators joined in, expressing their appreciation of Jeff's brilliant play, and the way he was handling what had to be enormous pressure. Most of the spectators knew of his past accomplishments, his long winless streak, and the hard work, dedication and courage that must be involved to get back into a position to win again. As always, Jeff touched the brim of his visor appreciatively and looked around, trying to make eye contact with a few onlookers, before he refocused on preparing for the next shot.

The last 10 feet of Jeff's approximately 20-foot birdie putt at the 10th were downhill, side-hill, and extremely fast. Sand Wedge was bent down, with his hands on his knees, his face positioned over Jeff's right shoulder, as Jeff sat on his heels "plumb bobbing" the line of the putt. The hole appeared off slightly to the right as Jeff closed his left eye and "sighted" the putt directly through the putter's shaft, which he held upright between the thumb and index fingers of his outstretched right hand, confirming the substantial break of the putt to the right.

"Just die it down there, on the high side... Don't be tryin' to make it," Sand Wedge whispered into Jeff's ear, and then rose to move off, out of Jeff's field of vision. This was not a putt for Jeff to go for aggressively Sand Wedge was thinking. If the ball was stroked boldly but didn't go in, it could run right off the green. The putt was going to be that fast.

Sand Wedge sucked in a breath of air and quickly clenched his teeth as soon as the ball left Jeff's putter. Jeff had given the putt a firm rap. Sand Wedge began to pray the ball would somehow find the hole. As the Titleist neared the cup, it began to take the left-to-right break, and headed straight for the hole. The anticipation of the crowd began to rise as the ball appeared to be headed for dead center. Jeff was standing with the putter held in his left hand, extended out toward hole, parallel to the green, anticipating the concussive roar from the crowd as the ball disappeared. But in the last several inches of the path leading to the cup, the ball inexplicably straightened and caught the top edge of the hole rather than the center. The pace of the putt was too fast for the ball to drop, and it spun quickly around the left top side, and released on down the slope of the green. The gallery groaned agonizingly in unison as the ball rolled... and rolled down the slick green. There was nothing to stop it until it came to rest up against the green's collar, some 15 feet below the hole.

Lowering the putter back down and standing motionlessly now in the same place from which he had stroked the putt, Jeff put his right index finger to his chin and gently rubbed it back and forth, trying to come to grips with what had just happened. NBC zoomed in for a tight shot of Jeff's face, and Johnny Miller commented to the TV audience that he saw some fear and indecision there, for the first time all weekend.

Jeff moved on down to behind where his ball had come to rest. It had trickled an inch or two into the fringe, so he couldn't mark it. He sat back down on his heels and started grinding again over what he now had left for par. He had gotten greedy, and he knew it. The issue, however, was what could he do from here. He had to somehow focus his concentration back on success. "T-e-m-p-o," he said under his breath, "t-e-m-p-o..." Sand Wedge was peering over his shoulder again. "Straight in and kinda slow; die left at the end," the caddie said, rising and moving away as before.

Assuming his putting stance, Jeff focused his thoughts entirely on the hole, and the vision of the Titleist tumbling over the right front edge as it disappeared from sight. Backstroke low and slow... accelerate through the ball... The contact between the putter head and the balata cover of the golf ball produced a solid click. The Titleist tracked back up toward the hole, as the crescendo of the crowd noise built again, and this time erupted thunderously, uproariously, as the ball disappeared from sight. Jeff instinctively reached to the bill of his visor and spun it around nearly backwards, celebrating the wonderful unorthodoxy of it all. On the card, it looked for all the world like a simple, two-putt par. But everyone who had witnessed it knew it was far from that. Johnny Miller was proclaiming over the air that Jeff had just made the stroke that would win the Championship.

Chapter 39

Jeff maintained his 2-stroke lead through the 16th, where he lipped out a 10-footer for birdie that would have raised his advantage to a more comfortable three shots. Up ahead at the 18th, Stillwell had converted a pressure-packed "sandy," getting the ball up and down from the left-side bunker for par. He had posted a fantastic 65 for the final round, and a leader in the clubhouse, overall score of 276, -12 for the Championship.

As he walked onto the 17th tee, Jeff knew that his situation was the exact one architect Pete Dye had in mind when he had designed the hole. Johnny Miller's thesis, which he was excitedly explaining to the TV audience, was that to win the Players Championship, Jeff had to get his tee shot onto the island green. According to Johnny, it was as simple as that.

Given the absence of any appreciable wind, the field staff had set the markers at the 17th at the very back of the championship tee. The hole would play right at 145 yards and the pin was set in its usual Sunday placement, to the right rear of the green, just over the tiny pot bunker located on the right side. Railroad ties encircled the green, defining it in the middle of the lake, beautifully or diabolically, depending upon your point of view.

Jeff and Sand Wedge agreed that the shot called for a medium eight, aimed, it went without saying, at the middle of the green. But as Jeff started into his pre-shot routine, Sand Wedge saw that something was wrong. Rather than focusing in on the shot, as was his custom, with a slow motion practice swing, while standing behind the ball facing the target, after teeing the ball Jeff simply assumed his stance, waggled the club a few times, and then appeared to be settling into his actual swing. To Sand Wedge's growing concern, Jeff was inexplicably changing his routine and quickening his tempo, at this most crucial of times. The caddie clenched his teeth again, biting right through the filter of his cigarette.

The sound of the club's impact on the ball indicated that the shot was marginal from the start. Jeff had caught it heavy and it was a guess whether or not it would fly long enough to catch the front of the green. The flight of the shot didn't look reassuring from any angle and the thousands encamped on the spectator mounds lining the left side of the Stadium Course's "signature hole" watched the ball's descent in eerie silence. Commentator Johnny Miller was the only person expressing any opinion about the shot as its outcome hung in the balance. "Uh-oh," he had said, "I don't think Taylor caught all of that. It looks like it could be short...," he had informed the TV viewing audience.

Incredibly, Jeff's ball came down squarely on the center of one of the railroad ties that encircled the green. Due to the silence of the crowd, the report of the ball striking the wood sounded like a home run being struck in a baseball game. Everyone watched in horror, as the ball bounced high into the air, and flew on over the left side of the green, splashing sickeningly into the water. Apparently not believing what they had just seen, the thousands looking on continued the deafening silence. Jeff looked across the tee to Sand Wedge in disbelief.

"Now what," he said bending down to pick up his tee and beginning to walk over to his caddie's side. "How are they playing this?" Jeff asked Sand Wedge as they now glumly watched Arlen play his shot, a routine 8-iron that hit into the center of the green and curled down to the right, stopping about 18 feet to the left of the hole.

Sand Wedge pulled out the book and began flipping to the pages that outlined the 17th. A note at the bottom of the diagram addressed the procedures for a ball hit into the water: "lake is played as a water hazard, provided that player has the option of either replaying from the tee or from the drop zone indicated at the front of the forward tee." More bad luck. Jeff was hoping the water at the 17th was being played as a "lateral" water hazard, as he knew it had been in prior years. If that had been the case, he would have been able to drop the ball on the green since, with the bounce off the railroad tie, his ball had last crossed the margin of the hazard over the far side of the putting surface.

So Jeff would have only two options for his third shot: he could play again from the tee, or go forward to the drop area, and play a 60-yard pitch from there. He elected to replay from the tee, requesting the 8-iron once again from Sand Wedge. Withdrawing the club from the bag, Sand Wedge toweled the leather grip vigorously before handing it to his player, saying, "Be patient now... watch your tempo now... don't get quick now... and make a good swing."

Jeff made a conscious effort to walk more slowly this time to the desired position, over near the right-side tee marker. Teeing the ball, he blocked out everything from his mind but the vision of his next shot, a smooth eight with just a touch of fade, coming down in the middle of the green and then curling down the slope of the green to the right-side pin placement. This time he proceeded through his routine, like some sort of precise, yet fluid and relaxed machine. The contact of the club on the ball was the unmistakable "thwack" of a perfectly struck iron shot, and the ball flew off toward the green, this time clearly destined for its center. Jeff's ball landed very near where Arlen's ball had come to rest, pitched forward two or three feet and curled down toward the pin, stopping some 10 feet away. The huge gallery cheered in relief, but not so exuberantly. They seemed to fear that Jeff was letting the Championship slip away.

The putt Jeff had left himself was another slick, downhill, left-to-righter. As he prepared to make his stroke, Jeff fully understood and agreed with the warning Sand Wedge had whispered to him as they were lining the putt up: "Keep it high, and just touch it, gonna be fast." Like the birdie putt on the 10th, this bogey putt was not one to be bold with. This time Jeff stroked the ball very gently, ensuring that it would die at or close by the hole. It was low all the way. But the distance was about right, the ball stopping a couple of inches to the right of the cup. Jeff tapped the ball in with the back side of the putter for a double bogey-5. He had fallen back to -12 and was again tied for the lead, this time with Rocky Stillwell, who was in the TV booth with Johnny Miller and Dick Enberg. Rocky's 276 was signed, sealed and delivered. Jeff still had the treacherous 18th to play. Johnny Miller summed the situation up for the TV viewers by analogizing to tennis: "Advantage Stillwell."

Chapter 40

After Jeff had tapped in at the 17th, minor pandemonium broke out, as the crowd stampeded toward the 18th tee. All of a sudden, the importance and drama of Jeff's upcoming tee shot had just gone from 8 to 12, on a scale of 1 to 10. Jeff had to raise his arms and ask the crowd to remain still, to allow Arlen to finish out his par putt. They obliged, sort of.

On the way to tee Sand Wedge was grim-faced and quiet. The irons in the bag clanked in cadence with his steps as he walked along. Jeff was wordless too, deep in thought about what was to come. The dominant thought he was trying to seize upon was the solidness of the second 8-iron he had hit some 10 minutes ago. That one had felt so good. He couldn't remember what happened on the first one, and repressed any efforts to try to recall it. He was trying to somehow turn the double-bogey into a positive.

When the players reached the 18th tee, it resembled a green raft, floating within a vast sea of humanity. Spectators were pressed up against the gallery ropes, sitting, standing, leaning and craning. Fathers held little children on their shoulders, so they could better see what they didn't really appreciate in any event. The marshall's repeated requests for "quiet please" notwithstanding, outspoken fans, and uninhibited ones holding souvenir cups full of beer called out what they intended as encouragement. "You're OK Jeff." "You the man Jeff."

Standing by Sand Wedge's side as Arlen prepared to drive, Jeff knew he was at the defining moment of his career. The three-sided Rolex on the practice tee, as well as the Rolexes on the wall in Sid's office, on the wall in Commissioner's Hospitality, and on Sid's wrist, all pointed to 5:25.

From the back of the championship tee, the 18th hole at the Stadium Course looks much more like a lake bordered on the right by a green pathway, than a golf hole bordered on the left by a lake. The hole works from right to left, toward the menacing water, and plays to the demanding length of 440 yards. Any hope of making par or birdie on the hole requires an aggressive and well-executed tee shot. Sand Wedge had his left hand on the 3-wood and was thinking about recommending it to Jeff. He was worried about the tendency toward quickness he had seen building in Jeff's swing as the round wore on. He knew if Jeff pulled the tee shot to the left with the driver, the Championship would almost certainly be lost.

But as Jeff looked over to him, Sand Wedge decided to say nothing about club selection. The last thing he wanted was to say "3-wood" if Jeff was thinking driver, or vice versa. Sand Wedge left it with the usual, "Make a good swing now," leaving the choice of club to the player. Jeff pulled out the driver.

As Jeff walked to the left side of the tee and leaned down to tee up the Titleist, the silence enshrouding the tee was complete. No one even dared to sip their beer.

As he stood behind the teed-up ball, focusing in visually on his target landing area in the right center of the fairway, inexplicably Jeff's thoughts turned to his father, who had shown him about the game, and encouraged him to begin playing some 35 years ago. Somehow he felt his father was watching him, although he had died when Jeff was just 18. "Low and slow, and keep your head down, dammit," was his dad's one and only golf instruction. Jeff decided to try it, one more time.

And it worked. The drive reported solidly off the face of the driver and bore gloriously down the right center of the fairway, bouncing and rolling into perfect position, 15 to 20 yards past Baker-Charles' ball, which he had hit pretty well. The cheer from the tee was a medium one, not wild, as many of the spectators seemed to be too busy sighing in relief to express much euphoria. Besides, they all knew much work remained for Jeff to do, if he was to match Stillwell's overall score. Nevertheless, the wink and the smile were back as Jeff handed the driver to Sand Wedge and they strode off down the 18th fairway.

Jeff's lie in the fairway was good, and according to the book he had 190 yards to the center of the green and 195 to the left-rear pin placement. The placement was what was sometimes called a sucker pin, since a ball working right to left back toward the hole, ran the risk of running through the green, as Rocky Stillwell's had, into the steep rear bunker.

But as Jeff waited for Arlen to play, sizing up what remained to be done, he had the vision of another kind of shot in mind. He saw a gentle fade, starting out on the line of the left-side bunker, and working slightly back from left to right, hitting the green below the hole and releasing up the slope to the pin. If he could pull it off, he would leave himself an uphill putt at birdie, and the Championship. It would be an aggressive play, but the opportunity seemed to Jeff to call for it, and he really believed he could make the shot.

Sand Wedge was standing silently by the bag. He had left the book in his caddie bib pocket, knowing this one was all Jeff's to decide. The caddie didn't want to say anything that might conflict with the shot his player was dialing into his concentration.

"I got 4-iron," Jeff finally said, reaching over for the club. Sand Wedge withdrew the four from the bag, and, as always, toweled the grip before handing it to his player. "Make a good swing now," the caddie said as he shouldered the bag again and moved a few steps away.

As he stood back behind the ball, focusing in on the line toward the left side of the bunker, where he intended to start the shot, Jeff's mind drifted to the notes of the song *One Moment in Time* that he had heard in a video of John Daly's PGA Championship victory several years ago. He liked the video, and the vision warmed him and he began to believe that this, right now, was his moment in time. The warmth and calm coursed out through his shoulders and arms, and into his hands as he methodically went through his pre-shot routine. His swing repeated the effortless grace that had characterized his game most of the weekend, and the impact of the 4-iron on the ball was dead solid perfect. The Titleist soared straight along the line of the bunker and then, as if controlled by some kind of homing device, began turning perfectly as it descended, straight on line with the waiting pin. The crowd began to roar as the ball impacted the green some 12 feet below the hole, hopped once, and began tracking up the hill toward the cup.

Back down the fairway, Jeff had assumed a classic "follow through" pose as he and Sand Wedge watched the Titleist release up the slope and then wonderfully, mystically and magically... disappear from sight, into the hole.

Jeff fell to his knees as the 40,000 people cramming the amphitheater around the 18th green jumped to their feet and erupted into the loudest roar the hallowed Stadium Course grounds had ever heard. The place was up for grabs.

Sand Wedge had fallen to the ground as the ball disappeared and was now sitting on the fairway with his arms clasped around his knees. "My man," he was repeating delightedly. "My man." Jeff had broken into a medium-paced jog, and was ambling toward the green and the waving spectators. He waved back at them exuberantly, holding his visor high in the air at arm's length, as he luxuriated in the blissful redemption of the moment. Every few paces he would click the heels of his Foot-Joys together, to emphasize for all to see his total state of celebration.

The roar of the crowd would not die down, despite Jeff's raised arm requests that they do so, to allow Arlen to pitch his third shot onto the green. When Jeff reached into the hole and withdrew the Titleist 3, holding it aloft to the admiring masses, the roar came up again, almost equal to the level of the initial crescendo. Jeff raised his arms again to request the crowd to quiet down for Arlen's last putt, and like they had at the 17th, they did, sort of.

Arlen holed out, and it was over. Jeff Taylor was the Players Champion. He had managed a final round 71, 1-under-par, and overall had finished at 274, -14. All that remained to be done was the formality of reviewing and signing the card in the scoring tent. As he made his way there, he brushed hands with the hundreds of fans who strained against the gallery ropes, reaching out to get one last piece of the dramatic history they had helped make, just moments before.

Jeff Taylor had captured in his mind's eye, and then seized his moment in time.

CHAPTER 41

After all of the hoopla on the 18th green, and the TV interviews, and the tumultuous scene in the media center the Players Champion is inevitably subjected to, the private ceremony in the Champions Loft in the TPC clubhouse is a welcome conclusion to a precious accomplishment. The only invitees are the Commissioner, the past Champions, and the Champion. The purpose is for the Commissioner to make the formal presentation of the exquisite Waterford Crystal Players Championship Trophy, already inscribed with the new Champion's name, to sip a glass or two of very fine champagne, and reflect on an especially memorable week.

In presenting the trophy to Jeff, the Commissioner said very simply, "Jeff, I have never in my life done anything that gave me more satisfaction than to present this trophy to you, the Players Champion. You are indeed a credit to your profession, and the game of golf. And after the dust settles a little," Sid continued, "maybe in a week or two, I'd like to talk to you about one of the Player Director positions on the Board. We need players serving on the Board who understand the demands of the business side of the Tour. We've probably only seen the tip of the iceberg on this world tour thing, and if they do bring something before the Board, it would be nice to have player representatives like you there to analyze things from a long-range perspective. Not all of your colleagues are inclined to do that."

His emotional and physical energy completely sapped by the incredible journey he had just completed, all Jeff could say in response as he accepted the trophy was, "Thank you Sid, I don't know what else to say, I'll get back to you about the Policy Board thing, as you say, after the dust settles."

"I understand completely," Sid responded. "Let's have a drink and a cigar."

"I'd love that," Jeff said, relieved that the Commissioner was apparently finally going to let it rest regarding business matters. "But I need to make a phone call first." He hoped he remembered Sandy's home phone number from last night, when he'd called it from the Sea Turtle.

Be my guest," Sid said, lighting up a cigar as Freddy Blake was pouring Moet Chandon all around. "Phone's over there on the wall, dial nine to get out."

Jeff went over to the phone and dialed the number, not knowing if he had gotten it right until he heard Sandy's unexpectedly weak and halting voice at the other end of the line. "Here's looking at you kid," Jeff spoke softly into the phone.

For a moment he heard nothing from the other end of the line, and wondered if maybe the connection had gone bad or something. Then he heard Sandy clear her throat and begin to reply, her voice shaky and thick with emotion.

"Congratulations... Jeff," she finally said ..."Where are you now?" Jeff was alarmed by the obvious upset Sandy's weak and halting voice betray d. He had expected her to sound happy and excited, like he was.

"I'm up here in the clubhouse with Sid," Jeff replied. "But I'd surely rather be there with you."

There was uneasy silence on the line again, and Jeff began to sense the difficult emotions Sandy must have been experiencing in the wake of his triumph, a triumph that she, in her own way, had probably agonized over, even more than he had. She had been through this cycle with him before: intervals of sweetness and light, when his competitive fortunes were on the rise, preceded and followed by longer periods of insecurity and self pity, when he was missing cuts. The despondent scene they had suffered through, exactly one year ago at the restaurant in St. Augustine had defined the lowest point of this uncomfortable and unhealthy pattern.

As the silence wore on, Jeff attempted to appreciate Sandy's apparent anxiety. She feared, he expected, that his newly stated commitment to her might be temporal, connected to his current professional euphoria. That had certainly been his track record in the past.

"You know Sandy," he decided to continue, "we've got some things to talk about. Let me finish up here with Sid, and I'll drop by later. Can you give me about an hour?"

"OK," Sandy responded, still weakly. "I'll see you then." The click as Sandy hung up the phone signaled something of a reality check to Jeff. As he replaced the phone handle in its cradle he realized that real people with real concerns populated the world outside the white-hot, competition-focused Zone he had been immersed in since last Thursday morning. Sandy had every right, he continued to think as he walked back to join Sid and the others, to be skeptical of the convictions he had revealed to her last night. He had a further obligation, he realized, to show her that his commitments were based in the maturity of an overhauled attitude, rather than the unsustaining support of a weekend of low scores. She deserved to know where she would stand with him if he had just shot 80.

CHAPTER 42

By the time Jeff had parked the Riviera alongside the TR6 at Sandy's place, night had fallen, and Atlantic Beach was enveloped in another partially moonlit and comfortable spring evening. Just as he had on Friday night, Jeff sat for a moment in the car after turning off the engine. But this time he had remembered to turn off the car lights first, so he sat with his thoughts in darkness, and nearly complete silence. The periodic rush of a wave running up to the shore some 50 yards away were the only sounds he heard.

Sandy's house was dark, and if it weren't for the TR6 Jeff would have begun to wonder if she was home. As he got out of the Riviera, Jeff began to reflect on the unhappy Sunday night he had inflicted upon Sandy exactly one year ago at the restaurant in St. Augustine. He acknowledged the polarity between the situation now and what it had been then, and thought again of Polly and her simple wisdom, as he walked up the cedar pathway toward the door. Jeff believed he would be at peace with himself at this moment even had he not won the championship a few hours before. He sensed again vividly that he was exactly where he wanted to be, where he needed to be. It seemed as though he had won the championship at the very time he had finally realized that among all its rewards it couldn't deliver happiness. Like Polly had said, the obtaining of happiness is a personal assignment each individual has to accept, independent of extrinsic factors.

Arriving at the house, Jeff depressed the illuminated doorbell, expecting to hear footsteps toward the door, or Sandy's invitation to come inside. But the house remained dark and quiet. After a moment, Jeff pushed the doorbell again. But like before, the quiet continued on. He decided to try the door, and found that it was unlocked. Beginning to feel some anxiety over the situation, Jeff turned the doorknob, opened the door, and let himself into the dark front foyer.

"Sandy?" he called out, but there was still no response. "Sandy?"... "Where are you?"

Off to the right, through the kitchen Jeff noticed a flickering, grey-blue light, apparently coming from the television which sat in the far corner of the house, near the sliding glass door that led out onto the deck. Walking through the kitchen and on into the great room, Jeff saw that the television was still tuned to NBC but that the sound had been turned off. The "mute" indicator flashed in the lower right hand corner of the screen while actors silently laughed and scurried about in what appeared to be some nondescript Sunday night sit-com.

"Sandy?" Jeff called out again, finding the TV remote on the top of the set and pushing the orange "power" button. The TV screen, and the entire room went dark.

"Out here Jeff," Sandy finally responded, her voice coming faintly, through the open door leading from the great room to the deck overlooking the ocean.

"What's going on out here, lady?" Jeff said as he walked through the doorway onto the deck. "I was beginning to feel like I was in a Hitchcock movie or something... You all right?" Sandy was standing at the far end of the deck, her back to him. She made no attempt to respond to Jeff's questions, continuing to look out at the vast, black ocean.

Approaching her, Jeff's concern refocused on the extreme difficulty Sandy was obviously having, sorting through the revelations, hopes and fears the weekend's events had uncovered. The fact of the matter was that despite his recent demonstrations of calmness, confidence and commitment, he was the same person who had wrecked her world, just one year ago, labeling her a distraction from the more important aspects of his life. He again realized that she had a right to know, once and for all, what had changed. Was it he, or merely his golf scores?

When he got to the end of the deck where Sandy was standing, Jeff reached out and encircled her shoulders with his arms and pulled her close to him, muzzling his face into her blond hair and kissing the back of her neck. Sandy relaxed under his touch and pressed herself back into Jeff's embrace. Feeling her respond reassured Jeff, and quieted his need to talk or question Sandy about what she was feeling. He could now feel how she felt. He continued to pull her to him from behind, also looking out at the ocean, through the wisps of her blowing hair.

The two drifted along in silence for several minutes, enjoying the beauty of the surroundings and the serenity of their togetherness. Finally, Jeff decided the time was right to take on the bigger issue which was obviously troubling Sandy and threatening what should be one of the most satisfying and defining times of their lives.

"You know Sandy," he said, gently releasing his embrace and turning her around so he could look into her eyes as he spoke, "I met this marvelous old lady last fall in Orlando. Ran into her in a bar late Friday afternoon after I'd missed the cut at Disney. I'm in there... drinking beers... feeling sorry for myself, when all of a sudden she speaks up... wants to know if she can join me 'for a round.' She must have been 75. But for some reason, she was very intriguing, so I said 'sure' and we started to chat. I can't remember exactly how it happened, but somehow we got to talking about attitude, and, after a while, she got me thinking about things differently. Somehow, in the matter of just an hour or two, she taught me how to focus on the good things life has to offer, and that happiness is a matter of personal choice... And Sandy, I'm making that choice every day now, and plan never to stop. She had this expression... 'Success is always an option,' she said. 'All you have to do is have the guts to choose it...' Well, now I truly understand what she meant. I choose you Sandy, and I choose here and now. I choose us."

Sandy turned away from Jeff's stare as she attempted to absorb his ambitious revelations.

Looking back into his eyes after a minute she finally said, "You know Jeff, that's kind of eerie, what you just said. My aunt used to say 'Success is always an option.' She was big on seizing the moment and never giving up. She's always been the example I've tried to follow when things have gotten tough."

The two grew quiet again as Jeff thought about the coincidence of Sandy having an aunt who had apparently passed along to her the same philosophy that Polly had imparted to him.

"Maybe the lady I met in Orlando was your aunt," Jeff said after a moment, wondering if the fantastic coincidence could somehow be true.

"No, I don't thing so Jeff," Sandy replied... "Aunt Polly died 10 years ago."

Now it was Jeff who was dumbstruck.

"Listen, Jeff," Sandy resumed after a moment. "Let's just take one day at a time... And let's never forget that right here and right now it's been a wonderful, wonderful day."

Jeff thought for a moment about asking Sandy if her aunt had sparkling green eyes, or wore gloves, or drank whiskey, but he thought better of it. This was not a night for pondering coincidences, or delving into the uncharted territory of the supernatural. Instead, allowing her to take his hand as she led him across the deck to the steps that led down to the beach, Jeff attempted to improvise his amateurish Humphrey Bogart impression, saying, "You know Sandy, I think this is the beginning of a beautiful friendship."

Sandy's wink back to Jeff over her shoulder indicated that she understood his *Casablanca* reference, from the film's closing scene. And they both believed, as they walked along the wide, low-tide beach, in the direction of the blinking red lights marking the jetties up in Mayport, that it accurately foretold their future, like all sentimentalists believe it did in the movie, for Rick and Captain Renault.

THE END

About the Author

Gary M. Crist practices sports and entertainment law in Jupiter, Florida. Mr. Crist has been around golf nearly his whole life, first playing the game as a junior in Indiana in the 50's and 60's. His involvement with golf has continued in his professional life, although his competitive skills, once regarded as formidable, have diminished to almost nil.

Mr. Crist is currently the General Counsel of the National Golf Foundation, and worked as the Associate General Counsel of the PGA Tour and the General Counsel of the PGA of America from 1982 through 1994. In addition to practicing law, Mr. Crist is a free lance author and lecturer on sports law and related topics. He lives with his wife Vicki in Palm Beach Gardens, Florida.